Relief

L. E. Butler

Regal Crest

Nederland, Texas

ISBN 978-1-932300-98-7
1-932300-98-8

First Printing 2008

9 8 7 6 5 4 3 2 1

Cover design by Donna Pawlowski

Published by:

Regal Crest Enterprises, LLC
4700 Hwy 365, Ste A
PMB 210
Port Arthur, Texas 77642

Find us on the World Wide Web at
http://www.regalcrest.biz

Printed in the United States of America

Acknowledgments

Thanks to Alan McDonald, Jane Vollbrecht, Cathy LeNoir, Gary Russell, and Jill Braden.

All song lyrics in this novel were written by the author. Some passages in this novel first appeared in the author's earlier works.

The poems cited are: "After a Great Pain, a Formal Feeling Comes" by Emily Dickinson; "The Panther" and "First Duino Elegy" by Rainer Maria Rilke (translation by Stephen Mitchell, in *The Selected Poetry of Rainer Maria Rilke*, Vintage International Edition, 1989); "The Lamb" by William Blake; "The Princess" by Alfred Tennyson; and "Candles" by Constantine Cafavy (translation by Edmund Keeley and Edmund Sherrard, in *C. P. Cavafy: Collected Poems*, Princeton University Press, 1992).

for A. P.

Chapter
One

WHEN I CAME here as a little girl, I used to imagine all of
Boston Common going still, becoming as static and airless as a
painting. I used to dream of slipping into the scene and moving
about undisturbed, pushing gently at the spattered green branches,
crossing a path of multicolored brushstrokes, wading into a river of
oily indigo.

"Care for an ice cream, miss?" A boy's grinning face
interrupted my reverie. He blanched as I stared. His older
companion looked at my black collar and cuffs and hurried away.
They were at least ten years younger than I.

"Ah, forget it," I muttered. It was too damned hot anyway. I
reached under my hat to scratch at my salty head, then gathered up
my easel and paper. When I turned towards Charles Street, I was
shocked at how crowded the paths had become. Men were in their
shirt-sleeves. Women wore sleek powder-blue suits and gauzy
veils. They were freshly perfumed, ready for the cool descent of
evening.

I wished I'd worn a veil. People turned towards me as I passed,
and I felt their glances like handfuls of pebbles zinging against my
skin. I imagined them turning to a painted scene, their slouchy
trousers rendered in globs of black, their faces in smudges of
cream.

The streetcar was crowded. I lowered my eyes and rested my
easel on the tops of my shoes. A man beside me ate contentedly
from a paper cone of popcorn, while a woman sucked at an ice. The
sunlight tipped through the glass. If I painted this, I'd have to use a
paste of gold dust.

It was such a short trip that I really should have walked. Even
after two weeks, I kept forgetting that I now lived on Beacon Hill. I
missed my stop and had to double back, peering around for
landmarks. The carriages gleamed in this neighborhood; the houses
all had the heavy burgundy gloss of wealth. At John's house, a
maid swept the front stoop, singing to herself. She stood tense as I

approached, watching her toes and wishing me a good evening in her uncertain Irish voice. I cast about, as always, for a decent response, coming up with, "Yes, thanks, and the same to you." She didn't smirk at all. She hadn't been with us long enough.

I tried to pass without stumbling. I could never get used to entering such a fine house. The parlor, with its half-closed blinds and ceiling fan, was cool as an icebox. My skirts chilled me. I sat down, twisting my gloves, breathing the blessedly empty air. Someone would be home any moment.

Just as I leaned back, the youngest housemaid walked in and glared at the couch for an instant before curtseying. Of course. I'd made the mistake once before of sitting on the leopard-skin throw while still wearing my grimy walking-skirt. I stood again and wandered to the window, picking up a stereo-viewer.

I rested the viewer against the windowsill and leaned in. Someone had put in a slide of a European city, with crumbling buildings like half-eaten cakes. Adele, Jeff, and I had planned to go to Europe. How strange that I could remember such a fact with perfect simplicity. We'd argued over all the Mediterranean regions, finally deciding on Italy. We'd had almost enough saved for a second-class passage.

I tilted the viewer, and from the dun background the shape of a silver palm tree leapt out, garlanded with roses fat as cinnamon buns. Water gleamed on the city's horizon, and there, in the foreground, too. A bridge, a long narrow boat. Venice. I licked my lips and imagined how briny the air would be.

My throat stung; in the same moment I heard the ticking of the grandfather clock. No. I always tried to block the sound out, but it was no use; once I noticed the tuneless swing of its pendulum, I could suddenly hear every last clock in the great house, each one ticking more and more loudly. They started in sync but fell apart into chaos. I felt all the rhythms twitching and stuttering through my nerves, shaking my cells apart.

I dropped the viewer and put my hands over my ears. "No, no," I whispered. "I'll be all right." The same thing I'd wanted to scream in the street. "No." There couldn't possibly be that many clocks in the house. I didn't want to take any sleeping powders. I tried not to think of them, where they sat in two neat bottles beside my hairbrush, three flights up in my attic bedroom.

A stomp and rustle echoed through the hallway. The maids murmured.

Mum came in, drawing the pin from her hat. Her round cheeks shone pink; her linen shirtwaist was dark with sweat under her arms. She rolled her eyes and hooted.

"I'm melting!" She couldn't resist a nervous glance at my

shoes, but soon smiled again. She'd been scrubbing her teeth every morning and they gleamed now, white as fresh-cut apple. "Out sketching today? Wasn't it close?" She looked at my waist, my smudged hands. "Did you make any friends?"

I turned away, reaching for the stereo viewer again. When she went quiet, I tried to reassure her with a short laugh. "No, Mum. Not in mourning dress."

"We're quite alone?" Mum crossed to the mantel and looked in the foxed mirror above it, resting her hands on her cheeks. I watched her reflection and nodded.

Her voice took on a studied lightness whenever she was nervous. The youngest maid sashayed by the open door and Mum cleared her throat.

"You've seemed restless lately," she began. "Now, I know you've made great strides towards recovery. The medicines help, don't they? All the same, I know when you're feeling off. Mm-mm."

She gave a little contented hum to herself, like a cosseted grandmother. I wondered where she'd picked up that habit. I never knew what a chameleon she could be until she moved here, into John's house.

As far as I could guess, John met Mum over ten years ago, at the 1900 Mystic Convergence, where they became Hindoos for a time. That following summer, they spent a month in a community called, I believe, the Vale of Bliss. They never wanted to talk about that afterwards. I didn't meet John until my wedding breakfast three years ago. He had looked anxious to leave, tall and fine-featured and bug-eyed with affront, as if he feared someone from my boisterous new family would clap him on the shoulder. His hair was clipped short like an orphan's, and you had the sense it must have turned white from shock. Mum had clung tight to his arm, tittering until she was short of breath. She had taken me aside later, telling me he'd bought a new house for himself and she was to live with him, finally, *all in cream*. Finally. Her eyes had looked exhausted.

I used to spy on John then. I heard him tell a friend that middle-aged partnerships were always the happiest, because women had learned to be calm.

Now Mum was fussing around the room, picking dead leaves from the ficus tree, wiping dust from the ormolu clock. I sat, feeling suddenly sleepy.

"Did you apply yet for that drawing teacher post?" she asked, laying a quick hand on the daily paper. "I'll take that as a *no*. Don't you roll your eyes at me. I know you are, even when your back is turned. Put that viewer down. Listen, Katherine, it's time to stop obsessing over Europe. It's only anarchists and perverts nowadays, anyway."

My temple ached. The room smelled strongly of camphor. I wanted a small sip of wine.

She hurried to me. "You're still nervous, aren't you?"

"You used to be an anarchist, don't forget," I said, trying to laugh. I didn't want to have a heartfelt discussion with her. I dreaded the turn it would take.

"Socialist," she said. She fixed a pin in my chignon and smoothed my hair. She'd never done that before; I wondered whether she'd seen a mother do that in a nickelodeon. I turned to her and she glanced towards the hallway. Her silver pompadour had fallen to one side.

"Listen," she said. "John's daughters are going to be home soon, and I need to really talk with you."

"I know you do," I answered. "I know. I have looked into those jobs, and some of them seem promising. They pay all right, too, and I have the money from Jeff's family. I'm not going to be a burden."

"They might have given you more," she said. When she frowned, her eyes darkened and her mouth looked flabby and bitter. "With you being such a close family friend for so long. And don't forget to give that money to John. He's going to see his banker tomorrow."

She bit at her thumbnail. I spoke quickly to calm her. "I've been trying to give it to him for days. He's always too busy to talk to me. I'll get a position soon, don't worry. And with the settlement, I'll have enough to buy all the paints I'll need. And I'll stay occupied. I'll be so busy, you'll hardly notice me."

She chewed her lip and gave her dotty laugh again. A bicycle bell rang, and she turned to the window.

"Is there something else, Mum?" She whirled back to me as soon as I said it. "I can find a place of my own to live, if that's what worries you."

"Oh, no!" She put her hand on her throat. "How would that look? And what kind of decent place would you be able to afford, for God's sake? No. John did say that you might stay here as long as you need to. Only—"

She picked up a vase of dried lavender. "John tells me that we need some help around the house. Someone to oversee and advise the housekeeping. It would really be so helpful. I'd do it, too, but I have those committee meetings, and I'm always slogging all over Cambridge."

"Of course," I said. I watched her exhale as she put the vase down. Dust motes hung in the air like tiny frozen butterflies.

"That is," she said, waving a gracious hand. "I say 'help

around the house,' but you know I don't really mean it that way, like *help*. Only few hours a day, when you've done with your drawing and painting. You'll have plenty of time for fun on the weekends."

"I had been hoping to prepare for a showing," I said. "There was that lady, you remember, from the Copley Society, who sent the card that time and asked about my newer works."

"Has she called at all since — since everything that happened, since you became ill? No," she hurried to add, her voice rising, "no, don't get all wound up, Katie. I'm telling you I know how they are, those art people. They promise a great deal, just because they enjoy having artists around. They don't care for your long-term prospects, not like your family does. And you have prospects. You can really get on. Look at you! You look much younger than your age, and your health is better. And this is a perfect neighborhood, a divine place to be. The best, best people. It can happen. You need only believe."

I stood and crossed to the window. I started to lean my head on the glass, then stopped myself before I left a greasy smudge. Again I heard the clocks ticking and I shook my head, just once, quickly.

"I can tell you're angry," she said. "Listen. Do what I do, when you want to be angry. Be grateful instead. John's been very generous to both of us. Who do you think paid for your all your hospital stay, and the medicines?"

I had a sudden memory of myself in the hospital. One night they'd given me a combination of powders with Latin and German names, and instead of sleeping, I was seized with the urge to write. When I ran out of paper I wrote on the bedsheets, the pillowcase, even my left arm. I woke later to the sound of the nurse scolding me bitterly. I hadn't known those bed linens were so expensive.

Mum was still talking. What had I written on my inner forearm? I looked down and saw that I was clutching the windowsill. One of my fingernails split.

"Mum…"

"Hush, don't." she whispered. There was laughter just outside. The maids' footsteps came quickly.

I turned and tried to make my face smooth. Mum breathed out as if getting ready to sing.

But John's two girls passed through the vestibule, panting, their shoes ringing. From the shaded parlor, we saw only their skirts, their bundles of peonies. The maids followed them as they went bumping up the staircase, all of them shouting with laughter.

AT MIDNIGHT, I stood at my window and leaned into the sooty wind. The darkness rumbled with streetcars and thunder. The wind brought the sharp scent of rain and I scratched at my tired neck, feeling cool for the first time in weeks.

I'd been listening as everyone went to bed, room by room. Now it was just me, and my lamp turned low, and my old sketches and watercolors strewn over the bed.

I looked down at the polished cobblestones. This was my cycle: each night I comforted myself with dreams of suicide, and each morning my body, cruelly innocent and stupid, wanted to wear pink, wanted chocolate bread for breakfast. I couldn't stop chasing pleasure.

I sat on the bed and rested my fingertips on the sketches. Their lines were faded. It occurred to me that they'd started to fade the day I drew them. "I can't," I said to them. I heard the clock ticking and I spoke louder. I put my hands on my ears and the ticking became a muffled pulse. I imagined the walls on mechanized tracks, sliding closer towards me. I fell face downwards into my pillow, sucking my tongue.

"Stop," I begged. "Stop. No." I thought again of the powders, sitting now by my washbasin. The one with the yellow label, the chloral hydrate, made me feel I'd stepped into a warm bath. The desire for it tingled now in the fleshiest parts of me — my thighs, my belly. I wondered whether I could take just a little, like soaking my feet. Then I might go down to the parlor, all relaxed, and look into the viewer again, holding it near a candle to make the Italian sunshine seem real. Maybe that would make me feel sleepy and good.

I had an image of a middle-aged woman, coming down from her attic hideaway, wandering about a fine house in her nightgown. She looked like me, twenty years hence.

I sat up and almost shrieked. One of the shutters slammed into the window frame. The wind had picked up, bringing the sounds of men shouting and horses squealing. I ran to the window. The first fat drops of rain fell on my hands. I leaned out to feel them splash on my eyelids and trickle into my mouth, soft and warm and tasting of the sea.

In the next instant, I was reaching under my bed. I pulled out my trunk and shuffled through the rest of my sketches, finding finally the portfolio with Jeffrey's settlement. Mum was right; it was too much money to keep at home. All at once the thought of it made me sick with worry. I leafed through it, counting. It was a good amount of money, enough to rent a couple of rooms, or even a suite in a different neighborhood. Maybe Quincy, or Malden. A small place with a gas burner and a private bath.

I pushed my hair from my eyes and looked again at the sketches around me. I had a thought that made me shake, that made the floor tilt. When I stood, the shutters banged again.

The house creaked in the wind. The floors and stairwells popped as if with restless footsteps. The rain hissed against the windows, sounding just like the rustle of a skirt.

THE RAIN STOPPED before dawn. It looked to be another stifling day. Once we reached the harbor, I paid the cab driver to go and purchase my tickets for me. I sat alone in the glass-windowed cab, watching the sky change from charcoal to a dull, crimson-streaked pus color. The horse snorted wearily. I peeled off my gloves and opened the window, meaning to wave the man down, to call him back. *There's been a mistake. I'm not well. Take me back. I'm so sorry for your trouble.*

But he returned, sweating and huffing, and then he was opening the door and saying, "If you please," because he knew you mustn't say *hurry up* to a woman in an expensive-looking hat. And then there was the taut, shuddering walkway like a trampoline and the sounds of whistles and bells and seagulls sobbing just over my head.

My tickets would bring me all the way to Venice. I lay on the bed in my tiny cabin, clutching the mattress as the ship's engines fired up.

Chapter
Two

I STAYED BELOW when we called in New York, listening to
the passengers board, venturing to the deck only after we left the
harbor. The New York buildings were taller than those in Boston —
a fortress of smoky blue and peacock green. The pier receded until
only the white waving handkerchiefs were visible, like a flock of
frantic tethered birds. Children raced and hooted along the deck,
ribbons flying. They pointed down to the steerage decks, where
immigrant women sat placidly in the sunlight, nursing their babies.

A clicking noise started beside me and I turned to see a man
with a kinematograph camera, its lens wide as a spooked eye. He
turned its crank, waving at me with his free hand.

"Aw, no, stay where you are," he insisted. "Such a rum scene.
The Statue of Liberty and a pretty woman looking out to sea."

I retreated to my room. For the next five days I dosed myself
steadily, only wandering out in the mornings, half-stupefied, for
breakfast in the coffee-room. The weather was wild. I'd packed a
little heroin, a bottle of Mrs. Winslow's Soothing Syrup, and some
paregoric that I'd been given in the hospital. I took so much
medicine that when I lay back and closed my eyes, the bed
dissolved beneath me.

On the sixth day, a pounding at the cabin door woke me. "Miss
Larkin, Miss Larkin! We're boarding soon." I opened one eye. A
blade of topaz sunlight lay across my bed. I rolled over to sleep for
just a little while longer. The pounding started again, more
insistently. I sat up and bathed my eyes, then gathered up my trunk
and grip.

I clanged up the stairwell and noticed with a start that night
had fallen. The passengers stood pressed together, unnaturally
docile, and a current of anxiety ran through the dark air. I strained
to see beyond the crowd. Were we really that close to land? But
where were the noises of the city, the pier? My eyes still ached for
sleep; I rubbed them with my palms.

Finally, the crowd rocked forward. We disembarked onto a

bleak yard, then went on to a hall that smelled of vinegar and sulfur, where steel fences separated us like cattle. I showed my passport and customs documents to a thin young boy in an oddly ornate uniform. He bowed his head and waved me forward; I saw others boarding a flat steamboat.

Ah, a *vaporetto*. I remembered Adele's voice, reading aloud to me from Baedeker's Guide. We were on one of the outlying islands. I boarded quickly, squeezing through the perfumed shoulders. The water was tranquil and satiny, seeming to slant upwards to the city. I'd expected Venice to appear as a burst of light—the Salute, the domes of San Marco's. Yet as we neared the city, the shapes emerged soft-lit, bulging like reflections in a rounded glass. Motor-launches sped around us, and sandoli emerged from the blackness, lanterns swinging. Gay, dark-eyed children waved up at us, offering candy and souvenirs.

We landed just before midnight. As soon as my boots touched the Venice pavement, a chill went through me as if I'd stepped on a block of ice. I looked around, rubbing my shoulders, unsure where to go. The alleyways formed an impenetrable maze. In place of roads, there were only ink-dark canals. No motorcars, no trolleys, not a single horse.

I walked only a few paces and stopped in the first hotel I found, where a pale girl with long black ringlets led me up from the lobby to my room, chatting languidly in English all the while. It occurred to me I was not an anomaly here. The Venice tourist business was a play of mechanized clockwork figures, and once I slid into a track, I would glide along with everyone else.

The bed smelled of bacon and had curling red hairs strewn over its pillow. I left the lamp turned up to scare away cockroaches, wrapped myself in my mohair shawl, and fell on the coverlet.

"Did I really do it?" I mumbled into the pillow. "Am I really here?"

I slept for maybe an hour, then woke in a crystalline fog. The lamp had burned out. When I sat up, the moon shone full in my face. The city was perfectly still and silent, as if we'd sunk into the sea. I got up and cut a few pages in my journal to sketch some ideas for a painting, but my eyes stung in the weak light; I finally lay back and gazed out at the mist again. If I watched it long enough I saw shapes in it, seaweed and shadows of giant oysters. I imagined the mist hardening at sunrise and then settling all around like glitter.

A breeze nudged the white curtains as I fell asleep again. "Did I really...?"

THE MACHINE OF the tourist business served me well the next day. The girl at the front desk seemed to anticipate my request for help in finding rooms to rent, and within hours I met a middle-aged, blue-veiled woman in the hotel lobby. Her English was so heavily accented that she sounded like someone in a burlesque. She introduced herself with a small curtsey—Signora Orazio—then took my arm and led me out to Campo Manin.

I wondered if it were a religious holiday. The air teemed with a cunning, deliberate sort of silence. A man stood by the wellhead and played a violin; the melody was pure but faint, as if the catacomb of alleyways drew the sound into itself.

As I followed Signora Orazio, I tried to memorize the street signs: *Calle Mandola, R. Terra Assassini, Calle Madonna*. Were there only *calli* here, no *strade*? The alleys twisted into ever smaller passageways, some that only had room for us to walk single file, our skirts catching on the damp stone walls. Signora Orazio was asking about me uneasily. When I told her *widow* she seemed satisfied, but she scowled at *artist*. Still, she walked me to a medieval-looking building with a front of faded brickwork and peach-colored plaster.

"Two storeys," she said, leaning her shoulder into the front door. She had to push three times before it opened.

Just inside the door was a miniature vestibule, and beyond it a stairwell leading up. Signora Orazio led me off to the left, into a dank oubliette of a kitchen. There was a rusty old oven that I decided was mostly notional, with pans and tongs that resembled torture devices. A tidy mattress was tucked under the window by the stone sink, with a homemade quilt—a maid's living space. A back door led to an outside privy.

I nodded and started up the stairs, impatient to see the second floor. She showed me the bedroom, where an ebony cross hung over the bed. The bedroom walls were painted an odd, pearlescent yellow; it would be like sleeping inside a closed buttercup.

Signora Orazio smiled as she showed me the parlor, with its windows overlooking a canal and a footbridge. In one of its casements sat a window-box, thick with untrimmed mint and oregano. The parlor's six walls were hung with panels of ashen silk, and in the center of each panel was a painting of a peacock strutting alone in a golden ring. There was a sofa, a sideboard, and a desk, all faded and smooth as driftwood. The ceiling was high, freshly painted white, with one gaslit chandelier that I could barely reach.

I took the rooms without any further discussion, and my landlady gleefully hurried away with three months' rent. I spent the evening cleaning out the spiderwebs and mopping up dust from the furniture. When the last rays of sunset washed over the floor, the rooms filled with pale copper light.

I sat on the parlor's sofa and decided this would be my studio. My hands tingled. I wanted to begin work right away, but where should I start? I knew I could never sit still, so I decided to go out and look for things to sketch.

I explored the alleyways — the *calli* — that I hoped to know someday as a kind of home. I tried to make myself invisible in a soot-colored veil, but no one seemed to mind another awkward foreigner. I heard more languages than I could recognize. I gazed around, feeling my lashes brush against my veil like trapped moths.

The square — *campo* — at the end of my alley was filled with café tables. I sat under an awning, ordered a glass of wine, and began to draw. One slender blonde ballet-girl saw me sketching and smiled, holding herself still for a while so that I could work. I caught something of the tired innocence in her grey eyes, and the glint of scarlet lamplight over her sinewy shoulders. With her stern jaw, she reminded me of a virgin martyr in an old French tapestry. I wondered for a moment whether I could introduce myself and offer her the drawing. A few other girls joined her and she left, still smiling feebly.

I tried to sketch a bit more, but I had to quit the café when the men wouldn't leave me alone. Night was falling, and one by one, the women retreated indoors. A beetle-browed young man grabbed my hand and I made a sound exactly like a startled chicken.

I could never understand why people felt the need to lean into my face and tell me I was lovely, with that same anxious glee you see in parents at Christmas: *But you're beautiful, dear. Isn't it wonderful? And what do you plan to do with it? Come up with something, quickly. Christmas doesn't last all year!*

I felt acutely foolish. What would I do here? Would I just end up going home in a month? What a hilarious story that would make. *She really went crazy, the old fucking bat. All the way to Venice. They shouldn't have let her keep that money under the bed.*

I lay down without taking powders and felt my heart pump unevenly. I imagined my blood growing hot and bright, bringing a rush of images to my mind. When I was careless enough to close my eyes, I saw again Jeff's blood spattered on the carpet. Those drops must have seared my retinas. I thought of Adele's screams, and then his, and then the sudden silence that sucked up all the sound in the world.

My mind seemed to swell until it stung the inside of my skull. The only comfort was to claw red crescents into my upper arms. No, I mustn't. Stop.

I went to the window and hugged myself in the dark. The city had gone quiet. I didn't realize I was saying *stop* aloud until a dark girl in a poppy-colored dress stopped walking and stared up at me.

The torchlight washed over her eyes until they shone like a cat's.

Chapter
Three

THAT NIGHT I walked in my sleep.

I'd thought that being in a new place would cure me of sleepwalking, that at least the unfamiliar doorways and corridors would check me before I wandered too far. I dreamt I was walking underwater. A painted dolphin swam by.

I woke outside, with my hands resting on an iron balustrade. My dressing gown puffed around my ankles. My braid slid down my forearm. I gazed in confusion at the water, listening to a distressed hiss that I soon realized was my own breathing. I turned. I was only a few feet from my front door. I ran inside and locked myself in my bedroom.

I sat shaking until dawn, when the light finally calmed me. I felt better once the day warmed and the canals filled with people. I resolved to ask my landlady about hiring a girl to do a little housework. She could sleep on the pallet in the kitchen, keeping me company at night.

I promised myself it would be a good day, as I got up to dress. I wanted to go to the Seagroves Gallery first, just to see how it looked. I had a useless map; after walking down five dead ends, I asked for directions in a hotel lobby, got lost again, and finally paid a little girl to lead me there.

The gallery was closed. The sign read that it wouldn't open until noon, yet when I walked to a side door, Amy Seagroves was there, overseeing a new delivery. I recognized her from the newspaper photographs, the Society Section that Mum always pored over. I approached, girding myself, doing my best to look lighthearted and slightly bored, like any other rich tourist.

"Are you staying long in Venice?" Amy asked. She was surprisingly tall in person, with a wide mouth, narrow eyes, and way of wrinkling her forehead in regretful distaste. Her hair was a deep, hennaed red. I looked like such a shopgirl beside her, in my serge skirt, my cotton gloves.

"Yes, I've moved here. I'm a painter." It was the first time I'd said that to someone here in Venice and I watched her carefully. She smiled. I supposed she was used to meeting American artists.

"That's fine." She had that drowsy, gracious New York drawl. "Do you really paint? You've studied?"

"Yes, I studied at the Museum School in Boston." She blinked at this and I felt smug. "I had a painting shown with the Copley Society once." I didn't tell her of the illustrations for a milliner's shop, or the children's serial.

"Lovely." She faced me full on for the first time and let her eyes travel towards my shoes, then back up to my face. "Mm-hm. Do promise me you'll let me see one of your pieces."

We strolled to the patio at the back of her gallery, where a shaking young maid brought espresso and lemonade. Amy lit a cigarette and held one out to me. It had been years since I'd smoked.

"I didn't bring a portfolio," I told her. I smoked uncertainly at first, in fussy little puffs. "I'd planned to create a new body of work here, to be honest. I needed a new perspective. You know, Boston..." My voice rose. I fidgeted with my collar, then willed my hands back into my lap.

She nodded vaguely. "Lots of artists here, you know. But that's all right." She looked at me again. In the shade, her eyes were an earthy, russet brown, the color of fallen pine needles. "Lots of patrons, too. Fine place for you to be."

Her patio had a view of the Grand Canal, like a tinted movie spreading before us. Terns skimmed above the ruffled water. As we chatted, she studiously avoided asking me about my family, my history. I surely had the nervous, brightly-polished sheen of the lower classes. Perhaps she was afraid I'd launch into a life story full of lousy rooms and ruined eyes and drunken fathers.

"You do portraits then?" She lit another cigarette.

"Yes," I lied, glancing around us. I hadn't seen a single still-life or landscape in the gallery.

"Thank God." She rolled her eyes as the white smoke curled round her face. "You have no idea how many amateurs come here with their seascapes or postcard views of the city. Portraits are what sell, lately. You can hire models at one of the theaters."

I'd wanted to ask about other galleries but when I took another sip of espresso she said, "Twelve-thirty already, is it?"

I left quickly, exhaling. Would she really want to see something I painted? I decided to act as if I believed it. I bought paints and spent the afternoon mixing them. The colors were oddly bland, like overcooked food. The only one that inspired me was the red. It seemed to grow warmer as I stirred.

I thought of Amy's suggestion. Could I hire a model to come

here, to my studio? Maybe I should buy a mirror, and paint myself. I imagined trying to sell twenty images of a pale woman with flat hair and a mopey expression. If I planned to be a painter, I would have to somehow manage hiring a model. I sat down and wrote a notice to post at the theater. In English, of course. I'd have to be able to speak with her.

I DREADED THE night but forced myself to lie down at a normal time. I was so desperate to sleep, yet each time I closed my eyes I heard Jeff's voice screaming, *how could you?* It wouldn't stop. *How could you?* I pulled my pillow over my head and tried to shrink into myself.

A moment later, I took three doses of sleeping powder.

THE NEXT DAY I slept late, waking only as the San Fantin bells struck ten o'clock. Pigeons shuffled and cooed along my windowsill. I'd slept so deeply that I hadn't moved at all in the night, and my back had left a sweaty imprint on the bedsheets.

At noon, on those hot days, everyone seemed to disappear inside. The sunlight was fierce, pounding over the stones. The only sound was the abrupt unfurling of my skirt with each step.

I found the Hotel des Artistes first, and made my way past it to La Fenice theater, an upright, severe building with a gate of iron spears. I'd expected someone to be on hand—a guard, maybe. I wandered round the side, where a door stood open. A clammy breeze came from the doorway, as if from the mouth of a cave. I let myself be pulled inside.

My footsteps echoed before me. Cats scuffled in the shadows. Every few moments I heard laughter, distant and muted. I followed it down a black hallway, past a row of open rooms, then up a stairwell to a felt-covered door. The laughter came from the other side. As I pushed through, a wide echoing space opened around me. I stopped short, letting my parasol drop.

I was in the wings of the stage. The inside of the theater was trimmed in crimson and gold. The box seats were a vast birdcage covered in sugar and jewels. On the frescoed ceiling, fat white children pouted obscenely. Stagehands chattered unseen in the framework above me. The footlights burned low.

I stepped again and my heel rapped the floor, loud as a gunshot. The laughter went quiet. I turned back to the doorway I'd come from, lifting my skirts. In that cool, empty air, sounds echoed so strangely that it seemed I could hear breathing and laughter right behind me. I wondered whether someone would see me and call a guard.

"Are you lost, ma'am?"

I turned and almost screamed. A girl stood not three feet from me. I covered my heart and she smiled gently, lowering her chin.

"Sorry, I didn't know," I said. "I'm leaving." I wondered how she knew to speak English with me.

"Have you come for an audition?" She curtsied. She was nearly as tall as I, but small-boned as a child. Her tilting eyes were so black they seemed to absorb rather than reflect light. Her mouth seemed to tilt, too—or that might have been her smile. Her hair was a sweaty mess, with pins poking out as if trying to work themselves free. She wore a ballet-girl's costume: a cotton shirtwaist and a grubby tarlatan that fell just above her knees. A red velvet ribbon was tied snugly round her throat.

"I needed—" I began. "I wanted to post this notice somewhere."

She stepped forward and held out her hand. "I'm Rusala."

When I took her hand I was able to talk. "I'm an artist. I mean, a painter. I was going to post a notice because I'm in need of a model."

"Oh?" Her eyebrows shot up, and I handed the notice to her. She gave it back to me without a glance. "Perfect. Perfect. I could do it if you like. I'm a good model."

She spoke with a strange, unpredictable accent, sometimes English, sometimes altogether foreign, the kind of accent I imagined someone would have after traveling around Europe for years. Her smile grew wider. She had a dimple in her left cheek.

"I see." I sounded businesslike. "Could you start tomorrow?"

"Tomorrow's Sunday? Certainly. Two hours of posing for ten lire."

She rose on her tiptoes, suddenly restless, glancing up. All the hidden voices had gone quiet.

"All right then." I turned away.

"Wait!" Rusala shouted. I turned back, and she was hovering six feet off the floor. Her feet swung softly. "Won't you tell me where you live? Oof! Wait!"

She scowled upwards, jerking like a spider at the end of a thread. A creaking sound came from the rafters.

"Wait! I'm still talking to the lady!" She struggled and thrashed. More laughter came from above. When I walked underneath her, I saw a few boys turning a crank, one of them guiding Rusala's wires in his meaty fist. They caught my eye and laughed even harder. Rusala scolded them in English, then in Italian.

"What's your name anyway?" she called down to me. A few

more boys appeared at the edge of the stage, moving potted trees out of the way.

"Katie. Katherine."

"Katie Katherine, wait for a little while. Would you care to watch us rehearse? Go on. Go down into the orchestra pit."

I looked up at her again. Her voice sounded sincere enough, but her throat trembled with suppressed laughter. As I clambered down and found a seat, a few more girls emerged from the wings and padded around for a while, bundled in their shawls, frowning at the scenery and arguing with the boys.

I sat in the semi-darkness. The lamps on stage were raised only slightly, giving the air a feeble green tint like the bottom of a lake. Someone counted purposefully and started to sing: *yee bump bahhh*...Then five girls dropped from the ceiling, one after the other. Each dove to her nadir, closing her eyes as the wires caught her and drew her back up.

There was a loud snap and one of the girls kicked forward. Her wires had broken. They let her down in clumsy, painful jerks. The other girls were lowered more slowly, and some boys came stomping out of the wings.

The ballet-girls wandered off, griping. Rusala took a cigarette from a blond boy's pocket and lit it, slumping down to sit before a footlight. The light there, so close to her skin, was harsh as radium. She raised her head and scanned the dark house, puffing and squinting. She couldn't see me.

"Katie?"

"Thank you. I ought to be going." When I stood, my chair squeaked back. I made my way towards her, feeling along the chair backs.

"You ought to see it when it's finished. We throw handfuls of glitter, and there are silk rose petals falling all around the singers' heads." She was frowning, turning her head in the cloud of smoke, but she smiled when she caught sight of me. "It's just that we need to work all this out before the general rehearsals."

"Aren't you frightened when they lift you like that?"

She scratched at her neck. The brighter light showed the tendons working painfully in her throat. She had mauve shadows under her eyes. "No! Vitya and the boys know what they're doing. It's rather like taking a ride in a carriage, or sliding down a snowy hill. You just enjoy yourself."

She swung her legs over the edge of the stage and drummed her heels. Her shoes were bright but her stockings were laddered and smudged.

"Maybe I'll come and see the performance," I said. She cocked her head and sucked at her cigarette. She held it the way working people do, cupped securely under her palm. I didn't like the way she stared at my clothes. I pulled off my gloves.

"And so, where do you live?" she said. She didn't need to speak so softly.

I still held my folded-up notice. I tried to pass it up to her but she closed her eyes, saying, "Just tell me, I've a good memory."

"An alley off Frezzeria," I said. "I think the house number must be 23. Anyway the house beside me has a 22 painted on it. It's two doors down from a second-hand book shop, and there's a jasmine-bush and a café chantant called The Daisy."

"Yes, I think I know that area, not far from the Hotel des Artistes?" She grinned. "Do you like the theater, then?"

Without waiting for me to answer, she slid down from the stage and stood near me. The cigarette smoke was sweet and thick, scented with cloves. I had the odd feeling that she was going to snatch something from me and I clutched my purse tighter.

Instead she curtsied with a flourish, and held out her hand. "Noon tomorrow."

NOT LONG AFTER I arrived home, a girl rang my bell. She said she'd been sent by the landlady. I supposed Signora Orazio had anticipated my desire for a maid. As the girl spoke, she gazed at my feet and took off her grey felt hat. Her voice was low and stumbling, although her English seemed proficient enough. She was Slavic-looking, with a wide heart-shaped face and hair so pale it glinted with silver and green lights. I guessed she was one of the girls who came here from Dalmatia to find work. Her eyes were porcelain blue. She said her name was Lovorka.

She ducked her head shyly when I tried to question her. In any case, I didn't know what to ask. Once I finished showing her the house, she disappeared into the kitchen, evidently pleased enough with the makeshift living quarters. I had the feeling she enjoyed solitude. We'd get along fine.

That evening I mixed paints in my parlor, reminding myself to call it a studio. The sunlight in Venice didn't fall in neat squares, as it did back home; it crept like a vapor. When Lovorka opened all the windows, I heard the sea rolling gently, a constant heartbeat.

Lovorka went downstairs and watered the geraniums in the courtyard, singing to herself.

I counted out my budget. I decided that if I economized hard, I had enough for nine months. I tapped my fingers, worrying, wondering whether I should have hired a maid after all.

I gazed at the ceiling. I imagined a quiet, hidden life in Venice, one so filled with light that all the sharp edges would dissolve. It would be a formal kind of life, arranged around the rituals of painting, the café where I'd have my lunch, the café where I'd have my supper, and sleeping powders at night.

After a great pain, a formal feeling comes. I'd be ceremonious and remote, no more extremes of elation and pain.

When I lay down that night, scrubbed and dosed and in a fresh nightgown, I saw only the soft-lit flying girls in the theater, with the darkness beyond them so deep I felt myself tilting towards it.

Chapter
Four

IN THE NEXT morning's post, I received a little fan made of gold vellum and blood-red lacquered wood. I unfolded it and read: *Mlle Amy Seagroves requests the pleasure of your company at a very very very casual supper on Friday, the twenty-first of September, 1912.* The address given was the gallery itself.

Lovorka must have read it before she brought it up to me. I put it aside straight away, as I wanted to resume sketching, but she found reasons to stay around my room, rearranging things, pushing a rag around the spotless windowsill. Her gait was hesitant, as if her body were uniquely fragile. I sensed that she was waiting for my reaction. I ignored her until she finally opened the wardrobe and asked which gown she should prepare for the supper.

I put down my pencil. "I don't know," I said. "This?" I looked at my lap. "Grey is always smart."

She cleared her throat, turning back to the wardrobe. "I can sew," she said. "Ma'am. I can—how do you say it? Mend, and fix things." She described a few foulards with her hand. "It's not for another week. I've plenty of time."

I managed to get some more work done that afternoon, despite her rummaging through my underclothes and stockings. Normally I would be annoyed with someone going over my things, but she seemed so genuinely contented that I couldn't bring myself to stop her. She stood up once, laughing with delight, her eyes so strangely innocent that I wondered for a moment whether she were simple-minded. She'd found one of Adele's pink ribbons. It must have been in the very bottom of my old trunk. She brought it to me and held it against my wrist.

I WOKE IN the pre-dawn light. Lovorka stood over me, her eyes huge and about to shatter.

I sat up. I was still dressed, even my shoes. I had fallen asleep sketching. Papers lay over my lap and chest. My blouse was streaked with charcoal. My throat felt rough, and the air rang faintly.

"Was I screaming?" I looked up at her. Her mouth worked silently. She grabbed handfuls of her nightgown.

"I was, wasn't I?" I said. Hairpins spilled across my pillow like dead insects.

"A dream?" Lovorka whispered.

"I'm sorry. You must have been terrified. That happens sometimes, if I don't take enough medicine."

She only turned toward the window, as if still expecting to see an intruder.

"Listen," I said. "I've had a bad year. I'm a widow."

She nodded. I heard her swallow. A cat meowed outside.

"But what's more is—I had a sort of illness. A problem with nerves. I was in a hospital." I felt sick, suddenly. Pain spiked through my temple and I winced.

"And," I continued, "and so I have to take these medicines, and try to keep myself calm. But I promise I am all right." I reached uncertainly for her forearm.

Her lower lip still trembled. Her forehead was incredibly white. "But you sounded so..."

"I know."

"—so angry. You scream, 'How could you, how could you.'"

"I know. Yes, Lovorka." I spoke more sharply that I'd meant to.

We both went quiet. There was the distant splash of boats, a dog barking, a girl's ringing laugh.

LOVORKA HAD A free day on Sunday. She left early, leaving me at my paints. I found an old cracked dish to use as a palette, and set to work stretching canvases. The morning sunlight made the room glow silver and teal, like a Fabergé egg.

Rusala knocked just as the noon bells faded. She looked smaller than I remembered her, nodding stiffly as I let her in and brought her up to the studio. Her gown was violet sateen, with a low neckline and short puffed sleeves. Her dark hair was braided with a messy parting; in the sunlight it shone with saffron lights, like old polished wood. She caught my eyes for a moment, then looked down as a blush flared in her cheeks. Her bravado of the day before had given way to restive bashfulness; she glanced around the small room as if in awe.

I was blushing too. I could feel it. I'd painted models before, of course. In the Museum School's summer lessons, we'd had models in every day. Men and women, mature and young. But that was always in a class, with at least ten other students, and a wide expanse of clean light between me and the model.

I willed myself to be gracious and blasé with Rusala, pretending I was used to having strange girls come undress for me. I was a foreigner after all. It was my job to be eccentric.

"How should I be?" she said, leaning against one of the silk panels to unbutton her boots.

"I thought I'd do some pencil sketches first. Just lie however you usually do." I sat straight-backed before the terrifying blank paper. Just at the edge of my vision, she stretched her arms above her head, and the purple shape of her changed to white, then gold. I listened to her climb up on the couch.

She sighed deeply, a little theatrically. "How's this?"

I looked up. She lay on her stomach, her ankles resting on one arm of the couch, her cheek cushioned on her forearms. Her back was slim and tense as a cat's, its long slope ending in a dimpled vale and then a swell of buttocks. Her legs were tapered, covered in soft black down. Her feet looked knobby and scraped as a scullery maid's hands.

"You did mean all bare, right?" she asked, and when I looked to her face, it was red again. Her shoulders were hitched up.

"Yes." I swallowed, knowing it made me look clumsy and strange. "That's just fine. I'll make some sketches and maybe start to paint. Relax. I usually work with one pose. I won't ask you to move about."

I took up a pencil, pared it, and started to sketch. First, the bias of her neck. The line of her cheek, very round, almost plump. Her eyes surprised me. I'd expected a ballet-girl to have cheap eyes, clear and empty, that anyone could look into. Not these dark eyes that pushed your gaze back at you.

She cleared her throat, watching me. I kept sketching. The hollow of her shoulder ...

"Are you a famous painter, then?" she said. "You don't mind if I talk?"

"Of course. Only please don't move too much." I whispered the last part, lost in concentration. Her half-hidden ear. I must have been scowling, or pushing out my tongue as I worked, for she suddenly laughed.

"No, really," I said. "See, your face changes shape when you laugh."

"I'm sorry. Now I'm perfectly still. Do people pay you to paint?"

"I've sold a few things, but that was nearly five years ago."

"I love art," she said. "You look like an El Greco. Yes, you do!

With your long face, your melancholy aspect."

"An El Greco?"

"You learn a great deal about art when you're posing," she said. "But the more I learn about—oh, form, depth, relief, all of that—the more I'm certain that it's the life within a painting that counts. Its heat."

"Mm," I said. My new pencils were soft and too smudgy.

"Sometimes," she went on, her head still cushioned on her arms, her blush fading, "I like to go to a gallery and stand before the paintings. I know it's good art when I can feel the painting, the heat or the vibrations coming from it."

"Vibrations?"

"That sounds buggy, I know. Yet it's true. Once—oh, sorry." She swung her ankles into the air, then flinched and laid them still again. "Once I saw a Van Gogh in Paris. Some bumpy mess, all lurid and greasy-looking. But when I stood close, oh, this heat, all through my bones, the heat of melting jewels."

"I'm doing the feet now, please keep them still. I never thought of it that way. You do know a lot about painting." I paused to look at her face, so she'd know I wasn't mocking her. "Really. Most people see it as expensive wallpaper."

"That's why I love being a model. I've learned so much, just lying on a couch listening to the masters lecture. People talk as if I weren't there." She giggled and her feet jumped. "Sorry. And I learn all the gossip, too."

"What? Painters' gossip?"

"Every idle rich man—and woman, nowadays—goes through an artistic period. They take a tour to Italy and settle here because Venice is the *gamest* city. There's almost always a salon of them gathering to paint or sketch. And they need models." I glanced again at her face. Her eyelids were heavy.

"I used to think that the rich never gave a thought about money," she continued more softly. Her eyes fluttered closed. "They hardly need to, right? But that's not so. Rich people talk about money *all* the time. Who's inherited what, who's bought which company, who's invested where and how much they've earned. They're rabid."

She went quiet. I was drawing the soft lines of her temple when she suddenly opened her eyes again.

"Are you rich?" she asked.

"Speaking of gossip."

"I'm sorry." She watched my pencil. "Shall I move now?"

"No. In fact, I like this pose. I think I'll start painting. Are you cold?"

"No, I'm warm." She rubbed her cheek against the cloth. "I

could fall asleep."

"You may, if you like."

Her breathing softened. I primed one of my canvases and set down a rough outline of her form, using first a dark pomegranate red, then blending it with yellow until I found a champagne color. As the afternoon lengthened, a patch of sunlight grew across the floor towards the couch. When she felt its warmth on her thighs, she murmured in her sleep.

I was putting the paints away when I heard her sharp intake of breath. She sat on her knees, blinking. Her face was marked from the cushion. I didn't look below. She stretched, grinning and clenching her fists.

I got up to open the window. The air was heavy with paint fumes. When I turned back to her she was fastening her gown. She looked shy again, with her gaze trained downwards, her foot nudging the edge of the carpet. I handed her an envelope of cash and she folded it so quickly that it crackled.

"Shall I come again?" she asked. "I don't live too far away."

"At the Hotel des Artistes?"

"No! Lord, I could only afford to live there if I spent all day on my back. No, I live just one bridge away from the Hotel des Artistes, in the grand boarding house known as Hotel B."

"I see." I wiped my hands on a flannel. "I guess I ought to paint some other models, too. For variety. But come tomorrow so I can finish this."

She said "yes" so awkwardly I half expected her to curtsey. She ran down the stairs before I could speak again.

I had to sit down after she'd gone. The room seemed different somehow, a subtle difference like music changing key. I shook my head and traced my canvas. I wondered what it must be like to be a ballet-girl. I thought it must be a life full of exhaustion, with moments of brilliance like mismatched beads on a thread: performances, suppers, unexpected gifts. I imagined her returning to her rooms, perhaps eating some warmed-over spaghetti with her pals. *A nice enough Yankee girl. I talked a bit about art and got some sleep, not a bad day's work! Pretty swank.*

It felt good to meet others. I imagined that my formal life could have room for friends, for walks, for faces I might recognize in the street. Of course they'd be peaceful, occasional friendships, with plenty of clear space in between. I flinched to think of how heedless and warm we used to be back home, crushing together until we seemed to share flesh, until any separation, however brief, left us frantic.

I took my last spoonful of Soothing Syrup and spent the entire afternoon mixing paints to get the color of Rusala's skin.

Everything I tried looked dull and artificial on the cloth. Her skin was the color of brandied sugar, with an amber glow in the sunlight. Yet there was a luminescence to it, tints of violet and pallid blue. Her skin needed the paints of the Renaissance, with their silver dust and crushed jewels and poisonous minerals. I wondered whether the wings of a beetle or the skin of a goldfish would make the flesh seem more alive.

I kept lifting my head to look around the room. The sofa was still rumpled. What was it about her that kept distracting me? I thought again of her face, stained with the city's colors. It was her desire, I realized. I rested my hands on my knees. It was her desire, her ambition, that I'd felt. She was holding her desire close, nursing it, looking each day for the beginning of her story, the story that would rise all at once like a swollen river and bear her somewhere.

I felt her desire pulling at me. I was sure that she scrutinized each new person she met, wondering whether this one... or this one...

She still believed in the delight of being alive, the animal delight of desire, of possibility, of stories beginning.

LATER THAT NIGHT, after falling asleep for a few quick minutes, I woke myself up, barking with sobs.

I saw Adele's body, and Jeff's, lying on the floor, heavy and still as sleeping children. But the memory was fading already. A chill, moldy fog crept over them, leaching all their color. Their greyness now tinted every object in my world. My own skin.

I'd hoped that they would haunt me, that Adele's voice would cling and whisper through my hair. Instead there was only the sound of my own breathing.

I wanted to tell Rusala that all hopes ended in this, that desire became want and want became lack.

The water-jug was heavy and slick, wanting to jostle itself out of my hands. I spilled half of my valerian and almost licked it from the floor. I watched its ashy powders dissolve in my tooth-glass. I took more than twice the dosage, then sat counting breaths.

Chapter
Five

A WEEK PASSED, with tightly-laced days and plenty of powder at night. Rusala came to pose twice, still making an effort at gaiety and seeming nonplussed at my inability to respond. On Friday I slept until noon, and even then the drugs were so thick in me that I could only lie, half-dozing, half-dreaming I was underwater.

I felt a hand on my cheek and started. Lovorka stood over the bed, smiling indulgently. "Coffee?"

She left me sitting stupidly, propped up by pillows. I had to drink the whole pot of coffee before I could open both eyes.

When I was awake enough, I rubbed my throbbing shoulders and got back to painting. I was afraid to stop working. A feeling was coming over me, the old feeling I used to get just before a painting took shape in my mind. A sort of tingling in my chest, that spread to my fingertips. I felt like a lightning rod at times like this; every thought I had, every color and shadow I saw, went through me and into the painting.

As the day wore on, Lovorka kept asking when I'd be finished, when I might begin dressing for the Seagroves supper. She stopped at my studio, even after I closed the door. She seemed to think I couldn't hear her crouch at the keyhole. She'd mended one of my older gowns, a pale cream muslin with ruffles along the neckline. It reminded me of a milk-maid costume. She'd promised to do my hair too, "nice and poufy."

At six o'clock I heard her purposefully mounting the staircase. I opened my door and tried my best to look delighted, to feign a genuine concern about my bracelets, about the ribbons of my hat.

I HIRED A gondola. I wasn't sure that I could find the gallery on foot, and I was terrified of becoming lost and wandering through the thyme-scented alleys as evening fell, a nervous milk-maid in tight slippers. I settled into the boat's plush black seat and watched the bank recede as we cast into the Grand Canal. In the fading apricot-gold of sunset, the moorish palaces seemed entirely unreal, buildings painted as if for a pantomime. I couldn't imagine people inhabiting them, sleeping, sweating, or quarrelling in those blue shadows. I wanted to push along forever, but soon we edged across the current to a white palazzo. The Seagroves Gallery looked more imposing from this vantage. A semicircle of ivory pillars stood in its garden, surrounding an iron statue of a pudgy little dolphin. I shaded my eyes and squinted, but couldn't see any guests.

"Seagroves?" the gondolier said, turning to grin at me. His molars were all gold; when he smiled the flash of it hurt my eyes.

"Yes." I let him help me to the bank, over the steps covered with velvety algae.

I wandered into the garden, a grove of olive and fig trees surrounded in rustling bougainvillea. Half-rotted lemons covered the path. The gallery's patio was filled with servants, laughing raucously as they worked. They were shocked at the sight of me and stood giggling until the oldest of them, a slim white-haired man, led me to a parlor.

Amy burst in, her hair wild. She wore pajamas of red Chinese silk.

"Miss Larkin! Katherine! Bless your heart, right on time." She smiled easily. "I ought to have warned you that nothing here starts before nine, no matter what the invitation says."

She seemed so changed, so full of energy. She stared at my hat as I drew it off.

"Sweet as pie, aren't you? C'mon." She opened the door for me. "Sit with me while I get dressed."

"You live here, then?" I asked. "Right in the gallery?"

"Of course, when we're not in New York."

Her room was at the top of a spiral staircase, a cosy mirador with windows over the darkening lagoon. Furred green cloth covered the walls. A few dog-eared Ouida novels lay on the floor.

She sat at her vanity table. I settled on the windowsill behind her.

"You look lovely," I offered. A vase of carnations sat just before the mirror, their petals tinting her face pink.

"This will be a good evening." She pawed through a drawer and took out a handful of jars and brushes. "Everyone's back in Venice this week. All the artists who matter. The Russians. Greta Morgan, of course, the old hambone. I've heard she's fallen heels over head for someone, all too literally. I still haven't found out who."

She paused and glanced at me. "What a sweet little gown on

you. It makes you look seventeen." Then, without waiting for me to answer, she started singing to herself: "*One and two and get on top, now...*" She snapped her fingers. She forgot that one of her hands still held a brush, and when it dropped in her lap she cursed heartily.

"All right, pardon me, I'm excited," she said. "And I've taken a few sniffs of this." She held up a round green bottle. "My white whale. It's been so god-damned hard to find this season, lord." She dipped her fingers in, drew out a white powdery lump, and rubbed it into her gums. "Mm. Just a tad more. Want some? Pure as Alpine snow."

"Oh, no. God, that makes me too nervous."

She seemed undisturbed. "You'd like some champagne instead?" Then her mood changed abruptly and she scowled at the door. "Lazy bitch-pie. I think she believes that if she acts stupid, she'll get out of working. How long does it take to let out a gown?"

She reached above the mirror and pulled the bell frantically. I heard it clanging far below.

"I'm dismissing her after tonight." She smiled at me, her face sunny again. "Servants here are worse than anywhere else. They're sneaks, too. Shameless. Mark my words."

I cast about for a different topic, finally asking, "Which artists will be here?" I knew I'd recognize some of the names. I wondered how I might mention my old teachers without revealing too much of myself.

"Hell. Whoever shows up. Everyone's an artist lately, anyway. But I've got performers!" She grinned with her perfect, small teeth. She held her head still while she lined her eyes with kohl.

The maid entered, carrying a gown of heavy turquoise silk. She stood awkwardly as Amy finished powdering her cheeks.

"I'd meant to have those Japanese dancers come. They're in Rome right now. Put it down, Mary, there—no, there! And get champagne, quickly. Go! But can you believe they declined? I was in a panic, but there are some dancers from Theatre Slav in Venice, on holiday, and I got a few of them to do *Talqis.*"

"Here?"

"Yes, we make the front hall into a stage. They just perform select scenes. You've seen the ballet, haven't you? You'll love the private version. The costumes, for one thing, are quite different."

She shifted in her seat, humming. The kohl made her eyes look darker, her skin paler. She brushed her russet hair until it puffed and crackled.

The maid came back with a bottle of champagne and poured a glass for each of us. As she did Amy's hair, I sat drinking until my cheeks tingled. Amy rouged her lips heavily and stood, letting

Mary take off her pajamas. She wore no corset, just short drawers
and stockings. When she lifted her arms into the turquoise silk, it
billowed around her. I'd never seen someone dress another adult
before, and I marveled at how patiently Amy stood; she looked
suddenly helpless, almost meek, as Mary crouched behind her and
deftly pushed each button into place.

Once the gown was fastened up, Amy took a breath and came
back to life. "All right, now, go," she said to Mary. "I'm sure they
need help downstairs. Bring us another bottle of champagne. And
oysters."

Amy sat again and turned towards me as Mary left. She closed
one eye and pushed out her lower lip.

"Stand up, Katherine."

"Katie." I stood, carefully. The floor rocked.

"Now, that's a pretty gown. A nice enough color on you. But,
dear." She leaned forward. "No one wears such high collars here.
Not in the evening. And those gloves? No."

She turned up the lamp, then approached me with her palms
upturned innocently.

"You just relax, kid." She squeezed my shoulders and ran to
her wardrobe.

"Wait, Amy, no."

"This red dress." She spoke quickly, almost chirping. "Look at
me. I can't wear red. You, on the other hand..."

She pulled out a satin gown that tinkled with gold beaded
trim. It was a deep shade of scarlet, cool and soothing as the inner
petals of a rose.

"I don't like borrowing things," I said, shrinking back.

"Please. For me." She held its hem near my cheek. "It makes
your skin look alabaster-white. Oh, for God's sake, don't be so
shy!"

Mary entered with another bottle and a plate of steamed
oysters. Amy threw the dress on the bed and took hold of one shell,
bringing it to her lips and smiling.

"Mary, put the dress on her."

I let Mary undress me with her quick fingers. I thought of my
unspeakable corset, patched and yellowed and trimmed with pink
velveteen, but it was too late; I could only close my eyes against the
humiliation as I stepped into the gown. When Mary finished
hooking it, she backed away and watched as Amy brought me to
the mirror.

I frowned. "Absolutely not."

Amy laughed gaily, but I was becoming alarmed. As I turned,
the beaded hem swished against my ankles. It was so snug around
the knees that my gait in it became louche and indolent. The satin

clung to my back and pooled just over my breasts.

"Now you look just wild. Everyone will wonder where I've found you." Amy smiled calmly while Mary brought in the waist with a few basted stitches.

"If it please," Mary stammered, straightening. "People are coming."

"I know, Mary, go on." Amy ran to the window and peered down. The sky was entirely dark now, with only a smudge of cobalt along the horizon. Gondola lanterns flared below us.

"Yes, here they are," she said, leaning out. "Have you met any of these people before?"

"I doubt it."

She looked at me then. "I was thinking your people are probably scholars, Katie, right? Not in society, really, but writers, teachers, maybe?"

"Not quite."

"Who's your father?"

Full of champagne, wrapped like a Christmas present, I felt suddenly bold. "I never met him."

"Oh, all right. Naturally." Amy's laugh was a dry little bark. "And your mother?"

I couldn't stop myself from speaking. I stared at her wide eyes, her fish mouth. I suddenly imagined pushing her away from me. "She had been a chorus girl, but she was a socialist when she met my father."

Amy stopped laughing and sat on the bed. My cheeks were hot. I felt as though something in me had broken, like the spring of a wind-up doll that's finally been turned too tight.

"She met my father during her free-love period," I continued. "He went back to Ireland before she realized she was expecting. And I believe he died there."

Amy covered her mouth.

"Oh, stop tittering," I said. "You suspected!" I heard a weird, sharp edge in my voice and I paused for another sip of champagne. "You knew just by looking at me that I had an interesting past, didn't you?"

"Right." She squinted at me again and I realized she still didn't believe me. "Don't stop there. So your mother raised you all alone, I suppose?"

"I went into the Boston Female Asylum—a girls' home—for several years. That was when my mother went into service."

"A maid? Katie, quit it. You're making this up. You see, I was believing you, but you went too far. That's right out of a novel I read last summer." Amy twisted her stained lips into a smirk. "It's always the quiet ones, isn't it?" She chuckled. "Earnest, bashful

Katie is either a heroine from a sensational novel or a gifted fabulist."

Music rose from the floor below. Amy paled and looked down.

"Good God. You'll stay with me, won't you?" she said. "These people can be terrible. They're my oldest friends, you know, my only friends, but some of the worst fucking people you will see anywhere. How is my hair? Damn that Mary with her pudgy little fingers."

She grabbed her bottle of powder and snorted loudly, then tilted her head back.

As we descended the staircase, she took my arm. A black velvet curtain hung before the entrance to the great hall. We heard laughter on the other side and the rushing footsteps of maids. Amy pinched her cheeks, then pushed my arm from her, suddenly spitting, "Will you stop hanging on me?" She took a step towards the curtain, paused again, and grabbed my wrist. Her palm was damp.

"Hello," she sang, pushing through.

I followed more slowly, stumbling in her agitated wake until she released my hand. The hall's chandeliers were lit, and smoking candelabras stood in each corner. At the room's center was a fountain, six feet high, with a cascade of dark water. A haze of perfumed smoke hung just under the ceiling. There was a blur of iridescent satin, weaving dyed feathers, the glint of jewels and crystal. I neared the crowd as stealthily as I could, straining my eyes to find Amy's blue shape, tasting cologne and hashish in the back of my mouth.

"You didn't hear it from me." A brunette woman waved her fan as she spoke. "It just happens that when the Russian artists come to a city, suddenly the art dealers have acquired diamond tiaras and all sorts of ancient robes encrusted with jewels."

"From the Imperial palace?" her companion asked. At their side was a leashed animal. I supposed it was a dog, but its head was round and its paws were fat and clumsy. It turned to glower at me with milky blue eyes, and I stopped short. It was a tiger cub.

"Yes," the brunette woman said. "It makes me almost want to go there myself."

"That's what I've been telling you. That's how the Russians do business. You just have a few drinks, and make all the deals on velvet. There's a fortune to be made."

A small crowd closed around them, while the tiger cub showed me its teeth. I stood for a moment, then wandered further to another doorway. A few of the guests glanced towards me. When I smiled they looked away.

"So everyone wins." A low American murmur came from

inside the room as I entered. It was cooler here, with a few lamps turned low, and French windows opening to the water. A table was spread with pastries and glasses of pale rose wine.

The woman speaking was tall and broad-shouldered, with a round face and a nose like a little ball of dough. She reclined on a low divan, surrounded by a few younger women, smiling dozily as if content to sit all night with her plate of sugared strawberries.

She looked me over as I entered. "People need art," she said, "precisely because they don't understand it. And the artist shouldn't be afraid to demand that her needs be met in return."

I took up some wine and leaned in the doorway.

"Some people," she went on, grabbing a handful of sugar and rolling her strawberry in it, "are good at making money. That's their talent, and it's wonderful. Really, what's wrong with that?"

She looked around at me before continuing.

"And some of us are good at art. Or at least, that's what we do best." A few of the women nodded at that. "And when we ask for some support, we needn't act like beggars. We're taking dirty old money and making it into something pure. Something everyone can enjoy."

I took a long draught from my glass. I felt warm all over, as if, one by one, my cells were lighting up. The soft-eyed woman leaned her head back on her pillow and gazed at me expectantly.

"So artists are just like socialists?" I asked. I hadn't meant to speak so loudly. A few of the girls frowned.

But the woman cackled. Then she heaved herself up and leaned towards me, pointing. Her smock hung loosely.

"That's right, comrade. Except artists have nicer parties. And we don't wear those dreary clothes." She motioned me over. "Who are you, anyway? I'm Greta."

Before I could reach her, a brace of serving girls entered, dressed in gauze tunics like hetaerae in old frescoes. From behind them came the ringing of a chime and Amy's voice, crying, "It's starting! Hey, it's starting!"

We filed into the hall as the maids put out the chandeliers. A spotlight illuminated an empty space before the fountain, where the carpet had been rolled away. A man sat on the edge of this circle of light, holding a violin and looking soberly at his lap. The floor glistened. There was the autumn smell of dampened wood.

An arm snaked under mine. Greta smiled in my face. "Really, what's your name?" She wore attar of roses.

"Katie Larkin."

"I want to talk to you more. I can see you're —"

But the chimes sounded again. The crowd settled and grew quiet; only a few men behind me whispered persistently.

" — but now he's got into arms manufacturing."

"Oh, my wife would throw a damn fit. I can just hear her: *warmonger*."

"Quite the contrary. Think of it: these new weapons are so deadly, no one will dare wage war again."

"Shush!"

The man by the fountain lifted his violin and began to play, softly at first, as though he were practicing on his own. I recognized the melody from *Talqis and the Slave*, a sensational ballet that had been banned in Boston.

The violinist paused for a moment, then burst into a march, his bow sawing along the strings.

There was a sizzling patter in the darkness and I looked towards the windows, wondering if it had started to rain. In the next moment, a group of women ran to the center of the floor. Their brief skirts left their legs bare from their thighs to their ankles, where pointe shoes were strapped on tight. Beaded halters covered their breasts. They wore their hair in loose curls, shining with pomade and twisted with silk vines. The breeze from their movement ruffled my skirt.

They danced tirelessly as the march changed to a ronde. Linking hands, they circled the fountain, their feet quick and precise. The music changed yet again — to an earthy, plaintive lullaby — and they all reclined on the floor.

As the melody rose, another woman ran before the fountain. She wore the same costume as the corps, but her black hair was gathered high on her head, spiraled like a conch shell, wound with gold chains. A thread of rubies hung just over her eyebrows. Her back gleamed like metal. When she turned to the audience, her almond-shaped black eyes widened, then narrowed. It was Rusala.

I gave a start, thinking she must have seen me. Yet she was deep in her character, reaching towards a man who rushed out to join her. The music paused, and for a few moments Rusala's breathing was the only sound. Then the melody began again. Their pas de deux was lush and daring; several times I feared she would fall, but her partner held her fast, gripping so hard that his fingers left red dents in her waist. Once he lifted her above his head and she held herself in an arc, her lips pressed tight.

The violinist stood and played an abrupt arpeggio. The dancers all looked towards the windows, wide-eyed with fear. Rusala threw herself into her partner's embrace, and they sank to the floor as the corps lifted a Turkish rug to shield them from our view.

Playing a slow, ghostly rendition of the melody, the violinist wandered behind the audience while the dancers continued to stare at us. As the last notes faded, they pulled the carpet away. The audience sucked in its breath. One man guffawed.

Rusala and her partner lay nude. He reclined on his back and she rested over him, her legs sprawled on either side of his hips, her belly covering his genitals. She was arched up to look him in the face, her back trembling only slightly with the effort. One of his hands cupped her cheek and jaw; the other held her breast. As she leaned forward to kiss his mouth, the spotlight was put out, and the dancers hurried away.

Chapter
Six

THE CHANDELIER WAS lit again, and the servants rolled the carpet back over the wet floor. The guests around me rose quickly, hurrying to the dining room, where a steaming buffet had already been laid out. Soon I was the only person left in the great hall. Sitting with my palm over my throat, I felt the pulse there, hectic and too warm.

The servant boys cleared away every chair but mine.

"Hey, Red." Greta came towards me, holding a plate full of pilaf. "Shall we go outside where it's cool? Red? Are you all right?"

"I think I just need a moment," I told her.

"Poor thing." She hooked her arm in mine as I stood. I was drunker than I'd thought. "Let's get some air. You, hey!" she yelled at a passing servant, "fetch some coffee for this lady, would you?"

I looked around for Rusala, but the dancers had vanished. I felt absurdly petulant; I'd wanted Rusala to see me in this dress.

I let Greta lead me out to a torch-lit patio. She sat me down and laid her cool palm on my forehead. The night was almost cold. The torch flames thrashed and crackled, giving off gusts of heat. Greta sat opposite me and settled into her supper.

"So," she managed between bites, "I hear you're from Boston? And a painter?"

"How do you know this?" The cool air revived me.

"That's the gossip. Mmh. Want some pilaf?"

"But whose gossip? No, thank you. Not one of the guests even said hello to me."

"Oh, Red Katie, that doesn't mean they didn't notice you." Greta waved her fork at me and opened her eyes wide. "That doesn't mean they weren't gawping at you, and needing to know all about this mysterious new woman."

"Honestly." I let my head fall back. My neck felt too loose.

"They think," she continued, "that you must be rich."

I laughed. "Now that is outrageous."

"They assume that because you're American, and here, and not someone's mistress..." She kept her eyes on her pilaf, assiduously casual.

"I am not at all rich." I fought to speak normally. "I'm here because I paint. That's all I wanted to do, and in Boston there were too many—"

"Amy's telling everyone that you invented some fantastic stories about being a maid, and a bastard child, and she's convinced that you're actually an heiress in disguise. And then I heard a lady say that you had a criminal's physiognomy."

I couldn't speak. Greta looked up at me and paled.

"Oh," she said. "Damn it. What made me say that?"

I swallowed. "It was my mother who was the maid, in fact."

"I'm an idiot. I'm sorry, you poor sweet kid. Bite my tongue."

"I only think if they found it so interesting, then one or two of them might have greeted me and spoken with me, and asked me themselves." My eyes stung and I looked down. I felt alone, as if I'd only then realized that there was no one in the world who cared for me, who felt interest in me beyond a passing prurient fascination. As if this were a revelation.

"Don't. Don't now," Greta said. "That's behind you now, anyway, isn't it? Better not to tell anyone else that story. Someone might believe it. Do you know, when I was your age, I had only a fraction of your courage. I was a chorus girl in a god-forsaken saloon in San Francisco. It wasn't until I was past twenty-five that I began to audition for theater—real theater. I thought I was insane for travelling all the way to New York, memorizing Juliet's soliloquies in the rattling second-class car of the train. And here you've come to Venice on your own."

"But, no. I thought you were from London."

"I bet you do. That was my agent's idea. I was born in London, the daughter of a judge and an actress, and sent away to a finishing school in New York, right? Ha! He was right, after all, people will believe anything. Hey, now we each know the other's secret, mum's the word." She looked at me intently.

A girl brought us coffee and cinnamon rolls. Greta filled her plate and leaned back on the stone bench, a replete goddess. The torchlight found seams of pure white in her hair.

"I intend to show you around Venice, Katie." She gestured towards the canal. "It's not a bad town, once you get away from San Marco's square with its electric lights and monkey parade. There are so many hidden spaces. And of course," she added, leaning forward, "we'll have to work on getting you a showing." Then she straightened up.

A tall young man stood in the doorway. His waistcoat and tie were dove-grey, and his light hair was so long that it curled around his collar.

"Why is it," he said, fussing diffidently with his cufflinks, "that the most interesting people at a party end up hiding somewhere?" He stepped out to the patio and sat down beside me on the bench, drawing a cigarette case from his pocket.

"I'm—" he said to the case. He looked up at me and then turned to Greta. "I'm—well, Greta, introduce us."

"Amy's brother, William."

"And you're Katie Larkin, right?" He pulled out a long slim cigarette rolled in blue paper. "Do you mind if I smoke?"

"Not if you share." Greta leaned over and kissed his cheek. "Welcome back, honey. Glad you decided to take a holiday."

"Miss Larkin?" He held a cigarette towards me.

"Katie," I said. "No, I shouldn't."

"You should." Greta lit two in her mouth, her round face glowing, then handed one to me.

I puffed, hesitant. An earthy, tangy flavor filled my head. "Oh, mm."

They burst out laughing. "Mm!" Greta sucked intently at hers, then smiled at me.

"Now you can't say that I didn't get anything useful from New York," William said. "Always, the best hashish anywhere. Katie, do you realize you're the talk of the party? May I?" He took up a cinnamon roll.

I shrugged and looked at Greta. "What is this? Is there nothing more interesting for everyone to talk about?"

"No." William loosened his tie and pulled at his collar. "And your story keeps getting more interesting as they tell it."

I groaned.

"One thing is true," Greta said. When she glanced upwards, she looked suddenly regal. "She is, in fact, a painter of rare talent."

"Ah," I said, then stopped myself. I took another pull at my cigarette.

"And," Greta went on, looking out to the canal, "though she's too modest to boast about it, several major galleries in Venice want to show her work."

"Really?" William leaned away from me and raised his eyebrows.

"I hope your sister doesn't pass up the opportunity to give Katie a show this season." Greta stood, serenely arranging her robes and shaking her head with regret. "That is, if Amy is serious about this gallery."

"Now, Greta," I began, but I couldn't gather my thoughts. I puffed again at my cigarette, surprised to find it already a tiny stub. When I closed my eyes, I was no longer interested in thinking.

And there was the sea breathing, if I listened closely enough.

"Steady there." Greta took my hand. "You need to eat."

We were still laughing aimlessly as we entered the smoky hall. A victrola played. A few couples danced, cleaving so close that their cheeks touched, singing along.

Snowbird, my snowbird
Can't I catch your gaze?
Flit on before me, snowbird.

The crowd parted, then surged around us. I lost hold of Greta's hand and stood still, hot in the midst of all that fragrant sweat, letting the music shake through me. I started to dance on my own. When my head fell back, some of my hair came unpinned. I couldn't remember why I'd felt so awkward before.

Ain't you quick, my snowbird?
Too quick for my poor hand.

A wiry man grabbed my waist and spun me until I shrieked. Another man, tall and gentle, cut in and glided me across the floor so softly that I felt I was being rocked to sleep. I squeezed my eyes shut and sang the song's refrain while I danced with four or five more men.

Flit on before me, snowbird.

"Katie! Katie!" I opened my eyes to see Amy waving at me from across the room. She wore a wreath of tiny wild roses on her head. I waved back and started singing again.

"Katie!" She was suddenly inches from my face.

"Look at her." I leaned my forehead on my partner's chest. "Woo, she scared me."

"Miss Larkin, a moment, if I may." Amy fixed her wreath of roses on my head and led me away. We settled in an alcove behind a potted fern. Amy sat cross-legged on the padded leather bench.

"Right," she began. "Business. Katie, will you let us show you this winter?"

I rubbed my eyes. The roses fell to my lap. "Show me? Ah, painting. I'm always painting, you know."

I looked at her, suddenly certain that she'd understand.

"Even when there's not a brush in my hand, I'm painting," I said. I waved towards the fern, towards her hair, towards the snow-colored Chinese urn beside us. "Colors. Are there in fact different colors or is there just one shade that changes, that eludes?"

"My word, yes. Listen," she said. "You might get some other offers, but you'll do well here. It's a newer gallery, true, but I'm doing good things with it. All the critics come here, and buyers."

I rubbed my eyes again. I longed for some water, a bite of food, something to help me think. I chewed softly at my tongue.

"Ma'am?" Another voice came from just above me. I looked up. Rusala.

She still wore her costume. Her make-up seemed strange so close up, thick black lines around her eyes and streaks of carmine on her cheeks. Sweat trickled down her belly. Her halter was made of tan tricot, sewn with beads of crimson, tiger-orange, pink. She held a tray of biscuits.

"What are you doing?" I said. I started to stand, but Amy clutched my elbow.

"No, wait, Katie, please. We're not done talking, are we? I do want to eat, though." Amy leaned over the tray. I looked up at Rusala but her eyes were focused on the wall just over my head.

Amy picked over the biscuits while Rusala's stomach whined and gurgled. On Rusala's bare thigh was a fresh bruise, a circle of mottled ruby and black, like a small face glaring out at us.

"I'll just have one of each, I guess." Amy took a handful. I couldn't stop staring at Rusala. Her eyelids twitched.

As soon as Amy sat back, Rusala turned and hurried away, glittering and tinkling. She still wore her rigid ballet shoes, with their squared-off tips.

"Wait!" Amy snapped, gesturing towards the crowd. "Where the devil are you going?" Her voice rose and a few heads turned towards us. "You may bring it to the other guests, if it's not too much trouble."

I followed Rusala with my eyes. She was so small and bare and shockingly vivid, a streak of gold leaf in a watercolor painting. Several of the other dancers had appeared as well, also in costume, serving drinks and pastries.

Amy grunted. "Damn it all. I swear they take the food home with them. Do I have to start putting locks on their mouths, like they do with fruit-pickers?"

"God, Amy." I shrank back. I felt queasy.

"Honestly, I think half of our household budget goes to feeding the servants and whomever else they bring to the kitchen."

"But those are the dancers, aren't they?"

"They are paid for the entire evening if they stay and help. And people enjoy getting a close-up view of the dancers, their costumes and their skinny legs." She slapped my shoulder. "Oho, look over there. Jim found a ticklish one."

I didn't look. I stood, then leaned against the wall. Stars sparked before my eyes.

"Katie?"

I tried to answer but I could only moan. My stomach stretched and coiled inside me. I sucked air through my teeth.

"I feel—I have to go—" Before I could say more, the floor

rushed up at me. I stopped it with my hands, then leaned my forehead on the cool parquet.

I cannot remember everything after that. Two people lifted me by the arms and helped me up the stairwell. I tried to tell them I was going to be sick and suddenly a perfumed kerchief was in front of my face. A moment later I was leaning over a basin. I felt as if my insides had been soldered into a black, smoking mess.

I was laid down on a bed. I blinked to clear my eyes and was then looking up at William's flushed face. I turned away, mortified, while voices whispered over me. I rested my eyes, just for a moment. I imagined warm stones lay on my eyelids. Then I took a deep breath and tried again to move.

Light fell over my face.

I gasped and sat up. Mary was pulling open a heavy drape to the mid-day sun. I lay in a dusty room, in the middle of a great bed that smelled of stale perfume. The ceiling was dappled green and violet, the reflection from the sunlit bougainvillea covering the windows. Outside, the sea was a flat expanse of buffed turquoise under a white-hot sky.

"What time is it?" I blurted, looking around helplessly. I was in a pink muslin gown.

"Are you feeling better, ma'am?" Mary curtsied.

"God. God. Mary, I feel awful about last night."

"I'm sure, Miss Larkin. I'll bring breakfast then, shall I?" The door slammed behind her as she finished speaking.

I could only sit shaking my head, muttering to myself. "Stupid bitch. Circus freak. At least everyone knows now. No need to try and impress them anymore."

I was wondering how to retrieve my clothes when a knock came at the door. "Yes, Mary," I said.

"No, not Mary." The door opened a crack. "Are you decent? It's me, William."

"No." I found a dressing gown on the coverlet and pulled it over my shoulders, swinging my bare legs to the floor. My head felt full of rocks, but my stomach was quiet. I looked at the door. "I'm going."

"Oh, no. Can I come in?" He stuck his head inside. His hair was flat on one side, fluffed on the other, as if he'd just slept the whole night in one position.

"All right."

"Are you feeling better, really?" He still whispered. Dust covers slumped over all the furniture, but he crossed to a settee and sat on its edge. He wore his trousers from the night before and a jacket of faded maroon alpaca. I couldn't meet his eyes for long.

"Yes, I'm fine. I'll just get my clothes and go. And oh! Amy's gown." Why had I worn it? It was most likely a Worth gown, so expensive its price would make you shriek. "If I've ruined it, I'll pay for everything. Just tell me how much."

He was silent and I risked a look up. His brows were furrowed.

"I came to say I was sorry," he said. "We were the ones who forced champagne and hashish on you all night, didn't let you eat a bite, monopolized you for the sake of curiosity. I should have guessed you weren't used to that kind of thing."

He drew his knees to his chest.

"It was terrible of me to keep drinking like that," I said. "I never do that, really." My head was starting to throb.

"Bwah-ha." William rolled his eyes and leaned back in the settee. "You think you're the only intemperate one? We won't see Amy for another two or three days."

I gave a rueful laugh at that, remembering her wreath of wild roses.

"And, don't worry," he went on. "The maid and I spirited you away before anyone saw...before you..."

I winced. "You were too good to me." I thought of Mary, having to clean my face and rinse out the basin. Her flat voice and slamming door.

I wondered if Rusala had seen me, dancing and squealing in a borrowed gown, drinking until I got sick, like a crazy old aunt who is rarely let out of the house.

"You're just too decent for us, is the thing." William rubbed his eyes and hummed to himself. "Mm-muh-muh. Now, let's get some breakfast. Will you come down?"

"No, oh no. Thank you, but I'd better go home."

"You sure? All right then. I'll call for a launch and have Mary come take care of you." He stood and put his hands in his pockets. "I hope you won't think we're awful after all this. It would be nice to have a real friend here in Venice."

He strolled to the door, then to the window, then back to me. He kissed my forehead — a loud, nervous kiss — and hurried out.

I wanted to dress myself, but apparently that wasn't done. When Mary returned, she dropped her tray with a clatter and hooked me into my milkmaid dress as I held the wall for support. She led me quickly through the silent house.

A motor-launch idled at the steps. The sunlight made me ache all over. I fished through my purse and found two unidentifiable coins, maybe five lire. When I held them to Mary, she sniffed and turned away. Then she turned back, snatched them from my palm, and ran to the patio.

Chapter
Seven

ALL THROUGH THE afternoon, in my shallow sunlit sleep, I dreamt of New England. They were memory dreams, whole and perfect. I felt the rush of cold surf around my feet as we ran along Hampton Beach. I felt Adele's stiff, briny hair under my hand. I saw a curl of plum-colored seaweed around my ankle. Past the dunes, the autumn trees were incandescent in the sun.

I dreamt of Jeffrey and Adele in their aunt's garden on a summer afternoon, both of them roaring with laughter. They sat beneath the trellis, under cascades of pearly wisteria. The Aeolian harp buzzed and chimed fitfully beside them. They hadn't heard me approach just yet, and I was silent, holding my breath, knowing that in a moment they'd sense me. In a moment, they'd look up and cry out with delight, the way they always greeted me.

I stood half-hidden in the shade, wondering how I'd ever imagined myself to be happy before I met them.

"Ma'am?"

My back ached. There was the scent of the sea.

"Ma'am Katie?" Lovorka's touch on my shoulder was soft and quick.

"Mm? Yes."

"You talked in sleep."

It was dark. Lovorka carried a candle. It could have been early evening or three in the morning. I tried to lift my head.

"Listen," I said. "I'll need to sleep a little longer. Do you need money? There's my purse. Under my hat, there."

"Only—"

I looked up at her. Her face blurred and jumbled in the candlelight.

"Only, ma'am, I'm afraid you will shout again."

"Never mind, Lovorka."

"Like last time."

Lavorka put her cool fingertips on my forehead. She smelled of cold cream and brown soap. Her skin was so unnaturally frangible and luminous that I had to look away. I felt as though someone had placed a priceless porcelain figurine in my hands, and I was overwhelmed with the perverse desire to smash it.

"I'll take some more medicine, then." I felt wretched. I wanted, unreasonably, to beg her to forgive me. Shutting my eyes, I heaved myself up, but she already had the spoon at my lips. My head fell back to the pillow as the medicine wandered down my throat, a cool, bitter worm.

For the rest of the night I dreamt of Rusala. Her stomach growled. She shivered in her costume. I called out to her, but she fled.

I WOKE LATER to the sound of rain. I rose from my bed to look at the transformed city. What a novelty it seemed: the low grey sky, the gunmetal gleam of the canals, the uncertain tapping on the tiled roof.

Lovorka had pushed some mail under my door. A grocer's bill in stilted English, and a strangely folded square of flowered tissue paper, evidently meant to suggest the shape of a crane. Inside was a wobbly script:

Katie, I'm sorry I couldn't see you off. I'm indisposed today, too, and most likely tomorrow. Did you say you had some portraits already? I'll come and see them whenever you say. Yours, Amy.

For the moment, at least, Amy seemed sincere in her offer of a showing. I looked absently about the room, uncertain whether to laugh or cry. I couldn't quite fit the thought into my head. A showing. My work in a showing at the Seagroves Gallery.

No. No. I forced myself to relax. When she came to her senses, she'd certainly rethink her offer and find some elegant way to rescind it. Or would she? I stamped my bare feet.

I was glad, in any case, for the impetus to work, the thrum of possibility and terror that always sharpened me. And I did need to work. I had no portraits, except the one unfinished painting of Rusala.

I was sure that Rusala would not want to see me again.

I turned up all the lamps and got to work. When Lovorka came in with coal, I asked her to post another notice at the theater, an advertisement for artists' models, well paid.

As soon as she left, my bell rang.

I descended the staircase. A cat wailed just on the other side of the front door. My feet slid on the vestibule carpet, and I looked down with a cry. An inch of water had seeped in from the alley. The door was swollen shut. I had to pull twice before it burst open.

Rusala held a man's umbrella, black and enormous. She was in her faded violet evening gown. She smiled at the ground, weakly. Her feet, in their drab canvas shoes, were soaked through.

"I thought you might need to work," she began, fidgeting with the umbrella's ivory handle. The alley behind her had become a brook, dark as cocoa.

"I didn't expect — come in — I didn't think — "

She stepped over the puddle and stood close to me for a moment.

"I'm so sorry I ignored you at the supper," she said.

When I shut the door, she turned away and leaned her umbrella in the corner. Her hair was pinned in a tight figure-of-eight, with wet tendrils snaking down her neck. She wore a necklace of coral beads.

"I didn't mean to be rude to you, ma'am. Katie. Really, I didn't." She glanced down again. "I had to, though. What would they have thought of you if we'd greeted each other like friends?"

"What? I don't care."

"You ought to care. They were sizing you up last night. If I had said hello, you would have stood and offered me a seat. You would have insisted I eat something, too. For God's sake, you would have taken my tray and started serving Amy yourself. And everyone would have seen that, and — "

"Why do you care so?"

She wiped her face with her dripping forearm. Her eyes seemed hot. "And, *ah*, they would have thought, *that's who she is*. You would have quickly become invisible, a nobody. You most certainly would not have been offered a showing."

Her feet shuffled and squished in her wet shoes. "I'm chilled," she said. "Shall I leave?"

I led her up the stairwell and built a fire in my studio, still not speaking. Behind me, her joints crackled and ticked softly as she undressed. I worked the bellows at the crimson coals until the heat made my eyes tear.

I heard her walking towards me. "May I hang my stockings by the fire? They're soaked through." Her voice was small again.

"Why don't we hang everything by the fire?" I fetched her dress and her warm chemise, her narrow corset trimmed with appliqué daisies.

When I turned back, she was bending over before the mantel. Her buttocks were red with cold as she pulled off her black stockings. Her corset had left pale pink stripes down her sides. A rash of tiny, angry bumps slanted over her waist and her breasts.

She rested her palms on her sternum, patting at the welts. "That costume is murder."

I didn't answer. She padded away into the evergreen shadows

and stretched resolutely onto the cloth-covered sofa. Her teeth chattered.

"The same pose?" she asked.

"Wait," I said, running into my bedroom. I pulled my coverlet from the tangle of linens. She lay obediently as I tucked it around her shoulders.

"The room will warm up as I mix the paints." I stood on a chair to light the chandelier. Its crystal tiers sang softly as it rocked.

"Aren't you good to me, you daft thing." Rusala's voice sounded warmer. She was completely hidden under the lumpy, oatmeal-colored coverlet; only her round face shone at me. "Why can't all my jobs be this plush?"

I could only think, *she doesn't hate me, she doesn't hate me.* All those resolutions to be formal and reserved, and here I was relieved to tears to find that she liked me after all.

I chose a paint brush and pushed it against my palm, loosening the bristles. Then I looked up at her. "Wait. How did you know I got a showing?"

The coverlet wiggled. "I told you, I know everything. No one watches what they say in front of someone like me. Around dawn, I heard Amy bragging about her new acquisition."

I clapped my hands. "What on earth? Rusala, this would be funny if it weren't so terrifying. I don't have a single painting finished. Look." I gestured around the suddenly vast-seeming studio.

"But you have got talent."

"I've done myself in. This is a disaster."

"I said you've got talent." She lifted her chin.

"You haven't seen a single thing I've done," I said. "Don't try to flatter me. I'm not stupid."

"No, indeed. And you're not bored, or vain, or rich. You wouldn't waste your time on painting unless you knew you had a gift for it."

I tried to open a paint jar. Its lid was stuck. "You know nothing about it."

She sat up and pointed towards my desk, with its ledger and abacus. "You keep a daily account of your expenses, don't you? Those paints are most likely one half of your yearly budget. You did not come to Venice on a whim."

"It's really none of your business."

"Why here, Katie? Why couldn't you paint in Boston? That's the only part I don't understand. Are you from a bad family, really? Or are you a sort of remittance girl?"

I put down the jar and rested my hands on my lap. The room was filling with heat. The grey wind pushed and moaned outside.

"I'm a widow," I said. "I was married, in Boston. When I lost Jeff, when he died, I also lost—I lost everything, my family, the place I belonged." I'd hoped to shame her but her face remained motionless. A stab of annoyance made me turn my head.

"Go on." Her voice was quieter.

"Maybe a stronger person could have coped better," I said. "With being alone, I mean. Because in fact, we're all alone. We're born alone, we die alone. I just—"

I can't stop remembering, I can't stop chasing pleasure.

She lay back down and curled to her side, holding the coverlet close.

"Now the only thing that makes me feel—" I realized how melodramatic it would sound, but I had to say it all the same. "Feel that any of this was worthwhile—"

"Is painting," she said.

"Yes."

I was still getting used to Rusala's quick-changing moods. When she flopped to her back, she startled me. She covered her face and gave an exasperated groan.

"I see how it is with you," came her muffled voice. "You haven't the faintest idea." She kicked off the coverlet and lay there for a moment, shaking her head softly, gathering her thoughts.

"Do you know," she said finally, "what I would do, if I had half of your advantages? Your beauty, your talent, your education, your connections? God!" Her hands were cupped tight over her face. She sounded angry, but when her face emerged, it was perfectly serene.

"All you lack is courage," she said. "You're the type of person who is only one step away from wealth, however poor you might be. You're someone who might really get somewhere."

I didn't notice her rise and walk towards me. It just seemed that her face came nearer to mine, warmer and brighter, a soft autumn moon.

"I watched you dance last night," she said.

I meant to answer, but my mouth was numb as if I'd just taken a spoonful of morphine.

"And here's me," she continued, "a lousy ballet-girl who can't even write her own name. Yet I'm not going to spend the rest of my life trying to convince myself that I'm happy with the scraps others want to throw my way. I have so many plans, and they're all immoderate and morally suspect."

She knelt. Her face was level with mine. I felt unsteady. I wondered if the hashish were still in me.

"I must have enough courage for both of us," she said. "At least, for now. Is that why we met, do you think?"

Then her lips were on mine, quickly. When she drew away, she tumbled backwards to the floor, landing on her bottom and giggling.

I was shocked for a moment, almost angry. But when I saw her face, I laughed too. "What on earth is the matter with you?" I said. "Have you been drinking?"

"No, but thanks for thinking of me. Have you got anything in your pantry?" She hugged her knees to her chest, nude and brazen on the threadbare carpet, her right side glowing in the firelight. "Mm. Mm." She shifted to a cross-legged position.

"If you would put something *on*," I said, but there was something about the way she sat, insouciant as a cat, that struck me as the most amusing thing I'd ever seen. I tried to speak more but I was laughing too hard. I laughed until I wheezed, helplessly, covering my mouth with my sleeve. It had probably been years since I'd laughed like that.

I jumped when I felt her fingertips on my cheeks. "Look at you," she said. My tongue swelled as if I'd just swallowed something sweet.

"Sorry," she whispered.

I felt a sharp pang of emptiness in my stomach. Her face neared, and her mouth was on mine again. This time her lips rested softly. I sat petrified, unable to breathe, unable to push her away. I felt her tongue creep along my lip.

There was suddenly a bite of pain behind my ear. I pulled away and sat up. My heart was pounding, shaking my ribcage.

"I didn't mean to tug so hard," Rusala said. She held a curl of dark brown hair. "Can I keep it in any case?"

"What did you do that for? What's the matter with you?" I rubbed my scalp.

The confidence sank from her face until she seemed awkward as a girl of twelve.

"I'm mad." She looked down. "It's the company I keep, maybe. I forget that not everyone runs with—I'm sorry, I'm sorry." She gave a shy half-smile. "I'm all right," she went on. "I was teasing, I guess. I really am sorry. Please, Katie, forgive me. Here, here." She stood, quickly, and ran to the sofa. "You must work."

My hands scrambled across my tray of brushes. I picked up a clean brush and laid it on my burning mouth. She reclined on her back.

"Turn on your stomach," I told her. Perhaps this was something she did to throw people off-balance, to gain an advantage. "The first painting isn't done yet."

I decided to give up trying to puzzle her out. I found myself deliberately acting calm, hoping to make her more tranquil. Then, when the colors oozed into the cloth, I became absorbed in painting. I recognized the old feeling of being pulled into a warm tide. The lamplight and the weak silver glow of the rain formed the perfect range of colors. I pushed my chair back and stood at the easel.

I decided to paint rough outlines of several images. Just the basic forms, to be finessed later. I had her change poses, roll to her side, then to her back. She ran to cut a sprig of mint from my window-box and knelt, holding the leaves before her stomach.

I couldn't stop. Just one more, I kept telling myself. While the paints are fresh, while the light is so perfect. My shoulders tingled. My eyes ached.

"Another?" she said softly, as I took down a fifth canvas. I'd spread the drying canvases around me on the floor.

She had fallen backwards, letting the mint rest on her stomach. It had become so dark I had to squint to see her face. That was why my eyes smarted so.

"No," I said. "I suppose I've done more than enough for one afternoon. Sorry."

"Lord, do you always paint like that? I'm knackered."

"Sometimes I get absorbed." I didn't know what to tell her. "Though I can't remember when I last worked so quickly."

She wrapped the coverlet around her shoulders before coming to me. "Let me see."

Before I could find a reason to refuse, she had lit the lamp and brought it close, kneeling on the carpet to inspect the canvases. I looked over her shoulder, trying to clear my head and really see what I'd painted. The lamp cast swinging disks of light.

She looked up at me.

"Brilliant. Ha. I knew it," she said, nodding sagely. "Original, dream-like. Once you polish them up, they'll be warm and vibrant and erotic. Yes, that'll do." She tightened the coverlet around her. Her shoulders were covered in goosebumps.

"That'll do?" I said.

She gave me a quick, sisterly kiss on the cheek.

"Did you say you had some wine?"

Chapter
Eight

"DO COME ON, Katie."

I followed more slowly down my staircase. Rusala had me
wearing a tunic of heavy indigo-dyed cotton, with silver
embroidery sparkling along its hem. It looked like something from
a biblical pageant. When she opened the front door, the rush of cool
air against my ankles made me nervous.

"No," I said. "I can't after all. I have to change."

"Oh, for God's sake." She smiled up at me. "You look like a
dream."

Her voice echoed in the alleyway. The anise-scented breeze
brought the sounds of a concertina. I stood in the doorway for a
moment, watching her rustle towards the canal. She wore a tunic
similar to mine, but of pale rose, and a stole of clinging black satin.
She'd rinsed her hair with rosewater and singed the ends once it
dried, and now it hung loose, a length of raw silk.

She didn't slow, didn't glance around at me. I had to run to
catch up.

"You'll get used to it," she said, waving to a gondolier. "That
kind of gown is meant to be worn without a corset, isn't it?"

I hugged myself, feeling my belly expand each time I breathed.
It was like wearing a dressing gown outdoors. Then Rusala was
pulling me into the gondola, and we rocked towards the Grand
Canal. She spread her stole over both of us.

RUSALA HAD BEEN staying with me for three days. After
that first night of painting, I'd found a bottle of Servian wine in my
pantry, and we drank until we fell asleep on the carpet. We woke at
noon, when Lovorka crept in with a pot of coffee and a loaf of fresh
bread. I'd sat up, and meant to introduce them, but Lovorka had
lowered her chin, making her face dull and perfectly blank. I'd seen
that same look in the maids of Boston homes. Rusala had only held
the blanket to her chest and faced the wall.

Rusala hadn't seemed at all surprised when I invited her to stay the next night. She apparently found it natural to use another's comb and toothbrush, and when I offered to lend her one of my gowns, she immediately crossed to the wardrobe and started brushing down my best grey serge. She explained that her room at the artists' hotel was crowded, and she was always glad of a holiday.

I was charmed by her ease. The house seemed to warm and expand around us. I sketched and took walks when she was at rehearsal; I read poetry to her — Blake and Dickinson and Tennyson — when she got home. She listened intently as I read to her, moving her lips, asking me to repeat phrases she liked.

Once I put down the book and stared at her. "You really can't read?" The question had been nagging me.

"I know some of the letters." She blushed, surprising me.

"You don't speak as if — Sorry, I mean you speak like someone who's read a great deal."

"I'm a parrot. I keep everything in my head. I prefer it that way." She shrugged. "It keeps my thoughts fresh, and moving. I can't imagine what it must be like to fix your thoughts into a book, like dead bugs."

I looked down at the book in my hand. I wanted to explain to her that the opposite was true, that in fact my favorite passages were constantly moving and changing shape. Blake, for instance: each time I read *Innocence and Experience*, I found the verses had changed. Yet for an instant I saw the book as she described it, a box of dead ants.

On the third day, I'd mixed paints, but felt too exhausted to begin another binge of painting.

Rusala had insisted.

"All you have to do today is finish those three canvases," she'd said, pinning up her hair. "Then it will be nearly sunset, and I'll take you out on a spree."

She'd lain back, facing me and crossing her ankles. I'd painted for hours, still in the same trance of the day before, feeling the paints as warm, slippery, ungovernable.

I don't know when I fell asleep. When I woke, she was standing over me, her cheeks damp with rain. She had run to her rooms, to fetch some clothes for us to wear when we went out.

NOW, AS WE cast out to the center of the canal, a sky of arabian blue emerged from the trailing wet clouds.

"You have to tell me where we're going," I said.

Rusala took my hand, smoothed her palm along mine, then

pinched my wrist. "You'll see," she said. Her breath smelled as if she'd had some wine before we left. "It's just the usual theater scuff. Dancers, maybe some singers. I thought it would be fun for you."

I smiled at that, as if she were a chaperone, allowing me a little social time. "Fun for me? Are you sure you're not just taking me along as entertainment?"

"You are something to look at." She gathered her loose hair and began to braid it. I thought she needed earrings, something gold to complement the warm tones of her skin.

We passed under the Academy Bridge, where the palaces stood right at the water's edge, their mosaics gleaming like banked coals. Someone played the piano inside the Academy, a Schumann melody.

"God, I'm sick of Venice," Rusala sighed.

"Sick of Venice?" I sat up. "It's the most beautiful city in the world, empirically. Everyone knows that. I knew that before I even came here."

"Diseased old town," she said. "No, I'm not joking. Venice has become a sort of asylum for the rest of the world, hasn't it? A swamp settlement that's been built into a great amusement park, filling up daily with doddering old millionaires, hysterical women looking for an escape from themselves, insufferable rich artists, insupportable poor artists, perverts, criminals."

She saw my face and laughed. "See," she said, "you can't smell the decay in the air. That's because you've only just arrived. You'll see exactly what I mean soon enough." She punched my shoulder, then threaded her arm through mine. Her heart beat against my ribs. I could sense that she was trying to relax. I was learning that these moods of hers passed as quickly as summer squalls.

"The decay in the air, honest to God," I said, drawing the stole closer around us.

"I'm sure," she said, "that in a little while you'll be as keen to leave as I am."

We were nearing one of the largest palaces. As we hit its stone steps, Rusala leapt off the boat and pressed a few of my coins into the gondolier's hand. I meant to follow, but the sight of the greasy, spoiled water below stopped me.

"Oh, Katie, Katie." Rusala reached out and took hold of my wrists. "I won't let you fall in. Come on—one, two, three." I jumped over the side of the boat, then ran up the steps.

"Your friends live here?" I'd never been in such a building.

"Yes," she said. "I camp here too, sometimes."

She pulled open the iron gate. The wooden door inside was shut. She pushed at it, closing her tiny hands round the handle, but it wouldn't give.

"Locked. Precious buggers." She reached on her tiptoes and pulled the bell-cord. "I suppose they've hired a butler."

She rang violently until there came a thump and clatter inside. I pressed my ear to the door and heard whispering: *She's brought her?*

The door slid open. The front hall had pink marble columns and a staircase that shone like a glazed cake. A few pale gas lamps shone in the corners. A chandelier trembled ominously overhead, a crystal sea-monster.

Two women stood before us. One of them was Greta. I reached out and grabbed her hand, impulsively. She didn't seem at all surprised to see me. She wore the familiar loose smock, this time with a red scarf.

"Hey, my foster daughter," she said, pulling me in and putting her arm round my shoulders. Rusala clung to my other side.

"I should just count on seeing you everywhere," I said, still staring around the hall. There were frescoes near the ceiling; I could barely make out a painting of a smug man surrounded by a cloud of bare-breasted angels who threw gold coins at his head. "This is your place, Greta?"

"Is mine," said the other woman. Her accent was formal, as if she'd learned English from an elocution teacher. Her chestnut hair was augmented with false black curls. Under her white dress she wore a severe corset, so narrow and tight that she could have worn a choker around her waist. Her features were sharp, and her grey eyes were heavy-lidded and sardonic.

"Welcome," she said, holding her arms wide.

"Katie, this is Olga Prelestnaya," Rusala said.

"Katie knows who she is," Greta insisted.

Olga shook her head. "No, probably doesn't. And, no, you don't have to pretend."

Rusala whispered in my ear, "You know, from the Maryinsky ballet?"

"Of course." I stared. Hadn't I seen that same face in a poster, at La Fenice theater? I searched my memory. "I missed your performance in — *Giselle*, wasn't it? It seems I arrived in Venice too late."

"You don't have to do that with me." Olga said. Greta was already pulling me into the parlor, where an oversized fire spilled ash on the hearth. The walls were decorated with a pastoral scene of fruit trees and red-cloaked shepherds. The floor was covered with sheepskins. A tin tub stood before the fireplace, and two girls sat immersed. Two young men sat by a bookcase, smoking and chatting in French. They waved their cigarettes at me.

Greta let go of my arm and lay on a white couch, pulling a quilt
to her chin.

"You don't mind if I get back to my resting, do you?" she said.
"I've accomplished a lot of resting so far today. I wouldn't want to
fall behind now."

Rusala lifted the other end of the quilt and squeezed in, resting
her head on Greta's ankles. "Yes, me too. Come on."

Olga patted my shoulder. "I get you drink?" She went to the
sideboard, leaving me standing at the room's center.

"Oh, stop staring at her," Rusala called out. She craned her
neck and glared at the others. "Come relax, Katie. Never mind
them. They're pigs."

I slipped in beside Rusala. The quilt smelled of sweat.

"Those girls are dancers," Rusala said. "I think you might have
seen some of them when you visited our rehearsal, remember?"

One of the girls turned to me. Her red braid slid sideways,
showing her pearl-white vertebrae.

Greta laid her head on the armrest and closed her eyes. "Katie
and I met already, at the Seagroves' place," she said. "God, they're
a pair of nervous monkeys, aren't they, Katie? William's nice
enough, but sheltered. A little water lily. Amy likes to think herself
a brimstone bitch. Why are rich people so wound up like that?"

"You needn't tell me that," Rusala said. "Christ."

"It's part of our trade, isn't it?" Greta said. "When you can
manage it, you have to get in good with the money-makers." She
nudged me with her knee. "But then you must also get away from
time to time, and be yourself."

"And who are you, Katie?" Olga had returned with a tray of
drinks. She placed one in my hand, a tall glass of something very
clear with soda bubbles still rising to its surface.

"She's an artist, a painter." Greta opened her eyes again and
pointed at me. "Yes, and you've got a showing, haven't you?"

"So a real artist?" Olga said, pulling up an armchair. "Not
another American woman with nerve complaints and restless
hands?"

Rusala cut in. "You ought to see the portraits she's made."

Olga's face brightened. "Mm, did your husband bring you to
Venice then? What's his name?"

I felt Rusala's hand on my hip then, just resting gently. She
tented the quilt so that no one would detect her movement.

"I went back to my maiden name, Larkin, when my husband
died in Boston. It's all right," I added quickly, watching Olga's eyes
widen. "It really is all right now. It feels as if it happened a long
time ago."

Rusala tensed beside me. "Olga," she said, raising her voice just a little, "I'm still waiting to hear about the performance you're working on." Rusala's tone was so genial and unhurried that no one noticed the sudden change of topic. She moved her hand from my leg and I exhaled.

Olga sighed. "We have tour to America in Christmas holiday, so we work on only most boring and Puritan ballets. *Swan Lake, Coppelia.* American cities won't allow anything else. I'm stuffed with them."

Greta covered her face with a pillow.

Rusala rolled her eyes at me. "You've heard of the Theatre Slav, haven't you?" she said. "The Imperial dancers escaping to Europe and America?"

"No." Olga leaned forward. "We don't escape. Just something for the off-season. We're just sharing art. St. Petersburg is always home."

"Naw, naw, stay in Venice," Greta drawled, rolling to her side. "Girls, help me work on her. Stay, you peach. Stay in Venice. Everything you need is here, isn't it?"

Olga leaned over and slapped Greta's wrist, cursing her in Russian. Greta sucked in her breath.

The red-haired girl stood from the tub and wrapped herself in a towel. The dark-haired girl sank deeper in the water, propping her feet up.

I wanted to be alone with Rusala. To hide my confusion, I tried to join the conversation. "I've heard of the Theatre Slav, of course. You've, um, taken Europe by storm." I may have remembered that phrase from a journal. Their dancers had cut-glass technique, but their ballets were full of naked nymphs and slave orgies. They toured with a devoted coterie, letting some of their most aggressive sponsors appear in character roles. I'd made a point of avoiding their concerts.

"Maybe, then, Katie, you can convince Rusala to join us?" Olga said, glaring at Rusala.

"No," Rusala said, fitting her thigh against mine. Her fingers found my bare wrist.

Greta clicked her tongue. "Now, really, Rusala. Do you want to get on or what? Theatre Slav would love to have you. Take time off and go with them to Monte Carlo. You know the Talqis role. See how you like it, at least."

Olga tucked her legs under her skirt and nodded. "You wish rather to stay in second-rate opera company, Rusala? And serve drinks? You have to get on. Don't wait invitation."

Rusala moaned and hid her face under the blanket. This was evidently an old conversation; they were performing a little for me.

"There's more opportunity here in Venice," Rusala said from

under the quilt. "I don't want to join another troupe. I like being independent. I can do private shows, and make a heap of money."

"She has a point," came an English voice. The red-haired girl stood just by the couch, holding her towel under her chin. "You can earn decent money here," she said, "at parties, and modeling, and everything."

"And once I have enough saved," Rusala said, "I'm going to leave here and get into movies. That's where the heavy sugar is."

"Heavy sugar," Greta said with a laugh. "Heavy, baby. Lord, those photos and movies you girls do now. If I were younger, I would do that in a heartbeat." She held out her arms and wiggled her shoulders. "Just sit there naked, maybe walk around in the garden in a pair of drawers, and make thirty dollars!"

Rusala waved her hands imperiously. "No, not just French stuff," she objected, "but long films, you know. Artistic films!"

Olga appealed to me. "Now, Katie, I try to tell Rusala that real artists aren't filmed. Can you imagine Theatre Slav being filmed, and everyone can look at it in a movie palace, and throw popcorn at the screen? I might as well perform at music hall. I could perform *Bluebird*, just after fat woman playing tuba."

"But then again, someone ought to film you in *Salome*," Greta said. "Particularly that version I witnessed last New Year's Eve."

Olga looked away. "Wouldn't Vova like that?" she snapped. "Bad thing."

A corner of the quilt was tossed over my face. In the sudden darkness, Rusala's cheek pressed against mine.

"Are you all right?" she asked.

"I'm all right. Did she say 'Vova?'"

"Oh, God, Duke Vladimir of Something. From Russia. He looks like a big poached egg. This is his palace. When he's away, Olga lets artists stay here. He would certainly never tolerate this company." Rusala took my wrist again. "Did it upset you when they brought up Jeffrey? Katie, what was his last name?"

Greta lifted her end of the quilt. "What's all this whispering?"

Rusala sat up. Her hair was tangled.

"Katie needs some air," she said. We stood and took a sheepskin rug into the garden. A grassy path led to an inlet from the main canal, where one could board a gondola in private. We sat on a gritty bench and pulled the sheepskin tight around us. In the fresh air, Rusala's scent was stronger.

"His names was Jeffrey Stites, I bet," she said. "The Stites Case, in Boston. That was your husband, wasn't it? I've been suspecting, but I didn't want to say."

I rested a hand over my eyes, somehow unsurprised. "Was it in the papers even here?"

"I wouldn't know that. But it was talked about a good deal, in some circles. I posed for a group of American students last June, and they kept discussing it. A murder-suicide? Fuck me."

My fists clenched. I waited for the twist of panic, yet I was only numb inside. The garden was close and soundless.

"Jeff didn't know what he was doing," I said. "He appeared with a gun, too distraught to think. Adele, his sister, was trying to stop him, was trying to take the pistol from him. I still don't believe he ever meant to hurt her. I'll never believe that." I knew I'd said that precise phrase before. All the examinations with the police had left me with a memorized script echoing in my head, something entirely removed from reality.

The water sloshed softly against the bank. "But here's what I don't understand," Rusala said. "Why would he come to his sister's apartment on a Saturday morning only to hurt himself or to bluster at her? The story simply never made sense to me." She frowned out at the darkness. Clearly, she'd wondered this before. I imagined the hundreds of strangers who had analyzed the story like a poorly written play.

"He wasn't himself then," I replied. "There was something about drink that would just take over a part of his brain. Adele could see that right away, I could tell. That's why she ran to him."

"Oh." She turned to me. "You were there when it happened?"

"Yes." An image flashed, just behind my eyes, of Adele's room. The morning sunlight through the crystal vase of dandelions.

"You were already there when it happened," she repeated. "You were there when he arrived?" I expected more questions, but she only leaned away from me, slowly, intently, like a bow being drawn. I felt the old sick tension rising in my body. I clutched the sheepskin around me, wanting to cover my throat.

"Katie." She gripped my thigh. "No. Don't start. I can see it, you know, when you start to give up. Soon you'll be at your medicine again, sleeping for half the day. Listen to me."

She rose to her knees on the bench and took my hands in hers. Her eyes narrowed into crescents of onyx. "Don't let it make you weak. You've got to learn that, and quickly. Don't let things make you weak. Everything has to make you hard. Otherwise it's impossible."

"I'm all right," I said. "I've been better lately."

She ran her hands along my forearms, leaving streaks of warmth. "You have been better. You're not the sad little pigeon that came creeping into the theater that day, are you? There's a spark in you. I've seen it. I bet you can get pretty mad."

Someone inside began playing the piano, a stumbling waltz. I sat up, suddenly afraid that we'd be seen.

"Wait, you." Rusala put her arms round my shoulders. She stared at my hair, my lips. "Wait."

Then her palms were on my cheeks and she kissed me, her small wet mouth nudging mine. Her hands slid to my throat.

"Rusala," I looked to the window. The hair rose over my arms.

"Don't you want to kiss me?" she said. She turned her head from side to side, keeping her eyes on mine.

"But won't they see us?" I asked.

I'd grabbed her hands away from my neck, and now she squeezed my fingers. "This isn't Boston," she answered. "You must act as though you don't care, anyway. You must."

She leaned close and kissed me again, pressing until I felt her teeth against my lips. I could scarcely move. Only my hands reached for her hair. I couldn't bear the thought of touching any other part of her, then.

The door opened. We jumped away from each other in the sudden light.

"Ah, I'm sorry." Greta backed away from us, turning as if she wanted to go back inside, but Olga stepped beside her.

"No servants and I can't cook." Olga tossed a sable at me and Rusala, then wrapped a white opera cloak around her shoulders. "We go to supper, out. Zeljko and Vitya went to call boat."

As the gondola rounded into the inlet, the party climbed aboard. I took Rusala's hand and felt her turn towards me. I didn't meet her eyes. I was paralyzed for a few nightmarish moments. Then I called out, "We'll stay here."

Rusala pulled me back towards the house. Once inside, she hurried to the fireplace and heaved another log on the fire. She shielded her face against the sparks, letting her black wrap fall to the carpet. I watched her, feeling something in me tilt.

"Do you want a palace like this someday?" she asked.

I neared her. When I kissed her cheek, she gave a nervous hum. She skipped away from me and wound up the gramophone. Her cheeks were febrile scarlet. She put on a Spanish melody, opening the speakers until the music stung my ears.

"I mean," she hollered, letting her arms rise, "a palace like this, that we own. Not one that's owned by some inbred, incontinent old pig, who lets us pay rent by washing his feet and sucking his prick."

The melody shifted and a woman began to sing, drowning out Rusala's voice completely. She spread her arms wide and turned, gasping up at the ceiling. She'd kicked off her slippers, and her bare feet stumbled over the flattened pillows.

She didn't sense my approach until I touched her hair; it was rough and knotted now, curling round my wrist like a spring. She stopped and stared at me, as if she'd forgotten I was there.

She covered her face and burst into sobs.

"What is it?" I tried to look into her face. She shook her head and pressed her cheek hard against my chest. The more I comforted her, the more she wept, sobbing so violently I feared she'd choke. I pulled her down to the couch with me and sat holding her small, hot head under my chin.

Her sobs turned to hiccups and moans. The front of my tunic was soaked through. A few moments later, she slumped into me, fast asleep.

Chapter Nine

"ARE YOU SLEEPING?" Rusala's voice echoed over the water.

"No." I snorted as I woke, and she laughed.

We'd been lucky to find a boat so early in the morning. The fog was close around us, pearly grey and so thick it condensed on our hair. I wore an old coat of persian lamb, and its high collar kept nuzzling me back into sleep. The world was silent and safe.

Each time my eyes closed, I felt I was back at Olga's house, on the white sofa where Rusala and I had fallen the night before. At dawn, she'd touched my hand. We'd had to tiptoe over snoring bodies as we left.

"I'm glad we escaped," Rusala said. Perched in the opposite end of the boat, she stretched and grinned at me. She didn't seem to feel the morning cold, although her ears were red.

I blinked to clear my eyes. "Why'd you want to leave so early?" I asked. The boat rocked wearily. The gondolier seemed unconcerned that we were pitching into emptiness.

"You've got that last portrait to finish," Rusala said. "And then I really ought to go to my lesson. No, that's not it."

She frowned, glanced up at the gondolier, and then crawled to me.

"I don't like being there in the mornings," she said. "There's no telling what sort of mood Olga will wake in. The last time I was there, she was in a frenzy about some performance, and she began to wail and cry at how old she'd become, how fat."

"Fat?"

"No, she's right. She's nearly thirty-five, and can hardly dance anymore. She makes it through performances with the help of cocaine and body-memory, but it nearly kills her. After Giselle, she did nothing but sleep and take ice baths for two days."

She yawned, and I squeezed her. "So why doesn't she retire?" I asked.

"She's the reason, you know," Rusala went on as if she hadn't heard me. "She's what made me decide I must find a way to stop dancing. She's a living parable. You see, ballet becomes so all-consuming, it begins to feel like a real vocation. You begin to feel that you have a place in the world, when in fact you're only a little sideshow."

"But she's so well known. Doesn't she have money?"

"Her own money, d'you mean? She's got money for a year, maybe. Then she'd be living in a cold-water flat, giving lessons in deportment to shrill, fat little heiresses who breathe through their mouths."

"No, she has her sponsor, Duke Something."

"Do be serious." She sat up suddenly. The boat rocked and the gondolier grumbled. "She hasn't seen him in months." She rolled her eyes and lay back on me. "One evening, she'll come home to find that he's stopped paying the rent. He'll write an elegant, irreproachable letter from his summer home in Livadia."

"Signora," the gondolier said. A flock of blue-grey pigeons swept overhead.

"She'll be a nice memory for him, though," Rusala went on. "When he's dozing after his Sunday meal, with his warmed slippers and his glass of chamomile tisane." Her cheeks were mottled and dark as plums.

I jumped when our boat hit a mooring. San Marco's Basilica suddenly appeared, glittering like dirty ice.

"Come on," I said. I helped her out of the boat and paid the gondolier. The square was carpeted with pigeons, bumbling and cooing drowsily as far as we could see. A flute sounded in the distance. A lone girl dozed on the church steps, a tray of flowers on her lap.

I turned, peering towards the edges of the square. "But didn't the gondolier take us too far?" I asked. "Or am I turned around? I'll never find my way in this city. These buildings keep changing places, don't they? They float and shift with the high tide."

"Yes," Rusala said. "We're playing blind-man's bluff, only there's no need for a blindfold. But aren't you hungry? I had him bring us here because I know where to find coffee and breakfast at this hour. Come on."

The fog lifted as we slipped through a fissure into a neighborhood I didn't recognize. The buildings here were dark maroon, packed tightly together, with stout grey shutters and barred doors. We ducked beneath swags of faded laundry, under tendrils of thyme and ropes of drying garlic. A sleepy milkman was the only other person in sight, dragging his cart over the footbridges, thunking up and down the stairs.

She led me under a bridge, where we passed single-file along a bank. I had to put one foot before the other and lift my skirts. At the canal's narrowest point, we leapt across and cut through a grassy garden full of rose-quartz statues. When we climbed up the steps to a square, we found ourselves at a low wooden carriage-house, not far from La Fenice. Rusala found a cracked doorway, hardly bigger than a coal chute. The passageway inside smelled of rotted seaweed.

Down a flight of stone steps, there was a kind of canteen or servants' kitchen, where a tiny ancient woman had laid out a tray of rolls and a pot of coffee. The ceiling was bare, and the walls were covered in carpets. A group of boys, some stagehands I recognized from my first visit to the theater, sat silently at the main table, drawing diagrams. We took some coffee and buns. The woman nodded towards us, rasping out some pleasantry before returning to her mending.

We sat at a corner table. The one lopsided window, high above us, showed the lightening, milky sky. Under the windowsill, someone had pinned up a soap advertisement cut from a newspaper, with a brunette woman dancing in filmy trousers and a girdle made of pearls and gauze. She covered her breasts with a palm branch.

"Hold on," I said, standing to see more closely. "Is that you, Rusala?"

She grinned over her mug of coffee. "I told you, I get lots of work as a model. I was in some movies, too, especially when I lived in Paris. You know that bit about the moon? That was my moving-picture debut. I played one of the sailor girls." She saluted me.

"Why, I went to the movie palaces all the time back home. Maybe I've seen you."

"No," she pitched forward and almost choked on her coffee. "Mm. No. I rather doubt you've seen my latest work. Unless you go sneaking into the men's washrooms in Atlantic City arcades." She gave me a searching look, pursing her lips.

I shook my head. "There aren't movies in men's washrooms," I said.

"Indeed there are. Little kinetoscope peep-shows with imported titles such as *Burning Shame.*" She nodded slowly, keeping her eyes fixed on mine, a glow of pride spreading over her face. "You know just what I mean. A lady is preparing for her bath, when—oh! Who is that at the window?" She lifted her arms over her head and arched her chest forward. "Mercy!"

"Shut up," I begged. Laughing made my temple throb. "But really, why did you stop and come to Venice? What brought you here?"

"I got sick of all the blue movies. They can be exhausting. In Paris they have no imagination about the cinema. They think it's

only good for magic tricks and burlesque and porno. I knew I could
dance here in Venice, and do private shows, sit for artists, make a
decent boodle. I knew I'd work out a way to really make my
fortune, once and for all. No more kidding around. I'll get myself
set for life."

"You're able to save up money, then, from all your work?"

"Not that much. Even the nude work doesn't pay well
anymore."

"How are you getting yourself set for life, then?"

"What I do get here is information," she said. "In Venice, you
see the richest families from all over the world, drunk and on
holiday, panting constantly about money. I've learned quite a bit
while lying naked on a rug, or tiptoeing about serving brandy."

She paused, letting her head fall back. "At first," she mused, "I
could only assume they thought me stupid. Or they thought I
couldn't speak English, maybe. Because they discussed every detail
of withdrawing funds, cashing bonds, selling art — right in front of
me. Serving makes you invisible."

She stopped, swallowing awkwardly and glancing about,
seeming to fear she'd said too much. "I say," she resumed in a
higher voice. "Isn't there a book about that? About a man who's
invisible? Yet another unfortunate book that will never become an
opera."

"No, wait," I said. "Tell me more. What is it you hope to learn
here? Do you intend to keep wandering from city to city until
you've found your best prospects? You've already lived in so many
places, and done so much." I trailed off hopefully, but she only
became more nervous, sucking on her pale lips.

She looked away, tapping her spoon on her saucer. "Is it true
that the man had to be naked, in order to be invisible?" she asked.
"Now, I'd find that much more shocking than his invisibility. A
naked man, running all about town, squeezing onto the streetcar.
The book should've been called *The Invisible Pervert*."

"Listen," I said, leaning over the table. "Stop being so slippery.
I want to hear about your life, I do. I don't know a thing about
you." She smiled ruefully, but I pressed on, putting my hand next
to hers, remembering the weight of her sleeping head on my chest.
"You needn't be shy or ashamed with me."

She became thoughtful again, slowly pouring sugar into her
coffee, watching it turn from crystal to caramel. "A few men have
kept me," she said. "The first one, a long time ago, paid for my
dancing lessons. And do you know, he was the one who helped me
think up the ridiculous name of *Rusala*? To be fair, some of 'em
were first-rate, really decent to me. They took me abroad. We had
some gay times. That's how I got to Paris, and then a few other

places. And it never bothered me, I mean working, keeping them happy. I was good at it. Yet all the same, I reached a kind of crisis three years ago. I can't say what it was, but it was astonishingly sudden, like a light being snuffed out in me. I woke one day and there was a different scent to the air, a different look to the sunlight. Do you know what I mean? And then that night, I found I couldn't bear it anymore. I mean I would shake with revulsion whenever they touched me. I became terrified I'd hurt one of them."

She traced a slow curve on the oilcloth. "I've felt that way ever since. Fuck me, their urgency, their sudden fits of whingeing and slobbering. Yet it's exactly like the urgent desire one sometimes has for a chamber pot: once the business is done, that same chamber pot is the last thing one wants to have around, isn't it?" She laid her hand flat on the table and watched it. "I was dismayed, at first, to lose my bread and butter that way. I really tried, but I simply couldn't go back to it. And then—"

She broke off. We both watched her hand as it spread open, then formed a quick fist. "Then," she continued, "I realized that it had happened for a reason. It made me face the fact that there were other, better, more daring, more lucrative aspirations, if only I could make myself brave enough. That's what I've worked towards ever since."

"What, then? I still don't see it. You're going to get better work, you're going to get into investments?" I asked, sucking on a spoonful of coffee grounds. I shuddered at their bitterness. My stomach had gone sour.

"Leave off, Katie."

She held my gaze for a long moment. It was hot and close in the room. She tapped her spoon again, more rapidly.

I put down my cup. "Sorry, leave off what?" My confusion tipped over into irritability.

"That willful naïveté," she said. "No, I don't intend to buy stock, I don't intend to—" she waved her spoon in slow, sarcastic circles, "—marry well."

"All right, *what*, then? You intend to steal someone else's money?" I believe I'd meant to shock her, but her eyes only widened with a kind of cold pleasure as I spoke.

"I shall learn to be happy with what I have. That's the Buddhist way." She looked at the ceiling. "There's loads of money in the world. No one's going to suffer if I get some of my own. And I don't mean to become a professional thief, that's damned tiresome. I just need a decent shot of cash, something to pay off my debts and get me out of Venice again, and on my way. Do you know, in America you could make a mad filthy pile in moving-

pictures. They mass-produce 'em. It's a real industry. The
Vitagraph in Flatbush is a kind of movie factory! Can you imagine
what they'd make of me? Hell, it's only a question of getting there."

She'd leaned forward as she spoke. There was that cunning
light in her eyes again. I almost suspected she'd burst into laughter
at any moment and give up the joke.

Instead she looked down. "What? Have I shocked you?" Her
voice had done one of its sudden shifts, and was now sweet and
girlish.

I took a spoonful of sugar but couldn't get the bitter taste off
my tongue. "You're really planning some dodge," I said, "and you
think you'll get away with it?"

"Do you know, you're right," she said. "Maybe instead I could
forgo my noontime sandwich. I might save a penny a day. Just
think how much I'd have saved by the time I'm forty." She slurped
at her coffee and licked her lips. "Sorry. It's only that you struck me
as someone with a bit of imagination."

"Can you imagine prison, Rusala? You struck me as someone
with half a brain in your head."

I couldn't bear even the scent of the coffee now. I put the cup
away from me.

Laughter came from above. Two young women walked briskly
along the alley. The fog behind them dissolved into pure ivory
sunlight. I imagined how I appeared to them: a tall angular woman
in a borrowed gown, with flat greasy hair and an over-eager smile,
hiding like a cockroach in a basement canteen. My mouth was filled
with a metallic taste. I swallowed, swallowed, but my teeth felt
coated and slick.

"I'm only playing, anyway," Rusala said. Her smile was easy,
but her eyes darted. "I like to scandalize you. Are you always so
credulous, you bunny?"

I stood.

"Aw, don't, Katie," she said. "I didn't think you would be so
sensitive, with all you've seen and experienced and been involved
with and been investigated about."

"Would you stop?" I took off the sweltering persian lamb and
laid it on the bench. "I suppose you find it all amusing." I tried to
continue but my thoughts swelled up hotly and crowded one
another, until my forehead ached.

She laid her hand on mine. I looked down at the top of her
hand, the squirming blue veins. For a moment her hand felt
unnaturally hot and soft, like something that had been slopped
over me.

"I need some air," I said. "I just feel a little sick." I coughed,
and she let go. I stumbled up the stairwell and into the daylight. I

felt self-conscious, some madwoman who'd been sleepwalking, who'd barely managed to put on slippers before leaving her house.

WHEN I ARRIVED home, my vestibule smelled of vinegar. The floor was damp and the balustrade had been polished until it shone like licorice. Lovorka came down the steps, wearing a kerchief on her head and holding a rag. Her placid, frank face revived me.

"I let them in," she said. "That was all right? I got some tea, some rolls."

"Tea?" I stared. "You let whom in?"

I smelled the tea, and heard footsteps overhead. I saw for the first time the coats hanging under my new mirror. A man's boater, a parasol.

"You want to change. Come, ma'am." She took my elbow and helped me up the stairs, smiling as if it were my birthday. As she led me into my bedroom, I saw two shadowed forms in my bright studio. Lovorka rushed me past the doorway before I could take another look.

"Hello, Katie," said a male voice.

"Yes. Hello," I called out as Lovorka closed my bedroom door. She'd already laid out my blue summer muslin, and she now pulled my arms over my head.

"Who's there?" I whispered to her.

"Those art people. Brother and sister." She unhooked Rusala's tunic from me. My skin smelled of rich perfume and coffee.

"God, not now. My studio's a disaster."

"Shh." She pulled a fresh chemise over my head. I shook my hair free as she put a corset round my waist. I relaxed into its familiar embrace.

Tugging at its laces, she said, "I clean this morning. Looks all right." She combed her fingers through my hair.

"Ow," I complained. She took my shoulders and steered me to the mirror, where I stood blinking as she twisted my hair into a knot.

"You have no idea how tired I am," I began, but she only hummed vaguely, putting a few more pins into my chignon. She backed away, nodding towards the door.

I found Amy in my hallway. She was pale, wringing her orange satin gloves in her hand. She wore a gown of starched linen, with a high flared collar and triangles of lace at its hem. I was learning that she liked to wear these ridiculous things, the mode of the week, as if to show she could throw her gowns away like paper after one or two wearings.

I cleared my throat. "Good morning."

She grabbed my forearm. "You." She looked almost annoyed. Her ginger brows were furrowed.

Then William came striding out of my studio. Despite my confusion, I smiled at the sight of him. His hair was still damp. His white collar was so tight that I winced to see him swallow.

He took my other hand. "Here she is. Your maid told us you were on your morning walk. And we rudely made our way to your studio here."

"I'll be damned," said Amy.

We went back into the studio. Lovorka had opened the windows wide to clear out the reek of turpentine. The canvases were neatly propped against the walls; a vase of fresh-cut daisies stood by the tea tray on my little table. I looked towards Lovorka, as she waited in the doorway.

"Sorry," Amy said. She sat on the sofa and tucked her legs under her. "I was just taken aback."

William squeezed my wrist. "See, Amy? Katie's so polite she hasn't even demanded to know what the devil we're doing here," he said. He looked down at his hand, still closed around mine, then let go.

"We really should have waited outside, but in fact I prefer it this way," Amy said. "When I look at an artist's work for the first time, it's better if I'm alone. I don't have to worry about insulting them."

"Ah," I said. Of course. These hectic paintings. "These are just some things I did quickly, for practice."

She looked away, resting her palm on her forehead. My heart sank.

"My gallery is going to be the best in Venice!" she said, turning back to me. "Where have you been? Why didn't you tell me you were a genius?"

"I told you so." William went to her and put his arm round her shoulder, shaking her gently. "It's the quiet ones you need to be careful of."

"So you like them?" I looked around at the paintings of Rusala. The forms seemed to move, to dance slowly. I could almost hear her thighs rubbing together, the soft thud of her hip-bones as she stretched. *I didn't paint them,* I wanted to confess. *It was something that went through me. I couldn't do it again.*

"Confound it, yes," Amy said. "When can we have the showing? I don't want to wait for next spring."

I sat on my stool and reached for some tea.

"And it will be my gallery that shows you first." Amy clapped her hands together. She stood and starting pulling on her gloves, pointing at William with one blazing finger. "My gallery, that's been called a vanity project, a ladies' club, premiering work like this."

"You can stop barking at us, Colonel," William said, pushing his hands in his pockets and going to the largest canvas. It was an image of Rusala wrapped in a shawl, her eyes downcast, her hair in a single braid.

"Let us take you to lunch, won't you?" Amy smoothed her hair; she'd hennaed it again and it was bright as orange pulp. "We want to bring you to our favorite place on the Lido. To celebrate." She wound her wristwatch, scowling around the room. "Why don't you have a clock?"

I swallowed a mouthful of syrupy tea. I was exhausted. I wanted nothing more than to stretch out in my own bed and sleep, then think things over, then sleep some more.

Lovorka coughed. She was still standing in the doorway. She fidgeted with her apron and raised her eyebrows at me.

"Lunch would be lovely," I said.

Chapter
Ten

A GROUP OF five gypsy boys stood on the beach, singing a ballad. The smallest of them wore a pair of short trousers and an oversized white shirt that fluttered from his shoulders. His black hair was matted and fluffed like the back of a wild sheep. He sang with his eyes squeezed shut.

I felt Amy's hand on mine. "Are you listening, Katie?" Her eyes were narrow, her face pink from wine. "Who was the model that you used, anyway?" she asked.

The luncheon room of the Hotel Lily was deliciously cool and shadowed. We'd sat for a long time over our lunch, and now the room was deserted but for a few waiters chatting near the piano. The walls were inlaid with mother-of-pearl and tinted glass. Our seats were cream-colored plush, as if we sat in a jewel box. Electric fans rattled softly, high overhead. Glass doors opened on the patio, where the balustrades were wound with white ribbon.

"Did you hear me?" Amy asked.

"Sorry." I took another sip of tea. "My model's a dancer, a ballet-girl I hired." I couldn't stop thinking of Rusala, of how much she'd enjoy this lunch. I wondered if she'd even been to the Lido. She was probably sitting on the edge of La Fenice's stage right now, eating an apple and a cut of brown bread she'd brought from home. What were her rooms like in the artists' hotel? Did she have her own bed at least? I thought of her bed, her pillow, and I felt a stinging in my tongue.

"A dancer. Nice, I thought so." Amy nodded sagely. "The dancer motif is perfect. Everyone likes that. I want to show you before Christmas. I daresay we'll sell most of those paintings."

"I think you're right." William was digging into his second piece of lemon cake. "People have been craving something new: risqué portraits, those deep colors. Simple forms, but not crude, you know? What paints did you use, anyway, something you brought over from Boston? Brilliant."

Amy drained her red wine and sighed impatiently. "We'll

need," she said, snapping her fingers and lifting her empty wine glass. I'd never seen anyone do that before. "We'll need to get more works from you, preferably soon. Stay with that style, the reds and the sparkly bits of metal and the nudes."

A waiter came over, and I had an excuse to bend over my plate and pick at my watercress. Money. How much money would I make? I couldn't bring myself to ask.

"You look pale," William observed.

I touched my cheeks and found they were clammy. "I didn't sleep very well. Do you truly think I'll sell the paintings? Someone will want to buy them?" *And for how much?*

"Oh." William leaned back in his chair. "Dear, that's the whole point, isn't it?"

"You see, this is all so new to her," Amy said. Her freckles darkened along her throat. "A fledgling genius."

She leaned forward and the silverware rattled. William lifted his plate. "Easy, Sparky."

"Hold on, Amy," I said. "I don't want you to become overexcited about this and set me up for a ridiculous and very public failure."

The singing stopped, and I looked outside again. A man in a grubby apron bolted out of the hotel kitchen, waving a wooden spoon at the boys, who scattered. The littlest one squeaked like a chipmunk and sprinted to the surf.

I imagined Rusala in a swimming costume, splashing into the sea. I imagined her free of worries, with money in savings. See, I'd tell her, life needn't be all strife. Adele had always tried to tell me that; I'd wanted to strike her when she said it.

I felt a terrible heaviness in the center of my chest, as if I'd swallowed a ball of lead that was now spreading through my shoulders, my arms. I'd been so cross with Rusala, but I had no right to criticize her. She'd been just a child when the first man snapped her up, and there was no telling what had come before that.

Amy and William were watching me. Amy paid the waiter and was about to speak, but I cut in. "It's become a little close in here, hasn't it?" I asked. "Want to go for a walk?"

WE SET OFF along a path of wooden planks on the beach. The day had turned so hot that most of the bathers had gone, and only a few determined Englishwomen ran from the changing huts to the sea. Pastel-painted sandoli floated near the docks.

Amy opened her parasol—stiff pink satin edged with freshwater pearls—and lifted it over her head. Her form was an oasis of rose-tinted shade against the expanse of sand. When she held out her hand, I took it. The tassels of her parasol susurrated all around us as we walked.

William strolled ahead. "I was hoping one of you would race me to the end of the beach." He pivoted on his heel and walked backwards. "But I see you're too dignified for that."

"Is that a challenge?" I asked Amy.

Her arm twitched, and she burst into a run, lowering her parasol before her like a shield. I took up my skirts and ran past both of them. When my hat slid I pulled it off, still running, giddy and nearly breathless. The boardwalk shuddered.

We reached the end of the walk, where a deer path led uphill into a pine forest. I wiped my cheeks with my forearm and shook the sand from my skirts. A rush of cool air lifted my petticoat.

"So, Miss Larkin, do you think this path is private?" William was panting.

Amy came up behind us. "Follow me. I think I know where we are."

She ducked under a branch and started up the path, her pink shoes scrambling over the red earth, her hair a fox-red glow ascending and fading into the shadows. I took off my gloves and tucked them in my sash.

"Are you coming?" I asked William. Before he could answer, I grabbed a sapling and pulled myself up. The breeze brought the scents of eucalyptus and pine and meaty smoke. We caught up to Amy as she reached a wider path. A tiny wooden shack stood, covered in colored glass beads. Amy ran to it.

"Look, look, look," she said. "It just reaches my waist! A dollhouse." The hem of her gown bristled with pine needles. She leaned her ear on the roof and stared at us. "I hear something— children laughing."

"Oh, stop it." William ran to join her, then knelt on its opposite side. "Katie," he cried. "You've got to see this."

He took my hand as I reached him. One side of the shack was open, showing a floor covered in carnations and lavender. Inside there stood a wooden cross, and a jade statue of a slim, smiling goddess standing in a gold hoop. The threshold was lined with sun-bleached shells and little dried seahorses.

I sank to a crouch.

"It's a shrine, isn't it?" Amy knelt beside me. "Someone must have been here this morning. See how fresh the flowers are."

"Is there water inside?" William bent over behind us. He reached past Amy's shoulder, brushing aside the flowers.

"A face." Amy pointed.

A man's face, carved in stone, was hidden under the flowers.

The mouth was stretched unnaturally wide.

"See, I thought so," William said. "It's a spring."

Water trickled from the tortured stone mouth. It looked delicious to me, so dark and pure. I leaned in and put my lips to it, sucking in two mouthfuls. The scent of lavender filled my head.

"What'd you do that for?" Amy asked. I sat up and she scowled at me, her eyes bright. "You'll get a disease now."

"Either that or have eternal life," William said. "You drink now, Amy."

But she wouldn't until William did.

We kept walking, and although the afternoon was ending, they seemed unconcerned about time. I supposed that they could always wander as they pleased, never worrying about keeping hold of a key, or a purse. Anyone on the island would recognize their names and take them back home whenever they wished.

Amy ran ahead while William and I walked more slowly. The water had left a rusty taste in my mouth. The sunlight fell in amber-colored shafts through the dark branches. Above the canopy, seagulls wheeled and cried.

My eyelids felt heavy. I sighed and William took my arm. "All right?"

I felt a spike of irritation that surprised me. I barely resisted the urge to pull away from him.

"I've told you, haven't I, Katie," he said abruptly. "How happy we've been since you've come. I mean besides the excitement about the showing. I mean you yourself."

He broke off, kicking at a pinecone. "I don't believe we've ever met anyone so remarkable," he continued. "I mean, I haven't. I haven't."

Silence settled between us. I swallowed and watched our feet on the path, his shoes like great beetles, my own like little white pig-hooves.

"Hey!" came Amy's voice. She had disappeared behind a hedge. "I was right. Here we are." She yelled something about a house.

"Whose house?" William bellowed.

My heart was thumping. I had a sense of circling, as if I were in a magic lantern that played the same story over and over again. Ah, here's how it starts: the man and the woman take their first walk alone.

Amy called again and I took my arm from William's. He turned his fresh face to me. A perfect simplicity, an adamantine gloss.

"Let's find Amy," I said. "She's going to wander into someone's kitchen."

I ran up ahead, towards the blue-green hedge. When I rounded the corner, I was blinded. We'd reached a clearing with a white cottage, whose red-tiled roof caught the sun like molten copper. Beneath it, two shadows came down a sloping, sun-frosted lawn.

"You two!" One of the shadows neared me. I saw a halo of silver. I approached, going into the shade. William was beside me.

I should have known it would be Greta. She embraced me. Her bones felt small and fragile under her plump flesh.

"My foster daughter," she said. "Are you all lost, or what?"

Amy lay on the grass, arms wide. William threatened to step on her.

Greta led me under a eucalyptus tree, where she'd set a white wicker table and chaise longues. She wore a tea gown of grey muslin that made her look taller and paler. "God, you shocked me when you came creeping out of the woods like that," she said. "I think I just got a few more white hairs. Want a little strawberry punch?"

"Yes, please," I answered. Twisted apple trees and pink oleander surrounded the lawn. I turned back to look again at the house. It was solid and squat, made of clean white stones, with birds' nests in its eaves and a trellis thick with kiwi vines.

"It used to be the groundskeeper's house for one of the Volpi estates," Greta said. She pointed down a stone path. "See that grove there? Golden plums, with the sweetest, mildest flavor. I've heard that particular variety grows only here, in this yard."

She moved a stack of papers from the largest chair. "Sit."

I sat and took a long drink of punch. "What were you doing?"

"I'm reading over this play, for God's sake." She sat opposite me and earmarked a page. "I'm to perform it in London this January. Six weeks at Haymarket." She took a long, shuddering breath. I imagined the role was a coup.

Amy and William stood and came towards us, punching one another. William was struggling to take off his collar.

"Heat poisoning." Greta was so different with them. She lost her Western drawl and sounded like someone from the Eastern states. "Honestly. Sit down and have some punch."

"Thank you," William said. He perched on the edge of a chair. "I love your house. It reminds me of a place I want to buy over in Spalato. Katie, you've got to come with us sometime. A jewel of a place, an old Roman villa overlooking Diocletian's palace."

"Yes, fine old place, filled with sand and overrun with goats," Amy said. Her mood had curdled.

"Tell me more about the play," I said to Greta. I rested my chignon on the chair back and watched her. Her movement always fascinated me; it was studied, yet not exactly false, more as if she were trying to keep her focus, like a tightrope walker.

"Yes, this play by London's best playwright? Look." She lifted a few crumpled pages. "I suppose the plot has a kind of hypnotic predictability, but this dialogue. A string of pompous aphorisms. Who talks this way?"

"Lots of people. Everybody at Harvard," William answered. "It's a whole steaming heap of pomposity."

Greta shrugged. "Granted, there are people like that, but they don't usually get as much — attention from the ladies — as this bum does."

Amy leaned forward and poured herself more punch. "Yeah," she said, lifting a vampy shoulder towards her chin. "It's that kind of play? A free love drama full of burly poets with whiskers and vegetarian sapphists?"

William covered his eyes, defeated. "Good God."

Amy brushed at her skirt, frowning at the dust. "Sorry, Petunia. Hey, I'm hungry. Have anything in your kitchen?" She stood and started towards the porch.

Greta watched her for a moment, then turned to us. "All right, there might be a vegetarian sapphist in the play," she said. "Most of the characters are sort of interesting. All the same, they're so eerily placid."

She earmarked another page. "It's difficult to explain, but I believe that's what makes the story so odd to me. The playwright's trying to render happiness, or enlightenment, yet the characters just seem to be in a kind of glass dome. A smug, airless paradise. One of them needs to smash out and do something reckless."

"I know exactly what you're going to say," said William. "Don't think I haven't heard it a million times before." His voice took on a garrulous, affectionate tone, as if this were an argument he'd had before, and its familiarity pleased him. "About glory and excess. And I appreciate your point, but what happens after someone's done all that smashing? Have they really found out anything new? There's nothing wrong with a little contentment now and then, is there?"

Greta moved her left hand to her skirt, painstakingly drawing up handfuls of cloth. William leaned back and cleared his throat.

I turned to the grove. When the wind rose up, the sunlit branches flared. Each leaf watched me like an adamant eye. The back door opened, and Amy strolled towards us, munching on an apple.

"Amy, I think you missed some of my own pompous aphorisms," Greta said.

Amy had found a merino wrap from somewhere in the house. She lay sideways in her chair, throwing her legs over one armrest and bracing her back against the other.

"I'm wrung out," she said. "Greta, could I convince you to read to us?"

"I've been reading aloud to the trees all afternoon," Greta said. "I guess I could see how it sounds to real people." She rifled through the pages.

I tilted my head back. Above me, the leaves darkened, like eyelids darkening with sleep.

I WOKE LATER to find Greta smoothing my forehead.

"I didn't have the heart to wake you earlier," she said.

I sat up. It seemed I could smell Rusala near. I glanced around the violet-shaded yard, confused. It was the scent of my own skin that reminded me of her.

William lay stretched out on the grass, his hat covering his face. His chest rose and fell steadily, and his hands lay flat on his stomach. Amy sat slouched in her wicker chair, her head thrown back.

"I'll tell the writer his play is as nice as the Gethsemane Gardens," Greta said.

"No, it was fine." I rubbed my eyes. "It's just that I was up all night. And I have to go now, I have to."

Her forehead wrinkled. "All night?" she asked. I wanted to tell her more, but she glanced away.

William woke, sitting up and ruffling his hair until it looked wild. Amy rolled to her belly, yawning.

"I'll send for a cab and have you brought down to the pier," Greta said. "Next time you may even use the front gate."

Chapter
Eleven

WE HIRED A motor-launch and went careening over the sea, passing the omnibus full of tourists. Venice greeted us gradually, drawing us in. The air was opalescent, just moments away from darkness. The cooling breeze bore the first stirrings of evening life: a bitter argument, the singing of gondoliers, a violin. I sat up impatiently as the city closed around us.

When we arrived at the Seagroves gallery, the maids coaxed Amy awake and led her, grumbling, into the house.

"Come in for supper," William said, turning to help me out of the boat. The water around us glowed with remembered daylight.

I tugged back on his hand. "I couldn't, thank you. No, really." I had to get back to my rooms. The image of Rusala returning to empty darkness was agony. I couldn't believe how late it had become. She would think I was still angry with her. Perhaps she'd go back to her boarding house, or to stay with some other friend. I was terrified that I'd waited too long already, that I'd missed my chance.

William still clasped my hand and I tugged, hard. The boat rocked beneath me.

"At least—" There came that stop in his breath again. "I know you're a spectacularly modern woman, but let me see you home."

"Of course." It wouldn't slow me down too much.

His arm was firm under mine as we walked. By some desperate instinct, I suggested a route that brought us very near La Fenice. I looked into each window.

William hummed the gypsy boys' melody as we neared my house. I glanced at him, just to see how smug his profile might look, but there was something about his lowered eyelids, the tension round his mouth, that made me pause. My tongue touched the roof of my mouth. What would happen if I confided everything to him?

I am sorry if I seem distracted. I might be in love, or about to be in love, with a wild, enigmatic girl. Since I've met her, the world is full of color and oxygen, and I can't bear the thought of being without her.

"Am I walking too fast for you, Katie? You seem out of breath."

"I am anxious to get home," I said, watching the cobblestones disappear beneath my skirt. "I have business. Someone might be waiting."

"Here you are," he said. We passed The Daisy and neared my door. "And it might be nice to call again some time, even when there's no business proposition."

"Yes," I said, opening my purse and shaking it to find my keys. He still clung to me. I pulled my arm from under his so quickly that my sleeve hissed like a struck match.

MY ROOMS WERE empty. Lovorka was gone. I sat for a while, restless, looking out into the dark. I decided it would be best for now to stay put, in case Rusala came in. Her gowns were still in the wardrobe, after all. Her half-mended stockings hung over my desk chair. I lay down without undressing, without lighting a lamp.

I dreamt that Rusala and I lay curled on a bed of sheepskin and velvet blankets. In the dream, I fed her morsels of cake with my fingers, watching her throat as she swallowed gratefully.

Tap. I rolled over and the dream dissolved. *Tap, tap.* I turned towards the open window just as a tiny round speck came arcing in. It bounced across my carpet and rolled to my bed. An almond.

What on earth? I sat up. It was still early, not even midnight. The cafés were full of lazy chatter.

Another almond bounced off the casement and I padded to the window. When I peeked around the edge, I met the eyes of a thin girl of perhaps thirteen, with a round pale face. She wore a green calico dress and a boy's jacket of purple and gold brocade. A silk carnation was tucked behind her ear.

"*Che fai?*" I called out, disappointed at how peremptory it sounded. I regretted not taking the time to learn more nuanced Italian. How would one say, for instance, *Why are you throwing almonds at me?*

"Madam-a," she responded. "You know Rusala?"

"Who are you?"

She struggled for the words in English. "I take for Rusala, she want skirt and shoes, that she forget here."

"Wait there, dear."

I glanced around the room, snapping my fingers. On an impulse, I scooped some cash into my purse before I thundered down the stairs. The little girl gave a start when I burst out to the alley.

"No," she said in a kind of screaming whisper. "She say you just give me her things. Not to come with, no."

"It will be all right." I wanted to rest my hand on her shoulder but she flinched, almost sobbed, as I drew near.

"Just take me to her, will you?" I said, bending to her and smiling. "I'll take care of everything."

The night had a splendid full moon, surrounded by a nimbus of cotton-candy pink. Each café awning covered an orange-tinted tableau, full of flushed young men in waistcoats and women in iridescent gowns. As the night deepened, these islands of warmth and activity seemed more isolated, more intensely vibrant, under the dark sky.

The crowd near La Fenice Theater was thinner but more boisterous. Before the fountain, a man played a melody on a row of wine glasses filled with water. The little girl walked ahead of me, her careless braid swinging, her anklets ringing with each step. When we reached the Hotel des Artistes, she took me down an alley, over a bridge, then stopped at a broken door, turning towards me and chewing at her thumbnail. A sign beside the door read *Hotel B.*

"It's all right," I said again. "Is this where she is? I'll tell her you've done a fine job." I handed her a coin and she gaped at my purse.

When I entered the front hall I was struck by the mixed scents of peppermint, camphor, and buttery fried bread. The walls were covered in greyed paper, mended in places with squares of newsprint. Along the stairwell, the balustrade was half-gone, as if the railings had been plucked away for firewood. A single tallow candle burned under a nacreous shade. Great thumping footsteps came from overhead, along with screams of laughter and the sound of someone bleating like a goat.

I listened for a long time, standing with one foot on the stairwell, my head bowed low. All at once I heard Rusala's voice, rising sharply. I gathered my skirts and took the stairs two at a time.

The upstairs corridor was narrow, carpeted with a strip of old canvas. Most of the doors were propped open, showing rooms festooned with drying stockings and tarlatans. Girls sat in their dressing gowns, playing cards or mending. In one room, two boys were trying to put a wig on a cat.

Rusala's voice came from the end of the hall, speaking Italian. I heard another voice, a man's voice, rough from smoking. When I rounded the corner, there stood Rusala, still in the rosy spangled tunic she'd worn the night before. Her tin trunk leaned against her legs and she held a soldier's rucksack over her shoulder. She gestured nervously as she spoke.

It wasn't a man she spoke with, however, but a woman, one with a grotesquely deep voice and muddy eyes. She was skeletal, and stooped like an old spoon that had been stood on one end. A yellow parakeet sat on her shoulder, watching me warily and shuffling as I stole through the door.

The woman didn't glance at me. Rusala continued with her supplication, holding out her palms. As I neared, Rusala turned and looked up at me with wild eyes.

"Confound it, what are you doing here?" she said. "I sent Jadranka to pick up my frocks."

"What's going on?"

"Nothing, nothing. You needn't have come. I'm only moving out, and—"

The woman held up three typed documents and started speaking again. Her gravelly voice made my teeth ache.

"Do you speak English?" I started lamely, and the woman closed her eyes.

"Who the devil is this?" I asked Rusala.

"The landlady. I refuse to pay rent twice for the same month. She tried this same trick last month. Claimed I never paid, hounded me until I came up with more money just to get some peace. I'm not going to do it again. I know I paid. She evidently believes she can just wave some stamped documents in my face and talk about the police, and that will somehow induce me to pay whatever sum she cares to name."

"You're quite sure you paid?" I asked. I held out my hand for the papers, which only made the landlady snap them to her chest. The parakeet bobbed its head at me.

"You mustn't get involved," Rusala said. "That's not why I sent Jadranka. I never thought you'd come. Damn me, what a nightmare. The landlady's saying she's left several notices for me, something about non-payment and property being seized by an official body. I know I paid her, though. Every first Sunday I leave some money in her box. She believes she can cheat me because I can't read."

"I don't suppose you got receipts," I said.

"No, indeed."

I opened my mouth, not knowing what I would say. Rusala and the landlady looked at me.

"Who needs this, anyway?" I finally said. "Why don't you come live with me? I don't mean just to camp, but for good. As your home."

Rusala gave a brusque shake of her head. "Stop, really. I have plenty of other places to stay."

The landlady gave a reedy sigh.

"But I want you to." I barely managed to stop myself from reaching for Rusala's hand. A strange feeling crept over me, a delicious emptiness in my chest.

"I upset you so, this morning," she said. "Playing with you in that way. I don't know what came over me. It's just my bad heart. You don't deserve it."

I did take her hand then. I spoke in a slow, deliberate tone, desperate to get the words exactly right: "If you only knew, Rusala, how much pain I've had, thinking of you today." I knew my meaning was clear, even brazen, but I was too far gone to stop. "How I ached, thinking you might leave, and you might never know—"

"You really want me to come live with you?"

She started towards me, but then jumped and turned away, mortified, pushing her hair from her flushed forehead. I followed her glance to the doorway, where a few dancers had gathered to watch. They scattered when I stared.

I faced the landlady. "How much does she owe?" I asked, taking out my purse.

"Thirty lire, including legal fees," she answered, in flawless English.

I counted out a twenty-note and five coins, laying them on the cracked windowsill. I was still unaccustomed to Italian currency; it looked like play-money to me, yet the landlady's eyes bulged at the sight of it.

"This," I told her, "is for rent and any other incidental expenses. Your lawyer may contact me directly with any further invoices."

Two of the coins slid to the floor. I took up Rusala's trunk. The parakeet shrieked.

"MELANIA PAZZO," RUSALA spat. "That's her name, the officious old bitch. It ought to be the name of a terrible nerve disease."

I lay on my bed, curled on my side, the coverlet pulled to my chin. Lovorka was fast asleep in the kitchen. The city had gone quiet. Even the sea's breathing had slowed.

I couldn't stop looking at Rusala. Once we'd arrived, she'd said she longed for a wash. I didn't have a tub, but I'd piled coal in my bedroom's brazier and given her a stool and a washbasin. Now she sat naked in the half-darkness, drawing the sea-sponge along her legs. The indigo moonlight lit one side of her, while her other side glowed with firelight. Her eyes were slitted with bliss.

She sighed and twisted towards the fire. "But she's never liked me," she continued.

"Who, the nerve disease?" I asked. I was nearly choked with happiness. Only hours before, I'd feared I'd never see her again.

"Ha, yes. She knows I can't read. That's why she's only left written notices. And she doesn't seem to misplace others' rent, you see."

"Why would she dislike you?"

Rusala leaned forward and swished her feet in the basin. "Nearly two years ago, I shared that very room with another dancer. Larisa, a Russian girl."

"Go on."

"She was from St. Petersburg. Such a soft-spoken thing. They raise them like nuns in the Imperial school."

Rusala lifted one leg and stretched it out in front of her, flexing her ankle. "I was all ready to hate Larisa, naturally," she said. "But she was so sweet to me, Katie. No one so beautiful and fine had ever been so kind to me. She sought me out that very first day, and we became fast chums. She taught me how to dance, to really dance. Technique, line, elegance. I was just a little brown circus pony then, all force and no grace. She refined me. And then I was able to teach her how to jump, beat, do the hops on pointe that I'd learned in Milan. We joined forces. We rehearsed day and night. We were going to be *étoiles*."

She lifted her other leg and rubbed her calf.

"I mean to say that I loved her." She spoke more quickly now. "And, no, not like a sister, or a best friend. You understand."

I held my arms tight across my chest. "And you lived together."

"Yes, we did. As if we were married, in a way." She glanced suddenly at my bedroom door, as if she'd heard something in the hallway.

"Oh, but didn't we have to be on guard," she went on. "It's strange. In some circles, particularly among artists, it was absolutely the norm. In fact it comes into fashion every ten years or so, have you noticed that? At least, it does here." She looked down shyly. "And of course rich women can do whatever the hell they wish and make it into an intellectual enterprise. Yet girls who work must be wholly discreet about their private lives. There's no telling when someone will decide you're an abomination and make your life hell. All the same, happiness can dull fear, and we were— what's the word—*elated*, when you feel you're made of air and light. We danced together here in Venice, and toured a bit along Istria. We planned to audition for Theatre Slav. We did performances at private parties, too. Once we danced a pas de deux wearing only some diaphanous smocks, at a summer party in Spalato. Duke Pejacevic wanted to set us both up in his palace. He called us his little dryads."

She looked towards me, and I realized she couldn't see my face in the shadow.

"We saved our money, and we had plans. Larisa longed to return to St. Petersburg. She regaled me with stories of white nights, the Hermitage, the troikas racing along the boulevards in winter. She was sure that the political situation was growing calm again. But I wanted to go to New York, as I've told you. Yet she had a prejudice against America. She imagined it was all yelling, shunting crowds."

She splashed water in her face and rubbed her neck.

"I do believe," she said thoughtfully, "that we were happier arguing over plans than we would have been enacting them. We had a sense, then, that we had found our ideal and were living it. I think that's when we began to be reckless, to incur suspicion. Our landlady kept muttering about indecency. Old Melania was glad to see Larisa go."

"But where is Larisa now?"

"Now? Hell if I know. She could sew a little. Maybe she's making dresses, or hats. Maybe her little arms are beefed up from carrying coal." She scratched suddenly at her thighs. "She had an injury, you see. I'd bought her a pair of pointe shoes from Milan. Niccolinis, hard as oak, perfect for turns. She was so thrilled that she put them on right away. And then of course she had to try fouetté turns on the polished parquet of the theater lobby."

"Oh my God."

"She shattered her pelvis. She dislocated her thigh. We paid all our savings for a surgeon." She took two long, slow breaths. "But I think that made it worse."

"Did she have to go back home?"

"She hasn't got a home. She was raised at the Imperial Ballet school since she was five. No relatives that she knew of. Duke Pejacevic took her in for a time while she convalesced. She lost her contract with the theater, of course, and soon the Duchess began to threaten her. Now everyone says she's gone back to St. Petersburg, or perhaps to Moscow. Not one of our friends has seen her or had news of her in all this time. I've tried to hold fast to my idea of going to America, yet it's become an empty obsession, one I'm not even certain I want anymore. It's become something to fix my mind to."

She lifted her shoulders and steadied herself. She turned her head towards the window and the blue light made her face unearthly.

"It astounded me," she said, "how I could go on breathing without her, waking in the morning, eating, walking about, when I felt that all my cells had hardened into plaster. It's remarkable, isn't it, how cold and hard you can make yourself. I thought I'd reached a kind of purity, an austere sense of purpose."

"I know exactly what you mean."

"Then I saw you."

"Me?" There was a surge of blood in my chest, like panic.

"Oh, fuck me. Fuck." She breathed heavily, her brow wrinkling. "Is there any way I can say it without offending you, or frightening you?" Her hands on her thighs slowed until the scratching became caressing. "I never thought I would like you so much. I mean, I like the generous you, the sweet you, the side of you that pleases and pretends. But it's the secret you, the part I see only glimpses of, that I adore."

I was sitting up then. I clutched the couch, fearing suddenly that it might fall away beneath me.

"I'm sorry." She spoke so low now that I had to turn my head to hear. "I won't say it if you don't want me to. But it's already happened. I love the genius painter in you, afraid of her own vision but obsessed with it all the same. The dreamer afraid of her own dreams, the beauty who fears she's ugly."

The fire had faded to a rusty glow. She clutched her elbows and shivered. "I'm cold," she said.

I watched her. *No,* I thought. *You don't mean me. You don't mean me.*

A coal tumbled in the grate and the firelight flared over my face, making me recoil. At the same moment, her eyes went terribly wide. She pressed her towel over her mouth. I knew she'd seen me in the sudden brightness and been startled from her trance. She had wanted to convince herself that I was an exotic foreigner, full of possibility. But then in the sudden flare of light she'd seen the look on my face, the desperate, gaping desire. I was some crazy old Yank who wanted to keep her, in a couple of musty rooms. She was repulsed.

I tried to stand, but my feet were unsteady and I sat again. I'd sleep, and fix all this tomorrow. I'd sleep.

She looked up and her face was wet. "I'm sorry," she repeated. "I'm such a damned roach. I have scared you, haven't I?"

"No, that's not it at all."

"I can see your disgust," she said, "although you're kind and you try to hide it. I'll leave. You needn't—"

"Hush," I said. The moonlight was brighter, showing the gooseflesh along her hip. "Hush."

My fear was giving way to a smarting warmth. Her feet twitched in the water.

"Rusala."

"I'm sorry. I'm cold. I'm cold, Katie."

There's a moment, sometimes, when you're sleepwalking. You begin to wake, but then you will yourself back into your dream. "Come here," I said.

"Do you want me to?"

I pulled the coverlet from me. In the same instant, she rose. Water trickled over her belly, her thighs. The hair between her legs glistened like seaweed. She stood fidgeting, holding the sponge to her chest.

"Katie." She let the sponge drop. "Don't let me—"

"Don't let you what?" I said. I never knew desire was so close to fury, a swarm of wasps rising in my stomach. In my mind's eye, I wrapped her hair in my fist and scraped her throat with my fingernails. She would cry out, half from fear, half from desire, and I'd comfort her.

She watched me closely, her lips parted.

"Oh, Katie."

She ran to the bed and curled awkwardly into me.

I whispered, "Don't let you what?" When I touched her shoulder, she lifted her head. Moods flickered through her eyes—alarm, tenderness, passion.

"Don't let me bite you, or scratch you," she said. She took my face in her hands.

She may have spoken again. I'll never know which of us moved first. In the next instant, our mouths were touching—a tentative, cringing touch at first, as if we were terrified of bruising each other. Her mouth was raw from smoke and gin. Her hands moved along the back of my neck and there was a rush of icy sweetness down my spine. Between my legs, my flesh prickled and stung, the way your eyes will sting just before the tears come.

"I'll bite you then first, then," I said, taking her in my arms, pressing her to me. Her bare back was slippery. I fought the urge to sink my nails into her skin, to keep her from sliding away.

Her breath was on my neck. She ran her fingertips along my collarbone and grazed her teeth on my throat. Her mouth had become warmer, and I sought it hungrily, feeling again the violent pull in me, the sense of circling round a vortex of terrible beauty.

I took hold of her shoulders and pushed her to the bed, harder than I'd meant to. She bounced, the breath knocked out of her. Her eyes narrowed.

"You mad fucking cunt," she said.

I let her pull my chemise from my shoulders. I grabbed her

wrists and she pulled back, not quite hard enough to break free. The struggle drew us closer than any embrace. When I reached one hand to her hip, she closed her legs. I forced my fingertips to the flesh of her inner thighs and she bucked, grunting.

"I'll kick you," she said. Her teeth flashed. "I'll bite you, I'll scratch at you."

I pried my hand from between her thighs and ran it up her belly, where her pulse thudded. I'd never touched anything so beautiful.

I'll wake soon.

"Go on," I said resting one knuckle at her lips. She writhed under me, her hips nestling against mine. When she sank her teeth into my hand, the pain moved through me like a flame. Her smooth leg bunted between my thighs, soft, insistent, irresistible.

"Harder," I told her, "go on, go on, go on, go on."

She bit hard enough to draw blood, and in the same instant my spine stretched. The pain became the sweetest lambent pleasure, a trapped fire rushing along my spine.

I couldn't stop coming. I panted into her hair.

We might have slept. The rest of the night I recall only in flashes of memory, like heat lightning: Rusala's black hair making a tent around us, or the feel of her shaking thighs under my mouth. Her scent was the scent of the sea, the scent of the edges of things, the scent of oblivion.

She fell asleep in my arms at dawn. My eyes ached with weariness, but I wanted to watch her profile forever. As she mumbled, not waking, I touched her trembling eyelids.

I WOKE TO the sound of whispering. Beyond my curtains, the sky was dull pewter. There was a scent of cinnamon rolls from the bakery, and the distant rattle of the milkman's cart.

Rusala was gone, but her pillow was damp and warm. The whispering came from the hallway. When it stopped, she stole in silently, her fingertips clutching at the door. She wore my dressing gown with its belt tied tightly round her waist. Her hair was wild around her shoulders, her eyebrows raised. When she caught my eyes, she jumped and pressed her palm to her chest.

"Oh," she laughed. She ran to the bed, letting the gown slide to the floor. She crawled across the mattress. Her shoulders were still marked from my teeth.

"I just gave your maid a holiday," she said. "Mad Katie, I intend to keep you here all day."

Chapter
Twelve

"SHALL I BE your maid, when you're a great lady in Boston?" Rusala asked.

"Oh, just a few more seconds," I pleaded. I was finishing a grisaille charcoal sketch of her as she sat in the windowsill. I drew swiftly to capture the soft light of the overcast afternoon, the watery sheen of her black China-satin gown.

She often spoke to herself when I sketched her. It was her way of letting me know she'd had enough of sitting still. I was so deep into my task that it was several moments before I realized what she'd said.

"What do you mean, my maid?" I rubbed my face with my clean palm.

"I mean if your suitor proposes." She looked down at the street, then jumped back from the windowsill. "I think he saw me."

"Who?" I ran to the window and saw a man's white boater hat just below us, the spotless twill suit of a foreigner.

"Don't let him see you." She pulled me back and clung to my arm. "It's that William Seagroves."

Gentle knocking came from far below, then Lovorka's halting footsteps in the vestibule. I'd told Lovorka I didn't receive while I worked. I wiped my hands on my apron and looked around. I wondered whether I should invite him up, after all.

"He's not my suitor." I said. "We're sort of vaguely friendly with each other. He's remarkably kind to me, in fact, given that I'm not in his caste."

"I know that, I've seen." She yawned, lifting her arms above her head. Her eyes darted but she stretched with careful nonchalance. "Kind William. Still," she said, "he's been calling nearly every day. His type doesn't waste time. He's probably getting pressure to be married or something, d'you think?"

She rolled her head to one side. My palms tingled to touch her tired neck. When the door slammed downstairs, I followed her to the window.

I stood behind Rusala and watched William's hat disappear into the crowd. It was a muggy, listless day; everything seemed covered in silt and cooking oil. Only a few mothers sat in the square, knitting, watching their children play at jacks. They stared as William passed.

I slipped my arms around Rusala's waist; she swayed towards me.

"Has it occurred to you that William and I might simply be friends?" I asked her. My breath stirred the hair at her neck. "As radical as that sounds. And what are you talking about, being my maid? Do you mean you think I'd marry him, and then whisk you off to America with the both of us?"

"He has got that stubborn, glassy-eyed naïveté of his class, hasn't he?" she said. "Yet, at the same time he's one of those peevish rebels. I bet he sees marrying a dubious frail bohemian beauty like you to be a romantic gesture. A great fuck-you to his parents. And then he imagines you'll be so grateful for a safe warm room, for a motorcar, for steaks."

She grew angrier as she spoke. Her back trembled against me, the hard shell of the corset and her hot shoulders.

"All right, then," I interrupted. "You'll never have to meet him if you don't care to. I'm not out for a husband." I kissed her neck. "Shut up, Ru."

"That's what we'd do, though, if we lacked imagination," she said. She went slack in my arms, and her head fell back to my shoulder. I kissed her ear, lightly, losing track of her words. Her effect on me only grew stronger with each day.

"Lots of girls would love to have a chance to pull that sort of trick," she said. Her voice sounded faraway and desolate. "The chance for us to be together, after all, in relative comfort. You'd have to fuck him sometimes, but then we'd get a safe place to sleep, money for the doctor, money for the dentist. Women age fast with no money."

The San Fantin bell rang, its sound pushing through the grey air. Rusala looked at the ceiling. "Doesn't the idea of it make you so exhausted?" she asked. "But you understand that there's not far to fall. And when we fall, we go under."

"I wouldn't know," I said. "I wouldn't know because we're going to live the way we want to. Just as we are now."

She jerked against me. "You truly imagine that fey, homey optimism makes you appealing, don't you?" she said.

My arms dropped. "How nice," I said. I wanted to be angry, but I knew that when she lashed out, it meant she was afraid.

"Fuck me," she said, whirling around. "No, no, don't look that way."

Then her head was under my chin. "I'm sorry," she said into my throat. "No, I won't start." I breathed in the smell of her hair.

"Rusala," I said, "listen. Don't be so fatalistic. There won't be any need for intrigues and schemes and desperation." I tried to sound as if I believed it with my whole heart, but already her words made my stomach twist with dread.

I felt her nod. Her hands moved along my hips, feeling for me under my apron and skirts.

"Women can earn money of their own, decent money," I said. Why was I becoming less and less convinced as I spoke? I looked over her shoulder at the paintings that lined my studio walls. Four weeks' worth of work. "Look at all this. And Amy really has been publicizing my show. I will sell some pieces, at least a few, and perhaps have some commissions. Hey, I know!" I pulled away to look at her face. "We'll move, we might move away from the city, as you said you wanted. Get away from all this nonsense. Would you like that?"

I held her cheeks in my palms, looking for something in her eyes that would make me feel normal again. Below us, something clattered in the kitchen.

"Yes, of course," she said brightly, showing her dimple. "You're right."

I stroked her temple. Tears caused her eyes to change color from black to brackish green. I saw the pale bubble of my reflection in her pupils.

"I'm terrible, I worry so," she said. "I worry so that I lose my reason altogether, sometimes. I just think of what might happen to us, if we don't get some money soon."

All at once, the truth of what she'd said overwhelmed me. I really didn't know whether any of the paintings would sell. I had no money to last past the spring, and she could never support the house and the maid on her ballet-girl stipend. Poverty makes your soul shrink. It humiliates you by making you worship the meanest fetishes: shoes with good soles, a half-jar of cold cream, a box of boric acid to keep away the roaches. I saw us in five years, ten years, twenty years, finding rooms in some boarding house where everyone listened in on us, squabbling over grocery bills and doctor's bills and church-donated clothes that smelled of pork grease and there's no money, there's no money.

I shook my head frantically. "Don't, please," I begged. "If you only knew how different I feel now. Don't, don't." Don't what? *Don't say such things, don't leave me.*

I tried to speak again, but my breaths shuddered into sobs. She moved out of my arms and I held my hands before me, weak and ineffectual.

"Look, Katie," she said. I looked up, then swiped at my eyes, forgetting about the charcoal until I felt it smeared over my eyelids.

She'd undone her gown and let it slide past her hips. She pulled at her corset, twisting like a snake shedding its skin, then tugged her chemise over her head.

I'd seen her unclothed so often, yet each time it was a sunrise to me. I don't know how much time I lost, gazing at her — the slope of her waist, her small round hips, her nipples shrinking and darkening.

She rested her hands on her cheeks. I realized that she'd never seen me weep so. She'd undressed out of some desperate, mute instinct, knowing it was the only thing she could do to numb the pain.

Her flesh melted under my palms like fine sun-warmed clay. My blood roared in my head.

I WOKE BEFORE she did. With a sense of relief, I felt the steel bands loosening from around my heart. Yes, the day was ending, the hateful sluggish light was fading. Soon the sky would be pure, bracing black.

Rusala rolled towards me, opening one eye. I traced a smudge of charcoal on her belly, drawing a pale arabesque.

"Now then," she breathed, and I saw her mood had lifted too. Her face was still puffy with sleep, her smile vague and indolent. She tickled my bare shoulder and pushed aside the strap of my chemise. "You're always so covered, aren't you? It's a shame. Beautiful you."

She pulled the chemise away from my right breast and lifted herself on her elbow. We both watched my flat, beige nipple tighten.

"Oh, she's shy," Rusala whispered. She licked her lips. Her eyes flickered from my face to my breast. "She doesn't want to be looked at."

She leaned closer and kissed the flesh just beside the nipple. Her hair slithered down, pooling on my shoulders.

I shuddered, watching the goosebumps ripple across my skin. "Don't." It was too sensitive, unbearably sensitive as a raw tooth.

She kissed the underside of my breast. "Some time," she said, "I want to dress you in something appallingly revealing." She moved her thigh between mine, and in the same moment touched her tongue to the very edge of my nipple, where tiny knots formed in the skin. "And bring you somewhere wild, where you'll feel everyone looking at you, men and women, staring. I'd let them touch you, too."

Her lashes swept as she looked up at me.

"I would," she said. "I'd hold you still while they touched your pale, pale skin."

Then her mouth fastened over my nipple and she suckled like a lamb. Her knee pressed and pressed between my legs. I clutched at her helplessly as tingling began in my feet, the crown of my head, my stomach.

She watched me come back to myself, afterwards. In my weakness, I could only stare. She traced my jaw. Her expression had become softer than I'd ever seen it. I could imagine how she'd looked as a young girl.

"I never thought I'd feel this desire," she said. "Do you think desire could be a kind of thread?"

"A thread?"

"Don't you feel it pulling at you? As though you were in a labyrinth, and there was only a crimson silk thread. When you tug on it, there's almost a tug back, and you wonder whether it's a way out..."

There was a breathless moment, then we both burst out laughing at the same time. She wrapped her legs around me.

We woke again after midnight, starving and chilled. We dressed quickly and descended the stairwell, shushing one another, as we knew how lightly Lovorka slept. When we reached the vestibule, Lovorka emerged from the kitchen, still fully dressed, carrying her lamp. She turned her stone-white face to us, then ran away so quickly that the lamp's flame went out.

Rusala held her palm to her cheek. Without meeting my eyes, she grabbed my wrist and pulled me outside.

We had supper at a restaurant with striped velvet wallpaper, where we spent half of the week's grocery budget on cold beef and wine. A Chinese woman sang, tilting her head sweetly, waving her hands as if she were in a garden of vines.

SOME DAYS LATER, I was to come with Rusala to her ballet lesson and rehearsal. She'd obtained permission for me to sketch the dancers at work.

She rose at eight to prepare, pulling on a practice dress that she'd rinsed out the night before. She fixed her low chignon with a net and twenty hairpins, then palmed some pomade along her temples. Bending from the waist, she rummaged through her rucksack, checking off the essentials: her three pairs of pointe shoes, jars of salve, and a packet filled with hard little twists of boiled cotton wool that she said she used inside her during her monthlies. She always carried something for the curse, she said. There was no telling when you'd have a red-camellia day, and you'd be fined if you ruined a costume.

When she'd put on my long tweed hooded cloak, she looked severe as a nun. She smiled at me. I'd been dressed for a long time, and sat holding my box of pencils on my lap.

We were the first to arrive at the studio, which was the entire top floor of a building near the theater. For windows, there were only the arched tops of the front casements, rising from the floor. The ceiling was all rough beams with two open skylights. The walls were also rough, yet painted clean white. A wooden barre was fixed at waist-height along each wall.

Rusala sat me on a green sofa and produced a table for my sketch pad and pencils. Sitting beside me, she took off her walking shoes. I hadn't noticed before that her stockings had openings in their soles, so that she could uncover her toes. She set to work, fastening a small patch of cotton wool just over her big toenail, wedging a bit of india rubber between her first and second toes, then wrapping a piece of old newspaper around all her toes before pulling the stocking back down.

When she saw me watching, she said, "Now you see why my feet look like raw beets." There was a ring of bravado in her voice. She pulled out her newest pair of pointe shoes, stiff and shining and already curved like little toy boats. When she bent them, they gave a loud pop.

She put them on and walked on pointe a bit for me, showing how she had to pull in her stomach and squeeze the backs of her thighs to keep from falling backwards. I blushed when she lifted her tarlatan.

"See," she said, rising again on pointe, twisting her back towards me, "you have to grip."

I reached for her skirt. She giggled and pulled away, lifting her arms and beating a tattoo on the floor.

We both jumped at the sound of footsteps on the stairwell. She smoothed down her skirt and tucked her rucksack under the sofa.

"It won't be a brilliant class," she said. "This is just an opera ballet, after all, so don't expect any *tours de force*. Most of the best dancers have left for the Theatre Slav. But the maestro is decent, and you'll see a real old-fashioned lesson."

She looked at the ceiling, rubbing her throat. "And don't mind the other girls. Every few months, they all decide they dislike someone, and lately that's been me. I have no idea why. I probably failed to share some chocolates one day, and there was some deadly scandal that escaped my notice."

A few girls came in, wearing oversized shawls, their hair

severely scraped back like Rusala's. They stopped chatting when they saw Rusala, and stared frankly at me. I recognized one of them, the pale red-haired English girl from Olga's party. She grinned at me uneasily.

Just after them came a slight old man, dressed in an old-fashioned black morning suit and an orange waistcoat. His purple cravat was tied meticulously as a child's bow. His face was long, with mournful dark eyes, and his hair and whiskers were snow-white. He walked slowly, leaning on a silver-tipped cane; I couldn't imagine how long it had taken him to climb the stairs. He took a violin case down from a shelf and opened it, talking to himself all the while.

I breathed deep and spread some paper over the table. I knew it would be a good session. I felt alert, as if colors and shapes were flying into me. I turned the pencil over and over in my fingers. I didn't know what to sketch first.

The dancers raised their legs onto the barres and stretched. Their silhouettes were sharp black against the sun-filled windows. Rusala rested one foot on the sofa.

"They're pretty used to artists, so don't feel shy about looking," she said. "There might also be some patrons coming along. A few of the younger girls used to have chaperones or mothers come to class, but they've left that off. See, most of the girls are foreigners. You met Hilda, I think, the English girl? And some Germans. I'll bet you can tell the Italian girls right off. They're the ones who cross themselves before a difficult step." Two black-haired girls caught Rusala pointing and glowered at her.

I nodded towards the man. "Does he play his own accompaniment?"

"He used to," Rusala said. She began rising and lowering on her pointes, looking into the distance. Her shoes creaked. "Now he just plucks out the rhythm of each exercise. And strikes us with the bow when he's cross."

Two of the dancers removed the canvas covers from the mirrors. Another dancer, a plump, black-eyed girl who seemed the youngest, paced back and forth with a watering can, sprinkling until the entire floor grew dark.

When the maestro lifted his bow and said, "*alors*," it was as if a brisk wind blew over the room. The girls, about ten of them now, went silent and started to their feet, lining up along the barre, each resting her right palm on the wood, heels together. The teacher paced alongside them, a general inspecting the ranks.

"*Et*," the maestro said, raising his eyebrows. He held the violin across his chest like a lute and picked out a faint, wandering melody in waltz time. The women bent their legs and sank to floor, a sort of straight up-and-down curtsey, their arms moving in slow arcs. All these different women—some light, some dark, some muscular, some frail as children—moved in perfect time, like musicbox figures.

More exercises followed. The maestro plucked out a brisker rhythm and the girls extended their legs, tracing circles on the floor with their toes, or beating soft rhythms against their ankles.

I watched for a long time before I remembered to start sketching. At first, I caught only fleeting impressions: the curve of their lifted arms, like the horns of gazelles; the perfect arch of a stretched ankle; the knitted brows of the smallest girl as she panted after each exercise.

They watered the floor again and moved away from the barre. The sun left wide swathes of light along the soggy wood. The maestro opened one of the windowpanes, letting in the sounds of the square below.

I sketched quickly, hardly even looking at what I did, tearing through the pages. I made a portrait of each girl, high in a leap or leaning pensively against the barre. In the last exercise, they did quick turns, spinning on their pointes like peg-tops while the maestro sang. He waved his frail hands, sometimes clapping furiously and shouting out "*genoux!*" or "*les pieds, Marta!*" When he finally stopped singing, the girls sank into a low, grave *révérence* before breaking rank.

The maestro lit himself a pipe and wandered out while the dancers gathered in a knot. Some lifted their skirts and sat on the floor, while others slid into splits, careful of their stockings. Rusala sat beside me and took off her shoes. The girls all gave off heat, like horses that had been in the pasture all day. Some of them were opening packets of fresh figs or smoked fish.

I put my pencils away, feeling a sudden awareness of their eyes on me. When I leaned forward to close the box, I saw their heads move to follow me, and when I spoke with Rusala, they ceased talking to listen. Yet each time I looked up, their eyes slid from my face. Only the youngest girl, the tiny black-eyed one, met my gaze for an instant, then tossed her head.

"This is our rest," Rusala explained, taking out a cigarette. I offered her some of my mineral water but she waved it away, mopping her brow with a flannel.

"No, no water yet. It weakens your heart. We usually have rehearsal now, but we hope he might dismiss us early." Rusala smiled as the women went quiet again. Their bitterness made her gay.

"Do you think that your friends would like to see what I drew?" I wasn't sure how many of the girls spoke English, but when I laid out the drawings, they all looked. A few of them consulted briefly among themselves before sauntering over. Hilda sat beside me on the couch. Some other girls crowded around, crying out when they recognized themselves.

"Katie may develop these into paintings," Rusala said. "And the paintings will be part of an exhibition, here in Venice."

The little black-eyed girl squealed, and a blonde girl rejoined, "Yes, yes, Frannie, your portrait could be hanging in a club someday, a posh one."

Frannie clutched her fists together under her chin, quivering all over in excitement. "I will be famous?"

"Yes," said Hilda, "but they'll have to cover your portrait when there's a woman present."

Rusala burst out laughing. The maestro came back in, making a great show of looking cross, of pulling slowly, slowly at his watch chain. He frowned as he checked the time, glancing up at the women. When he gave a shrug, they gathered up their things. Hilda and Frannie stayed near us.

"No rehearsal then?" I asked.

Rusala put her hand on mine. "So come on, we'll go to lunch," she said, looking at Hilda and Frannie. The other women chatted in Italian and German as we all descended the stairs. When we reached the square, they hurried away from us.

"What were they saying?" I turned to Hilda, who shrugged. Frannie looked down. Rusala waved her hand.

"It's just as well you and Hilda can't understand them," Rusala said, taking my arm. "They were saying the usual nonsense. Never mind those bitches."

Hilda covered her mouth and giggled.

A crowd of women and children strolled back from morning mass, but otherwise the square was silent in the pale sunlight. The air was crisp, almost wintry. Frannie was Venetian; as we walked, several old women greeted her in the soft, lilting Venetian dialect that sounded so different from the Italian I tried to learn. We continued towards the Hotel des Artists, but then turned down a lime-streaked passageway that ended in a stairwell. At its lowest step there was a gate of rusted iron, and a wooden sign that read *Loredana Ristorante*.

"It's closed, though," I said. Hilda pulled the bell, holding her shawl around her shoulders.

A young man with dark skin came to the gate and leaned his forehead towards us with a bemused look. "*Buon giorno*," he said, pulling the gate open. "I thought we might see you today." His accent was Carribean.

We passed into a hidden garden, a startlingly wide green space with dark grass and tall cypress trees. Bocce balls lay scattered throughout the lawn like Easter eggs. A trellis shaded a row of empty tables, where we settled. Frannie sat with a thump and stretched out her legs. While I took out my sketches again, Hilda and Rusala went into the kitchen. Starlings squeaked and crackled overhead.

"Right." Rusala came back into the courtyard, carrying a pot that was almost as big around as she was. A blond boy jogged behind her. I stared for a moment before recognizing him as Vitya, the stage hand. Hadn't I also seen him at Olga's palace?

"This is the left-over macaroni from last night," Rusala explained. Hilda came out with a stack of bowls. "They always warm it over for us. They can't re-use it for the patrons, but it's fine with a little garlic cream sauce." Rusala used both her arms to stir, scooping spoonfuls into bowls.

"Vitya?" Rusala held a bowl to him, but he shook his head.

"Baptiste and I are eating all morning," Vitya said, with a slurred, Slavic-sounding accent. "So many oysters delivered, we help manage overstock. They would have be — would have *been* — spoiled otherwise." Vitya's eyes were grey, set wide. His face was freakishly beautiful, the face of an antique statue, but his mouth looked bruised and smashed, as if he could at any moment spit blood.

I guessed that Baptiste was the Caribbean man. He came near, throwing a towel over his shoulder.

"Are you a dancer, too?" Baptiste asked me, turning a chair around to straddle it.

"No, I'm a painter," I said, "or working at being a painter."

"No, does she look like a chorus girl?" Hilda said.

I twirled my fork in my macaroni, then looked up. Baptiste was smiling at Rusala, his brown eyes sparkling. Did he know about us?

As if he'd heard my thoughts, he turned to me. "A painter?" he said. "Then you must be Katie. And what do you think? I bet you're shocked to find a garden in the middle of the city."

"But do you know, there are lots of secret places like this in Venice," Hilda told me. "There's one garden where the trees have monkeys in them."

"I feel that we've left Venice altogether," I said. Something in me expanded. The sky grew brighter and softer, as if it wanted to draw us in. I hadn't realized how tense I'd been in the shifting maze of the city.

Rusala looked around the group. "Do you know," she said, "in the spring, after Katie's finished her first few shows here in town, she and I shall move to a house in Istria, peaceful and quiet along the coast."

For those seconds, the world grew quiet all around me. All at once, I saw the cottage she described: white-washed stucco walls, an herb garden, a goldfish pond. I saw Rusala and me, lying in a garden like this, listening to the sea.

Rusala lowered her eyelids and I breathed in. The image dissolved but the happiness stayed, warming my blood to my fingertips. I didn't normally believe in clairvoyant visions, but the house seemed so real to me that I felt I might have already been in it, run my palms along its sun-warmed walls. Frannie broke in. "And we may visit?"

"This is the plan now?" Baptiste said, looking at me, then Rusala.

"Vitya, will you?" Rusala was already helping herself to another bowlful of pasta, but she pointed her spoon towards a covered piano and then gave Vitya a pleading look.

"Yes, come on." Frannie squirmed in her seat.

"Ah, no," Vitya lifted his hands innocently, but everyone insisted until he stood and ambled across the grass.

"If insist," he said. He pulled the cloth from the piano and sat before it. "Only if insist."

"He says he taught himself," Hilda explained. She'd pulled her chair closer to mine. "But he can play the piano like someone from New Orleans. Listen."

Vitya leaned in and pounded out the most remarkable music. Its melody was full of yearning, but its rhythm was rollicking and infectious.

Frannie jumped up and did a little shuffling dance. The starlings rushed to the sky.

Chapter
Thirteen

I ONCE HEARD of a man who tried to cut off his own legs because he couldn't bear how restless they were.

When I painted alone, I imagined how he must have felt. I stood uneasily, rocking in time with the rhythm of the brushstrokes. My shoulders would finally tingle with weariness and anxiety, yet each time I stopped moving I felt a sort of fog gathering behind me, a low teeming fog that crept closer until I began to move again.

One afternoon, I felt the fog rising just behind my shoulders. I brushed my hair out of my eyes. I was overtired. Just a few more moments and I'd stop.

"Mmmh."

I wheeled around to stare at Rusala. She stood watching me quizzically, munching on a currant bun. Her gaze bounced to my feet, then up again to my face.

She swallowed. "You were in a trance. Want a bun?"

She'd come home early from rehearsal. Her brows were pencilled into arches and her lips were still rouged. Her half-eaten bun was stained with red as if it bled where she'd bitten it. She wiped her chin.

"You remind me of a Gorgon," she said. "D'you realize you're sweating?"

"I was on a streak."

"You're streaked in war paint. You'll have to soak those hands in turpentine." She popped the rest of the bun in her mouth and pushed gently at my shoulders, turning me back towards the canvas. I placed my brush back in its jar. When she massaged my shoulder blades, I tilted my head back. She ran her thumbs along the back of my neck.

"These shoulders, good God," she said. "You're getting the muscles of a prize fighter."

"Don't stop," I pleaded, untying my apron. She kneaded my

upper arms.

"But won't you get dressed?" she said. "Come on, Bruiser. There's a kick-up at Vitya's place, with drinks and what-have-you."

"Is it already suppertime?" When I pulled her arms around my stomach, she rose on tiptoe to rest her hard chin on my shoulder.

"Oo, hold on." She whistled. "This is fine. You went wild with this one, didn't you? It reminds me of a Klimt, but with nicer colors and a better form."

When I shut my eyes, I saw the painting in shades of phosphorescent green. I suddenly felt so exhausted that I wanted only to slump to the carpet and stretch out like a cat.

"I can't look at it anymore," I told her. "It's sucking me dry. Here, I'll place myself in your hands. You just tell me what I must wear, and what I must to do my hair and my face, and then lead me off to where ever."

She squeezed me.

VITYA STAYED IN two rooms above a Chinese grocery shop off the Campo Carita. The stairwell smelled of mold and cat piss. I lagged behind Rusala, drawing up my skirts. As she opened his door, she glanced back at me with a smug grin. Beyond her was a mass of color.

"You like it?" She took hold of my fingertips. I heard laughter and saw, very dimly, some half-reclining figures. "Don't forget that Vitya works in scenery," she said. "When I first helped him move in here, I just sat down and sobbed to think of him living in such a tomb. There were beetles, and plump rats, and a kind of green jelly all over the walls."

She drew me further in. "And now, look," she said.

I felt I'd entered a room at an exhibition, or the rococo stage of a private theater. The walls were draped in heavy satin, dyed in shades of lavender and periwinkle blue. Metallic vines were pinned along the corners, their copper and silver leaves twined stiffly together. The floorboards had been painted deep indigo, highlighted here and there with scallops of white. I moved my right foot and saw a saucy, winking goldfish drawn in oil paint. I guessed, then, that the carpets could be thought of as rafts.

"Now look up." It was Hilda's voice. I looked to where she lay back against the wall, but she pointed upwards. "Up."

The rough ceiling was washed in cobalt, fading into teal and pink streaks at its edges. Tiny cream-colored angels, nymphs, and goddesses were scattered throughout the sky, etched in meticulous detail. I stood on my tiptoes to examine them. Old-fashioned oil lamps hung from the rafters, covered in Chinese shades.

The only furniture the room was a trunk that served as a tea table and washstand. The bed beside it was just a pallet covered in quilts, with a bearskin rug and square silk cushions spread around it. Baptiste and Hilda sat in their stocking-feet, surrounded in books and dewy bottles.

"Welcome!" Vitya came from his balcony, wearing a smoking jacket and a matching velvet cap. He snapped his heels together and bowed. His hair was tufted where it showed, like rabbit's fur.

"Pardon me, we start without you." He winked and lifted a glass of clear liquid. "You like my town house? I was just enjoying my new toy, look." He lifted a framed photograph of a dour-looking man.

"Ew. Who is that? He's got a lot of wax on his whiskers." Rusala leaned close, squinting at the image.

"Don't know. But look." Vitya pulled a lever in the frame, and we saw that the picture was cut crosswise in tiny slivers, like louvered blinds. They flipped over, showing an image of the same man, smiling maniacally.

We drew back. "Oh, fuck me! Why did you show me that?" Rusala yelled.

I couldn't help laughing. I looked again at the terrible stretched smile, so forlorn and raw that it was probably the most frightful thing I'd ever seen, and I laughed until my stomach spasmed. Rusala looked at me, shaking her head.

"That damned ugly thing," Hilda said. "Cheers, you two. Sit, sit. The chow mein's almost ready." Just by the head of the pallet, Vitya had set up a gas burner, where an iron cauldron almost bubbled over. Hilda rose and stirred the chow mein, then lifted the spoon to her lips, blinking and huffing as she tasted. "Mm, ow, mm."

Vitya ducked his head again. "Come—oh, wait." He offered each of us an elbow. "Allow me." Together we walked the four steps to the pallet, where Rusala and I sat. The gas flame warmed our skirts.

Baptiste leaned against the wall, stretching his legs along the rug. His glass of red wine cast garnet-colored reflections over his face. "Vitya finds in that photograph," he said, "a sort of philosophical allegory. He's been trying to explain it to me, but thus far I find myself only dazzled by his intellect." His eyes shone as he watched Vitya approach.

"Now then." Vitya sat by Baptiste's legs and refilled his glass from a vodka bottle. He looked at his drink carefully, laying the glass against his flushed cheek before continuing. "What I mean is this: the happy photograph looks aggressive, doesn't it?"

"Maybe someone's pinching him," I said. I felt a hand on my

shoulder, and Hilda passed me a tiny cup of something that resembled pond water. I sniffed it.

"Absinthe," she said, patting my knee.

"He's — Baptiste, help me, what's the word?" Vitya turned towards Baptiste, who shrugged and looked mystified. Vitya snapped his fingers. "Determined. Determined to be happy."

"Good for him," Rusala said. She downed her drink and leaned back so that Hilda could refill her cup.

"So you see, you must be determined, in a way, to be happy." Vitya saw that I was the only one paying attention, so directed his remarks at me, swinging his drink for emphasis. A little vodka sloshed over the sides of the glass and I drew my skirt back.

"I do see," I said, reaching my tongue into my cup.

"He knows," Vitya continued. "This fellow knows you sometimes must force yourself to be happy, not search for reason. People think too much. Thinking always creates sadness. If God had meant us to think..."

Vitya paused and glanced from side to side. Baptiste covered his mouth while his eyes shone even brighter. Hilda and Rusala whispered about the day's rehearsal.

"But I know precisely what you mean," I assured Vitya. I believed I did. I sipped at my absinthe and felt its warmth on the back of my tongue. I was so tired and hungry that I knew the drink would either make me faint, or make me feel like an angel. I let it trickle down my throat.

A few moments later, I felt it burning all through me and I laughed harder than ever. Vitya was still trying to explain about happiness, and determination, and the delicate balance between hope and regret, but my laughter drowned him out.

Rusala brought me a bowl of chow mein, patting my knee again like a solicitous nurse, but I only wanted more absinthe. We lay back, watching the goddesses on Vitya's ceiling. I stared hard at some of the more vivid ones, then closed my eyes tightly to see what colors they would change to in the darkness behind my eyelids. I kept laughing, until Rusala stroked my forehead.

"She's wrung out," I heard her explain to someone. "She paints as if she were possessed, sometimes." I lifted my head to finish my drink. The floor rocked gently, and above me I saw Rusala's eyes, soft and dark as the petals of a pansy. She clicked her tongue at me and helped me sit up, saying, "It won't do to get so fly, so early in the evening."

I hefted myself onto the pallet. "Your room is lovely, Vitya," I said. "I never knew you painted, too."

"Is nothing. Just old props and extra paint from theater. Only looks nice with old oil lamps, and when you're drunk." He was still engrossed with his framed picture, switching its lever back and forth. He pressed his full lips together. "Real artist like you, Katie, could make something magnificent. Ah, but I forgot, you will retreat to lovely house on sea, and create masterpieces."

"But Ru, how will you become a film star if you retire to the sea with her?" Baptiste asked, looking at Rusala. She clenched her fists.

"Oh, I've given that up," she said sharply. "All that scheming to get on. I just want a peaceful life now." Behind her, Hilda looked at Baptiste and raised her eyebrows.

Rusala gave an impatient twitch and stood. "I find I need some fresh air," she said. "At the bottom of the stairs, right?" When the door shut, Vitya put down his picture and stared at the ceiling. Baptiste shuffled his feet.

"What happens with her?" Vitya finally said. Hilda turned towards us, drawing her knees to her chest and fiddling with her bracelet, a bit of seashell on a chain.

"She's wound up tight lately," Hilda said. "I'm afraid she'll bust." They all turned to me and looked expectant.

"She's been working a lot," I said, pressing my temple. "And I understand she's had a hard time, these past few years. May I have a little water?"

Baptiste picked through the bottles until he found some mineral water. "Rusala has had to endure a great deal of hostility," he said, handing me the whole bottle. "As I've heard."

"In the year I've been dancing at the Fenice, I've only ever seen her be kind," Hilda said, her voice rising. "I can't imagine why those bitches are so horrid to her. They were a bit sweeter when you were there that morning, Katie, because they love to be drawn and painted. They were preening for you. But otherwise, well, they seem so suspicious of her."

Baptiste leaned forward and scratched his neck. "There's persistent talk of —"

Vitya cleared his throat.

"No, of what?" I said. "Vitya, don't *ahem* me." I didn't feel the least bit drunk, but the floor continued its gentle lilting. I wondered whether the earth were always cradling us so, and we were too distracted to notice. How lovely.

"Of her old pal." Hilda said, glancing at Vitya.

"Some years ago —" Vitya began.

"But I know all about that," I said. "Stop looking at each other that way. She's told me."

"About Larisa?" Baptiste seemed relieved. "Terrible story."

"Do you know that some of the other girls blame Rusala for Larisa's injury?" Hilda asked.

"That's just cruel," I said.

"They fell out so suddenly, and so bitterly," Baptiste said. "That is what caused the rumors."

"They quarrelled? Rusala and Larisa?" I took another drink of water and squinted at Baptiste. "About what?"

Vitya only shook his head. Baptiste opened his mouth, then closed it. When we all looked at him, he glanced out the window.

"I never quite understood," Baptiste said. "And what's more, I have heard that Larisa is still around Venice. Someone saw her in a vegetable market."

"I've heard those stories too," Hilda said. "But, really, that's too absurd."

Vitya was about to speak again, but there came a thump and creak from the stairwell, and the rustle of Rusala's skirts. I thought she made extra noise, as if she guessed we would talk about her.

"Oy, oy," Rusala cried, bursting through the door. "Have we restored ourselves? Shall we advance?"

The night was warm. The stars were low and sugary; I wanted to tilt my head back and taste them. The streetlights' reflections fizzed and shone in the water, like drops of metal in a crucible. I took Rusala's arm. Baptiste and Vitya resumed their debate about happiness, becoming increasingly decorous and nonsensical until Hilda covered her ears and begged them to stop.

Baptiste cried triumphantly, "And thus, old man, thus concludes your argument."

Vitya waved his cigarette, all stumbling hauteur. "Thus concludes," he said, "damn it—and good *day.*"

"Good day to you, sir," Baptiste replied, clutching his stomach and cackling, while Hilda echoed, "I bid you good *day.*"

We debated our destination in a vague sort of way, letting the crowds ripple around us, finding ourselves finally along the Fondamenta Nani. I closed my eyes and hummed as we walked.

"Hey," Baptiste nudged me. "Might this be the last time you walk with us?"

"What are you talking about?"

"When you're famous artist," Vitya said. "Will be pet of rich people. Won't have chance to walk with us, like this."

I wanted to be indignant, but the absinthe had given me a strange kind of peace. "Don't joke that way," I said. "That's not me."

Rusala watched us silently, drawing a lock of her hair across her mouth.

Vitya rested his heavy arm round my shoulders. "All right, true. You won't be completely tame pet. Half-tame, half-wild. You'll spend time with those rich people, and then report back to us. You'll be our canary in a goldmine."

"*Mais ça suffit.*" Baptiste stomped ahead of us. Hilda threw her head back and brayed with laughter. She had a surprisingly loud laugh for such a frail girl. Vitya trotted to catch up with Baptiste, and Hilda ran between them, linking her arms in theirs and letting them lift her. She squealed as her feet thrashed above the pavement.

Rusala's silence pooled around us. I wanted so to kiss her, to nuzzle her forearms.

"Rusala," I said. She turned to me.

"Hey!" came Vitya's voice. Rusala kept her eyes on mine. Our skirts slithered and clung.

"Hey, hey." Vitya ran to us. The ground beneath me tilted suddenly.

"Look, is that the Seagroves Gallery?" He pointed down a narrow canal that ended in a burst of light.

"Yes," Rusala said.

"Do let's walk by. The gate to greatness. Good *day*." Hilda laughed again, a little vein wiggling in her neck. She was very drunk.

Rusala sneaked a kiss on my cheek. I leaned to her, but she stepped away, shaking her head at me. She dug her nails into my palms before she let me go, and the little shocks of pain made my mouth flood with saliva.

The ground pitched again; I had to step backwards to keep my balance. "Oops," I said to a man who'd walked into me. Instead of apologizing, he scowled at us and stomped off. Baptiste grabbed my elbow and suggested we all stop somewhere for a moment, just to enjoy the evening view.

We turned to see Hilda's retreating form. She was running to meet a couple coming out of a saloon: a slim, harried-looking man with brilliantined hair and tragic black eyes, and a young woman wearing an Indian sari. The woman's face was heart-shaped, with a tiny chin and round eyes; she reminded me of a Valentine's Day card. Long pheasant feathers were fastened in her hair, quivering high above her head like a moth's antennae.

The man hung back, sucking dejectedly at a pipe, while Hilda and the Valentine woman came running to us, hand in hand.

"Whoop!" The woman jumped into Baptiste's arms, then Vitya's, then Rusala's, kissing each of them loudly on the cheek. She took a step back from me and then bowed low, while Hilda introduced me as a painter.

"No! A painter?" the woman cried. "Why, I'm a muse." She spoke with a German accent.

"Her name's Sincere," Rusala told me, smiling.

"I should love to talk with you about art." Sincere was still panting, holding one hand to her unraveling hair. "I am a type of artist too, am I not? I try to practice a woman's art, something true to my nature. Don't you think a woman's art is in inspiration, in desire?"

She pronounced *Muse, Art, Inspiration, Desire* as if she would write them with capital letters.

"I suppose that's cheaper than paints and canvas," I said. Right away I was sorry for my sarcasm, but she nodded blithely.

"You're right. Today I made a portrait of Tomasso, all in flower petals. The wind scattered it as I worked, so no one ever saw the completed work, not even me." She wiggled her small hands, looking wistfully past her fingertips. "It was a perfect artistic moment, ephemera and melancholy, passion and loss."

I realized Tomasso must be the dark young man who watched us, smoking and grimacing. Sincere followed my glance, turning to wave at him.

"He's such an *enfant terrible*. Crowds make him nervous. Ach, come!" Sincere cried. Rusala strolled forward, drawing the rest of us in her wake. Tomasso rolled his eyes and followed at a distance, while Sincere took Hilda's arm and told us of a new drama she was creating.

We stopped before a café with a navy blue awning. Vitya saw a friend of his, another Russian, a boy so curmudgeonly and gothic he reminded me of Raskolnikov. Vitya's friend wore a sailor's wool sweater and carried a pet starling that ate from his palm and said little phrases in Russian. Hilda was delighted with it. She laughed with her mouth open wide, leaning forward and closing her eyes and finally just wheezing "ah-ah."

Baptiste brought me into the café, where the air was spicy and hot. A woman in a green cap looked at us twice, and her glass slipped from her hand.

"All right, Katie?" Baptiste said, shading his eyes. "We need a nice big table for everybody. Keep an eye on the kids out there; don't let them wander away." He looked around for a waiter.

I leaned against a stool and caught my own reflection in the brass-framed mirror above the bar. What red cheeks! I looked like a tomato, waiting to be bitten. If I tilted my head, I saw the reflection of the fondamenta behind me, and the bright shapes of Sincere, Hilda, and Rusala against the darkness. Sincere's gold-edged sari floated around her slowly. Hilda and Rusala were dressed like ballet-girls tonight, with noisy taffeta skirts — Hilda in lime-green, Rusala in cherry-red. Hilda's hair-combs had silver chimes attached to them.

Rusala held Raskolnikov's starling now, and was coaxing it to perch on the stem of a rose. The tip of Rusala's tongue showed between her lips; her hair was coming loose on one side. A group of men came along behind her, all of them tall and wearing the boxy jackets and wide trousers of Americans. Two of them looked like brothers, with bulging weasel eyes. They stopped just behind Rusala. I saw her eyelids twitch, though she kept coolly chatting with Hilda. Vitya was arguing with Raskolnikov and didn't notice the boys crowding round them. The starling spread its short wings.

All at once, Rusala cried out, stepping forward and clutching her skirt away from the men. A corpulent boy joined them, wiping his moustache and shaking his forefinger in Rusala's blanched face. When she tried to turn away, he rested his fingertip in the hollow of her throat.

I was about shout for Baptiste, when I caught sight of William. Or at least I thought it was he. It was the same delicate face, the same pale hair, yet he looked shrunken somehow, like a fruit with the pulp sucked out.

He approached them, looked at Rusala, then closed his eyes. His friends called to him but he turned and walked away, pulling almost violently at his collar, shivering and curling his upper lip.

I watched his mouth moving, and, as if by a trick of echoes, heard his voice in shocking clarity: "Christ, you're on your own if you want to play with filth. Get a disease just looking at 'em."

The world went very dark for a moment. The rocking beneath me suddenly stopped, and a creeping agitation spread through my limbs. I felt my fingers fidgeting. When my vision cleared, I saw Rusala entering the café. Her flesh looked subtly changed, bright and repellent, as if all the fine golden hairs on her skin had changed to poison spines.

I could only think of the boy's fat finger, pink as an uncooked sausage. I didn't want to harm him. I just wanted to make a deep gash in the tip of that finger, to remind him that he must never, ever do that again.

Rusala's eyes went wide with alarm as I thought this. She stepped to me and took my hand, shaking my arm as if to rouse me. She kissed my cheek. I knew she was trying to hide the confusion of the moment in an insouciant gesture.

She cupped her hand around my ear and said, "My mad cunt."

A WHISPERED VOICE is no one's voice, is anyone's voice.
Asleep? Asleep?
Rusala wandered my rooms at night. I would half wake, my drugged hands heavy on my chest, and see her at the window, absently stroking a piece of mink. I'd blink, and then open my eyes

to find her gone. When I blinked again, she stood by the bed, pulling my dressing gown around her.

I willed myself to move, but the drugs held me like cooling wax. I thought if only I could lift my head or take a swallow of water, I might shake off the heaviness and comfort her. *Here, we might ride a gondola in the moonlight, or go to the café you like. There's a little money. Don't leave, don't leave. Can't you see my eyes are open?*

She would take a candle with her, its light shrinking and pouncing along the walls as she left. I watched my hand uncurl like a starfish.

One night I woke from a dream of solid darkness, and heard a whisper.

Asleep? Keep sleeping. You know there's no love. There's who wants to fuck you, and who's tired of fucking you. Do you know what they used to tell me, all of them, when I was little? Women are made of love, they said. Women will love whatever fucks them.

Rusala's hair in my face, rough and musky as the hanging moss of a swamp. Her eyes, glimmering like orchids.

Chapter
Fourteen

I WOKE EARLY one morning, my hands grasping the sheets. I'd dreamt that my paintbrushes were too hot to touch. I slipped out from under the coverlet, dressed silently, and built up the fire, turning to watch its orange glow spread over the bed. Rusala slept heavily, her braid wound around her throat like a collar.

I found Lovorka in the kitchen, lifting the covers off the stove, filling a new copper kettle. She looked up quickly at the sound of my footsteps.

"Going out so early?" she asked.

I nodded, coming into the kitchen. We'd made it more habitable for her with a carpet, bedding, a dressing table, and even a changing screen covered in red paisley cloth. Once Rusala had moved in, I'd suggested to Lovorka that she could perhaps spend her nights at her own home, and just be our *midinette*. Lovorka seemed alarmed at this prospect; I guessed she didn't have a proper home, so I never mentioned it again. She did her best to keep out of our way, timing her few chores around our comings and goings. The area behind the changing screen became her own private space, and in the evenings I saw her silhouette moving slowly in the expanse of firelit cloth, like a figure before a desert sunset.

"Are you still happy here?" I asked her, holding my gloves over the stove.

"Yes," she answered. The fire clicked softly beneath us. The rain pattered outside. "Yes," she said again. "Only — yes. Of course I'm happy here, you're a nice woman." She reached for the kettle.

"You seem disturbed lately," I said. "Nervous." She exhaled quickly as I spoke, but I persisted. "Lovorka, you can tell me."

"Must she live here?" Her hand tightened around the kettle's handle until her knuckles went white, then blue. "Must she *live* here?" she said again. "It's too much."

I felt as if she'd slapped me. "I asked her to," I said. I put on my gloves and took a step back from the stove. "I invited her to live here. Why shouldn't I?"

She turned from me. I watched her miserable back, her hunched shoulders. "Of course," she said, with a derisive laugh. "All your idea."

I was about to be angry, but when she turned towards the window I saw her profile—her wrinkling forehead, her jutting lip. All at once I understood.

"Lovorka," I said gently. "Listen, is she cross with you sometimes? Does she scold?"

"Cross with me?"

"You know, impatient. She's had a hard time. She's been so unhappy in the past. And she shows it through little explosions. But, dear, she doesn't mean any of it. She doesn't." I took a step closer. "I know Rusala likes you very much," I continued. "I'm sure she'd be sad to think you'd taken something to heart."

I'd meant to reassure her but her shoulders only sagged more.

"And," I went on, "what's more, she's accustomed to flophouses, artist hotels, that sort of thing. You know how it is for ballet-girls and theater people. They're not used to having a boring old domestic life. It makes her feel nervous, and out of place. So can you help me? She needs our patience, so that she can really feel at home."

She rocked slightly on her feet. I stepped to her and almost rested my hands on her arms.

"But," I said, "is that it? Is there something else? You can tell me."

Then she stopped moving altogether. Her stillness was so eerie that my heart stopped for a moment.

"No, ma'am, thank you. You're very kind," she said in a rush, as if she only wanted me to leave. She let go of the kettle and crouched to check the fire. I turned back to say goodbye as I reached the vestibule, but she looked into the flames.

Outside, the rain was measured and lyrical, crenellating the water and turning the dust to froth. I wore a purple cloak that Rusala had inherited from one of her theater friends, and carried Rusala's oversized umbrella. Frannie had taught me a bit more Venetian, but the voices around me still seemed more like music than speech, falling through my mind like birdsong.

I strolled towards the art-supply shops and watched the red sailboats glide along the Giudecca. It was too early for anything to be open, so I knew I would have to sit in a café for a while. I fumbled nervously in my pockets, counting the coins as they clinked. I hoped to find some gold powder at one of the art shops, and perhaps I could ask them where to get crushed indigo and ochre.

When I heard feet shuffling behind me, I turned. Greta was

reaching for my shoulder. Rain slithered over her black felt hat.

"Hey, I saw you from across the square," she said. "Sorry if I frightened you. Where are you going?" The rain fell harder and we moved under an awning.

"I don't know. I felt restless and went to buy some paint, only I think nothing's open yet. I'm sort of meandering."

"Come see Vitya with me, then," she said, tucking her yellow muffler into her coat. "I'm bringing him food and tea. He's ill."

As we walked, the wind grew fiercer, with bitter gusts ricocheting through the alleys. Vitya's building seemed smaller in the daylight, and the piss-stained stairwell seemed even more precipitous. Greta knocked lightly and opened Vitya's door. Baptiste sat cross-legged on the rug, while Vitya lay swaddled in quilts.

Vitya smiled. "Now I want always to be ill. This is fine." He sat up and waved us in. Baptiste leaned back with a cup of tea.

"What's the matter?" I asked, sitting beside Baptiste. Greta unpacked a baked potato and a jar of soup from her basket.

"Cold, or something," Vitya said. He propped himself up on his pillow and lowered his eyes for a moment, the best bow he could manage. His face had a thin film of greenish sweat.

"He never takes care of himself," Greta said. She took off her hat and knelt before the bed, shaking her hair from her eyes. "So stoic. And he insists on living in this drafty place."

"I like it here," he answered lazily. "Privacy." When he closed his eyes again, I looked around. Rain washed over the windowpanes, leaving streaks of sallow grime. The paint on the floor now looked thick and uneven, and under it I saw gouges and waterstains and skid-marks, evidence of all the nameless people who had lived here before and moved on. On the wall beside his bed, Vitya had drawn an entire piano keyboard in charcoal, and beneath it was a stack of sheet music.

I turned back to Vitya and caught him looking at me.

"Are you from Russia?" I asked, embarrassed.

"I was serf," he said. "I worked in fields." Greta handed him a mug of tea. "I wore—" He gestured around his throat. "Metal collar, with spikes."

"What?" I touched my own throat.

"So can't lie down," Vitya explained. "*Barin* can't watch you all day, so you have collar on you, with spikes long enough to keep you from lying on grass and sleeping. But I was very handsome and blond, so later I worked inside beautiful house."

"Doing what?"

"Being handsome, being young. Englishman visited, and took me away as sort of valet. We came to Venice."

"You left him to work in the theater?" I asked.

"I left him because I was afraid I'd kill him. I was maybe fourteen. Then I was working on the alleys, then some theater people took me in."

"God," I said, looking down at my hands. I'd twisted my fingers together until they went pink.

"Never mind, Katie, it was long time ago." Vitya's laugh turned into a cough. "You looked for a moment like you're ready to strike someone. Reminded me of other night, when men talked to Rusala."

Baptiste nodded. "Looked like a thundercloud, then."

"Listen," I said to Greta, "that William was on the Nani the other night, and I heard him call Rusala and Hilda *diseased*. And yes, they heard him. He didn't see that I was around, I don't think. Strange how they might serve him food in his own house, yet he can talk about them as if they're animals, on the street."

She closed her eyes. "The thing is," she said, "William might be decent enough, if only he got in better company. He's sensitive and squeamish, and it makes him mean. So many of the Seagroves' friends are toadies anyway, who crowd around them begging favors. I think that's why they've taken to you so well, Katie. You're a marked exception. Anyway, I'm trying to salvage William's good sense."

Baptiste watched me closely, finally patting my wrist and changing the subject to the next performance. Soon they were all chatting brightly, boiling another pot of tea, but I could hear only the rain outside, bouncing and refracting throughout the city, an urgent hushed code. I imagined Rusala sitting on our bed, stroking her bare calves as she watched the rain. I thought of her small fingers tapping against our windowpane.

Somehow I said goodbye and kissed Vitya's cheek. He promised he'd look after Rusala and me.

Then I was stumbling through the alleys, the rain drumming on my umbrella, my hem dragging around my ankles like a fishing net. The canals swelled until water spread over the cobblestones. I passed a garden gate and looked down to see the hydrangea blossoms submerged.

I came up our stairs two at a time, my umbrella tumbling behind me. Our bedroom was hot, glowing in the firelight like a thieves' cave. The bed had been made haphazardly, strewn with parcels, a gown, an overcoat. Rusala sat bathing in a new tub, washing her stockings and watching me with her chin lowered.

"Like the bathtub? I got you something else too," she said. She stepped to the mantel, splashing water over the carpet and her scattered underclothes. On the mantel stood a potted plant, still in its paper wrapping. She tore at it, smiling.

"I had to buy them," she said. "They matched so perfectly the color of your skin."

As the paper fell away, she held up a pot of white orchids. The largest bloom curved its face towards me like a curious insect.

"Don't you think they're gorgeous?" she said, coming closer. She left a trail of spreading, glittering footsteps.

She stopped just before me and rested an orchid bloom against her damp cheek. The petals trembled at the touch of wetness, almost curling away. She turned her head and closed her eyes, resting the tip of her tongue on the very center of the blossom.

When my hand closed around the back of her neck, her eyes flew open.

Soon I lay naked under her. She unfastened her hair so that it spread around my thighs and belly. Then her face was at the center of me, nursing gently. I reached above me and grasped the headboard, moving faster and faster beneath her, until I felt myself dying. In the end I left my body and had a dream of plummeting to the very bottom of a sea, holding my breath as long as I dared in order to gather the treasures there.

I surfaced, gasping for air. She was still wet and bright as a peach. I wanted to suck all her flesh but I was too weak. I could only lift my arms towards her and pant, "Ru ..."

"Don't say you love me," she said suddenly. "Don't."

I took her in my arms. When I kissed her mouth, she wrapped her arms around me until I felt her heart pumping against my breasts.

A WEEK LATER, the weather turned cold. The strange limelight of the autumn sun finally gave way to shifting dun mists that lent depth to the landscape, that brought into relief the everyday comings and goings along the alleyways. I was in the habit of waking early, when Lovorka came in with coffee and cleared away the chamber pot. I always intended to begin work right away, yet I spent a long time sitting by the atelier's windows, drinking my black coffee, watching the people below.

Rusala slept late one chilly morning, having been at a rehearsal until eleven the night before. I turned away from the window as she rolled over. She lifted her naked arms from under the coverlet and rubbed her face, smiling at me, stretching until she shuddered. As she slipped from the bed, pulling on my dressing gown, the sun broke through the clouds.

"Will you look," she said, pointing outside. A tabby cat stalked along the courtyard wall and settled among some purple asters, tucking his legs beneath him and flattening his ears. "We've got a ginger loaf, baking in the sun."

The cat did resemble a sweet little loaf. Some mornings Rusala woke in a lighthearted mood; her acuity was now tempered with whimsy. I noticed that her eyes had become gentler since she'd been living with me. Her throat had grown plumper.

She turned to the sunlight. My heart stopped as I stared at her profile, her small nose and her spiky lashes. I felt a wave of tenderness, and then a violent desire. The two feelings seemed always to be repelling and chasing each other within me. Once again, I imagined myself circling and falling, yet the sensation no longer frightened me.

"How might you assess the probability of my attending rehearsal today?" she asked.

"No chance whatsoever."

"Absolutely correct." She stood and spun in a circle, arms wide. "Let's go somewhere plush for breakfast."

The cold air stung our mouths. Rusala wore a mink hat and cape she'd borrowed from Olga. I told Rusala it must be even colder than this in Boston, with snow already turning to a gritty slop all over the streets.

"You so rarely talk about Boston," she said in a careful voice.

Florian's had just opened. We claimed a table with a piazza view and ordered coffee, taking off our gloves and flexing our pink hands. Outside, the wind picked up, and we watched the pigeons lift in a lead-colored cloud.

Rusala hadn't spoken since her remark about Boston. She watched my face. I turned the sugar bowl on the marble table-top, saying finally, "It's just that Boston seems so far away."

"Like a dream now?" she asked. The coffee came and we warmed our hands on the blue porcelain.

"It's more that Venice is the dream. Being here in Florian's, and with you, is the dream."

I'd said it to make her smile, but she only kept watching me. Then she said simply, "You were in love with Adele."

Just as she said it, a memory flashed behind my eyes: an image of Adele and me in the kitchen of the girls' home. We were standing on a bench, doing the wash-up on some bitter January night. The carving knife was already clattering on the flagstones before I realized I'd cut my forearm. The gash was a white tingling thread that changed, as I watched, to electric crimson. I stared stupidly, wondering how to staunch it; my hands were raw with soda crystals, and I'd be beaten if I ruined another pinafore.

Adele had bent her head swiftly, closing her mouth over the wound. I'd felt a violent tug under my ribs. I'd shocked myself by thinking, *I will always remember this.* The reeking dishwater, her hot mouth, the moment before she lifted her pure eyes to mine. It was the first time I'd imagined memory, and loss.

I blinked at Rusala.

"I didn't meet Adele's brother Jeffrey until we'd finished school," I told her. "I stayed with them at their aunt's for a summer. Everyone said Jeffrey and I would marry. Really, from the day we met at their aunt's parlor."

"Weren't you worried about how much he drank, though?" Rusala asked.

"It wasn't the amount that he drank," I said. "It was the way he seemed to become another person when he drank. Sober, he was an angel. The warmest, kindest man. Then when he drank..."

"I know," Rusala said.

"And of course we thought that, with enough forbearance and care, we'd pull through. We planned to travel, maybe even settle somewhere abroad. None of us imagined that anything could go wrong. We loved one another so. How could anything go wrong?"

The café was deserted but for a lone woman at a table near the kitchen door. From the corner of my eye I saw her half-turn towards me.

"Did he know?" Rusala asked, biting her lip and leaning in. "Did he know about you and Adele? Did you and she—?"

I felt myself blushing fiercely. "We did. I mean, no, he didn't know. Adele and I had always—how can I say it? We never told a soul. I don't believe we gave words to it. But it was such an essential thing to us that we could never really feel guilty. Can one feel guilty for breathing, for being hungry?"

"I'll bet he did know," Rusala said.

"No, really, for a long time he didn't. Haven't you noticed how blind people can be, especially when something is right before them? The proximity makes it impossible to focus, just as when you hold something close to your face, or when the light is too plain."

"Yes, exactly," she said. "Until just the right shadow falls, and provides just the right relief."

She leaned back in her chair.

I whispered, "I didn't mean to—" but I couldn't remember what I'd intended to say.

"I know you didn't mean to deceive him, Katie." I looked up as Rusala spoke; her vehemence shocked me. "You only did the best you could. And, even if the courts never knew the entire story, they were, in the end, correct. Simply, the drink made him insane, and when he saw that he'd killed his own sister, even by the purest accident, what else could he do but kill himself?"

I still felt the pull under my ribcage. The sight of blood, bright and pure, came before my eyes. A widening pool on Adele's white fur carpet. I squeezed my eyes shut to dispel it, but the vision only sharpened behind my eyelids, and the blood changed its color from red to violet to green.

"No, no," Rusala said. "Here." Her face seemed to flare quite brightly, then go dim. Everything was dissolving, floating away from me. I went rigid with panic.

"Here," she said again, holding something to my mouth.

There was powder on my lips. I licked it away as Rusala watched.

"Put a pinch of it under your tongue," she said, and I did. She turned and put a red lacquered box back into her purse. Her hands were pale, transparent. I thought I could see through them to the table beneath. I almost screamed.

I covered my face and heard her continue, "It'll fix you, you'll see."

I took another breath and the air felt powerful and clean. I was warm again. I could hear the sounds of the square outside, the tink of Rusala's spoon in her cup.

When I looked at her once more she appeared blessedly solid. Again the room brightened and went dim, but I realized it was only a cloud passing swiftly over the sun. The wind rattled the window panes. A waiter glided to our table and said something. When Rusala nodded, he bowed and stepped away.

"I was ill," I said, looking down at my coffee. "For over a year, and I was in a sort of hospital. They don't call them lunatic asylums anymore, you know. And all the drugs, for my nerves."

"Ah," Rusala said. She touched her fingertips to mine.

"I changed," I said. "I became desperately timid, afraid of everything, shaking all the time, cold as a wet cat. I only found ease in powders. They can bring you such peace, you know. First, a pulling sensation all through your body, and then weightlessness. You can imagine you're rocking in a tree branch. And then your heart slows and all your thoughts fall away. I wonder sometimes whether death will be like that. Perfect love and bliss. Lord, that really sounds awful, doesn't it?"

"We all do what we must," Rusala said. "We all take whatever comfort we can find. Why fault yourself for that?" The waiter brought two more coffees and my stomach growled.

"And," she leaned towards me again, her voice low, "when we have our house on the sea, perhaps you'll have no more need of the powders. You might paint all day, in peace, and teach me to read. We'll leave all our nightmares behind us."

I'd never seen her look so grave. Her lower lip went pale and her voice faltered with emotion. I wondered whether she'd ever

spoken with such candor before, ever laid her heart so bare. I felt a
spark in my womb, and squeezed her hand. At that moment the
woman in the corner rose and came to us.

She was tall, and moved stiffly, holding on to the backs of
chairs for support. She wore a veil of heavy black crepe.

"Have you heard?" she said without preamble. She lifted her
veil and there were Greta's brown eyes. She looked ten years older.

Rusala and I sat dumbfounded.

"You haven't heard about Olga?" Greta sat beside me on the
bench. "She couldn't even read French."

"What are you going on about?" Rusala snapped.

"Olga saw some dreadful review in *Le Figaro*, saying she'd
become fat, that she should have left the stage ten years ago. They
said she looked pregnant. Of course none of us would translate the
review for her, but still she sensed something was wrong. Then she
finally found a god-damned stage hand, who didn't know any
better, who translated it all to her, so helpfully explaining the
nuances of each phrase."

"For fuck's fucking sake. I'm fed up with her. Who hasn't had
a bad review?" Rusala began sharply, but she looked at Greta and
suddenly trembled, pressing a hand over her mouth. "No, what?
What?"

"Girls, she's killed herself. A parlor-maid found her in her
bathtub." Outside, the wind knocked over a chair.

THERE HAD ALREADY been a short service for Olga that
morning, and there was to be a supper in the evening, at the
palazzo Olga had shared with the Duke. Rusala begged me to come
along with her. She couldn't decently stay away, yet she feared that
the other girls might be cruel to her, and she needed me to shelter
her, or even take her home if they were too awful.

It was a miserable gathering. About twenty of Olga's friends
sat in the great hall, whispering in the weak glow of kitchen
candles, as the gas had already been shut off. The furniture had
been covered, and servants rushed to pack away the paintings, the
lamps, the *objets d'art* Olga had collected. The Duke had
telegraphed that afternoon, ordering that the place be vacated
within two days.

Hilda and Frannie sobbed together. Baptiste paced. Greta
stood before the fire, warming her hands, sometimes leaning her
forehead on the mantel and shaking. The dark wind roared in the
chimneys.

Rusala and I sat on a drafty windowsill and gazed at the
ceiling's fresco, the painting of the fleshy, smug man in a shower of

gold. Someone handed us cups of punch and we sipped dutifully. After an hour or so, a dark boy stood and picked up a violin. He played a few waltzes and polkas. Then he played aching melodies that made us all stop drinking and look at the floor.

He came to Rusala and me and held the violin very close to our ears as he played the softest notes.

Chapter
Fifteen

RUSALA SANK INTO a depression after Olga's death. She moved heavily, like a worn-out animal. For several days she did nothing but sit at a low stool and watch the coal burn down to ash.

She took no notice of me as I sat around in a dressing gown and apron, smoking and putting the last touches on the paintings. She stayed home alone whenever I went out, saying she preferred to rest and look through the trunk of bric-a-brac Olga had left her. She kept the shutters closed tight, and soon my atelier became so dark that I could never tell day from night.

I tried to cheer her with gifts: hyacinth bulbs in tight little glass vases, or candied apples, or a pink chiffon wrap that I'd found in a second-hand clothing stall. She would smile at the presents, not quite lifting her eyes to mine. Then she would put the trinkets aside and go back to her reverie. Her lower lip was chapped and bruised.

"Don't you want to come out, Rusala? To lunch, at least?" I asked one day. I knew she would shake her head. Her hair was in a loose knot, held by one of Olga's tortoiseshell combs.

"Do you want to invite some of your opera friends here?" I pressed. "Wouldn't that be a nice change? We might ask Lovorka to go and buy a cake." I was dressed to go out, in a cloak and a muff of rabbit fur, but I sat on the carpet by her feet.

"No!" she cried, and I leaned away. "No," she said again, trying miserably to smile. "I mean, no, I really wouldn't like to have them here, at all. You mustn't invite them, ever."

"What, all your friends? I don't believe our friendship is a secret to them."

"We can't risk it," she said, her voice still strident. "Promise me that you won't ever invite them. Promise."

"Of course," I said, reaching out to touch her shoulder and half-expecting her to flinch. She didn't, but she held herself stiffly, the folds of her shawl kept close around her throat. Her face was still; only her eyes moved quickly, the way a baby doll's eyes will rattle after you shake it.

I stroked her cheek and she smiled again, that pale, tight smile, like a crack in china. She was trying to act happy, I knew, for my sake.

"Are you staying in again today?" I asked.

"Yes, for a while longer. But then I have to go and teach private lessons for the Croyden sisters. Hey, do you know them, from Baltimore? Filthy fucking rich, lousy with it. They saw the Theatre Slav last year and decided ballet is an *art form*, and their calling. These same bitches would never be caught dead talking with a ballet-girl on the street back home, but here, of course, they've become so avant garde. They make such a production of receiving me at the front door, and insisting I sit and take tea with them at their table."

Her complaining actually heartened me; I thought it meant she was returning to normal. More color had come to her cheeks.

"All right, then, Ru, I'll be home tonight, and we'll see how you feel then." I stroked her snarled hair and she tilted her cheek towards me for a kiss.

I left her by the low fire and the kerosene lamp, working her hands restlessly as though she were telling a rosary.

ONLY A FEW months before, I'd got lost trying to find the Seagroves' gallery. I'd wandered until my cheap mincing slippers were tattered and I nearly wept in the street.

Now I knew the shortcuts: along the bank where women did laundry, under the bridge near the Moroccan tea house, past the tobacconist's with the mean brindled dog, then the narrow alley with art supply shops and the blood-stained fountain. There was a sharp grey wind, the scent of smoke, and an urgent feel to the air.

When I rounded the corner, I saw that the Seagroves had put in a new front gate of blue-painted wrought iron. Its center showed a peacock, its tail and neck forming an elongated *S*.

Amy had hennaed her hair again, and had it cut short so that it swung round her shoulders.

"Hey!" she said, skipping down the stairwell. A nervous young girl held out her hands for my hat and cloak. A potted gardenia tree was in full bloom, and the first floor smelled of gingerbread.

"Hey, Artemisia!" Amy was in an elated mood. "Come here."

She led me through the main hall to the gallery. Several girls polished the floor; they parted and eddied around us like the pigeons at San Marco's square. I couldn't recognize any of them.

Amy's cheeks were white with bright red spots in their centers. Her pupils were so distended that her eyes seemed to have turned black. "Tell me what you think of the set-up in the gallery," she said. "We've two weeks to change it if you don't like it. But you ought to like it. The new thing is to have everything simple and plain."

Our footsteps echoed once the doors closed behind us. I looked around.

"You took down all the drapes?" I asked. The walls and floor had been painted white. The thick carpets had all been removed, and the windows were half-covered with Japanese paper shades.

"It looks like a hospital," I said.

She didn't blink. "No, it looks like a modern art gallery," she said mildly, in the same tone she often used with William. She crossed to the other end of the hall, where a ficus tree made a keen-edged shadow against the window. Her green velvet skirt was tight around her hips. "All the best modern galleries in Paris have this décor. Stark and powerful. Your paintings will stand out. This is the way to do it. Trust me."

Again something in my throat swelled. I swallowed twice before I felt normal. "They're finished, Amy, all of them. Well, as finished as I can make them. Damn it, I'm nervous."

"There'll be lots of dealers coming, you know." Amy stared out the window. The canal plashed outside, reflecting a soft mother-of-pearl light into the room. "They like the fact that you're a woman, too. Be sure to wear something pretty. Something red."

She folded her arms and frowned at the walls. "Don't act all soppy either, as you sometimes do. You know what I mean. Take some cocaine drops with me beforehand."

I should have rallied myself to be offended, but I was too distracted and nervous. And I knew just what she meant by soppy. My mother used to call it my hang-dog look, when my cheeks went slack as cutlets of bled meat.

I was trying to think of some brisk rejoinder when she took my arm again. Her hand fidgeted over my wrist like a crab. "Someone wants to see you anyway."

Their sitting room, where I'd sat with Greta on my first night here, was overheated and rank. A wood fire burned behind a brass cage. A vase of honey-colored lilies stood on table. William lay on a leather sofa, a notebook propped on his knees. His hair had grown longer, waving away from his temples. He reached behind him with an ink-stained hand and turned up the lamp.

"Should we have some chocolate?" Amy asked. "Now that Katie Larkin's here." She pulled a bell-cord over the mantel. Behind the drapes, the sky had become a dark algae green.

William scooted his feet tighter in, to give me room on the opposite end of the sofa. Amy sat on the carpet by the fire. They both looked at the empty spot on the sofa until I sat down. The cushions were plump and soft as marshmallows. William shuffled his papers and put the cap on his pen, still looking up at me, still smiling. My skirt clung to his trousers.

"Right. What're you working on?" I said, maybe a little too loudly.

"Have you been to Duino?" He looked at the fire. "It's not far from here, a beautiful place near the Adriatic. There's a poet I know, Rilke, who's moved there."

"He's strange." Amy yawned. "Rheumy eyes."

"He came to dine with us a few times, this past spring," William said.

I'd wanted to ask William more about Duino. Could one rent a red-roofed house on the sea there? Yet the name *Rilke* brought an intense memory. The fire popped behind the grate.

"But I have heard of him," I finally said. "Haven't I?" *Behind the bars, no world.* I had heard his poetry, in a reading at the Braintree Chautauqua Society. A man had read some of Rilke's works in German, then in English. Adele and I had stood towards the back of the room, sweating in our overcoats. I was always dragging her to readings.

"*A great will stands paralyzed*," I said, feeling the words rush by like a flock of birds. "*A hundred thousand bars.*"

"Yes," William said. "The Panther: *His vision, from the constantly passing bars, has grown so weary that it cannot hold anything else. It seems to him there are a thousand bars; and behind the bars, no world.*"

I smelled that lecture hall as William spoke. I'd wanted to cry when I first heard the poem. I'd been afraid that Adele would be embarrassed by me, so I'd sneaked away to the lavatory.

"Katie," William said, "why does it not surprise me that you know it? You know, if I weren't so dignified, I'd confess how the poem moves me."

Amy shifted on the carpet.

I tried to answer, but the memory pulled at me. The poem had made me so weary, that first time I heard it, as if I'd been wandering for days and someone had finally offered me a place to sit down. I'd cried in the lavatory, helpless, thinking of Mum and her nervous shrieking laughter on the day she brought me to the girls' home, the neighbors who would never let me in the house even though I'd only had lice the one time and the sulfur had cleaned them all away. The way people looked at you when you sat in shabby clothes in the streetcar; they gawped as if they wondered mildly whether you were, in fact, as mad and awful as you looked and maybe you'd do something to amuse them.

I stared at the fire, pretending to be mesmerized by the flames.

"Wait until you hear this, then," William said. "Do you understand German?" I felt him looking at my profile. I pretended my collar scratched me so that I could turn away.

"No."

"He's given me some work to try and translate. I'm trying not to butcher it. Here's what I have so far:

For beauty is nothing
But the beginning of terror, which we still are just able to endure,
And we are so awed because it serenely disdains
To annihilate us."

"That's enough," I heard myself say. Again I felt something in me circling and falling.

William was silent. Turning back towards him, I said, "Whoops, now I'll cry." I sounded light and I must have looked normal, for he exhaled and smiled again.

Amy stood and said she'd see about the chocolate. She closed the door carefully behind her.

"Katie." William leaned forward. He still held the pen, and he tapped it against his leg.

"Want to read me some more?" I said quickly. I knew I couldn't suddenly stand up without seeming coy, so I forced myself to settle back into the soft, soft couch.

"I haven't met anyone like you," he said. His hands rested on the paper. On his white thumb was a heavy gold ring, like an emperor's ring in a fairy tale. I wondered how it must feel to touch everything through that ring.

Amy came back in and I jumped.

"Sorry," Amy said, looking down. "Are you—"

"No, I'm sorry. I was thinking of Boston," I said, covering my eyes.

"Ah," said William. "Ah, I see."

"You know," Amy said, lying on her stomach and resting her chin on her fists, "I'm so damned glad we're not in New York anymore. Lord, it's stifling there. All your life is swallowed up in joyless rituals. Getting the right sort of dress made, seeing insipid operas, cultivating the favor of brutish old ladies."

I stared at her dully. I remembered being eighteen and longing for soap, for some tooth powder, for a gown without moth-holes. I'd wanted so badly to look clean and decent, so that people might give me a chance. Someday, I used to think, I'll look nice, and I'll sit in a parlor with the finest people, acting interested in whatever they said. They would smile right in my face.

Amy's eyes crinkled. She wore a fine powder, full of saccharine sparkles. "I feel so much freer now that I've escaped from that farce," she said. "Look, here we are meeting poets and painters. In the arts, none of that matters."

I wanted to tell her how lice torment you, when they bite. Yet you daren't scratch; someone might see you.

The chocolate came.

"Here, but I've got to leave," I said. The maid ducked her head at me.

"Oh, no, just as we were getting cozy," Amy said, glancing at William.

"All the more chocolate for you," I said. I smoothed my skirt.

"Let me take you home," William said.

"No. I have to pick up parcels."

"Everything's closed now."

"Brushes, and a milliners."

"I don't mind going with you."

"You'd be so bored. No, really."

He put his papers on the floor and stood. "I'll see you to the gate."

I knew he would clutch my elbow tight. A shower started, and the brim of my hat drooped. He walked with me to the end of the alleyway, where a gypsy man sat rocking and begging. It was the quiet hour, when children were napping, just before the cafés turned up all their lights.

He kept silent for a long time before he spoke.

"I can wait, Katie. I'll wait. I know you were married, and he died, and there was an awful case. But when I see you, I can't help feeling that..."

I felt a sinking dismay. "No." What could I say? Reluctance would only seem like a slow concession. "I wish you'd stop." My voice sounded peevish. "When did I ever give you those ideas?"

We came to the end of the alley and the scent of the sea reminded me of Rusala.

"You'll let me wait, though, won't you?" he asked. "And see you sometimes?"

Wait for what? I looked into his face, wanting to think of something cynical. His eyes looked plaintive. In spite of myself I felt a surge of pity.

"It will be all right, William," I said, wondering what on earth I meant. Before I turned away, I kissed his cheek. I had no umbrella so I had to run through the rain.

RUSALA'S HUGE UMBRELLA almost blocked the door. I called for her as I came in, as if I'd been away for a week.

Raised voices came from my studio. I thought of Rusala, and

how she'd begged me not to have any guests. Her voice became shrill. I pounded up the steps.

"*You mustn't!*"

When I opened the studio door, there was only Rusala leaning against the windowsill, dressed in a new walking suit of chocolate-brown wool. Lovorka faced away from her, shaking out a rag.

I stepped in, panting. Lovorka looked up and met my eyes for a second. Her nose and eyes were pink; her mouth seemed to be frozen open. She threw her rag on the floor and hurried from the room, stumbling on the stairs.

I saw myself in the window's leaded glass, gasping like a stranded fish.

"What's going on?" I asked.

"Why don't you sack her?" Rusala spat.

"What?"

"She was looking through my things. That chest, the one that Olga left me—she had it open when I came home. She was putting her little chapped paws all over those treasures. Can you imagine? After she'd wiped out the chamber pot, she came in and simply helped herself."

I crossed over to the chest. It stood open, filled with silks, furs, portfolios, tiny brass figurines. "You don't mean Lovorka took something?"

"No, but she might have done. I don't know." Rusala put her hand on her forehead. "I just would like to think that poor Olga's things might be respected." She started to weep, silently, in that tired way children sometimes weep.

I threw my hat on the floor. In three steps I was at her side, taking her in my arms. She rested her cheek on my jaw and sobbed while I kissed her hair.

"Now then," I said, when she quieted down. "I'm sure Lovorka was only curious, or wanted to unpack it for us. She'd never steal from us. You know that."

She nodded and clutched at the back of my gown. I stroked her back, feeling her head rest more heavily on my shoulder. After a time, I lifted my head. Something in the trunk kept catching my eye.

"Ru? Are these what I think they are?" I asked. A sequined cape half-covered a stack of notes. I knelt and fished one out. It was stiff as starched linen. A pink eagle spread its wings across the top, and below was a pastoral scene of deer grazing along train tracks.

"Bearer bonds," Rusala said. "Have you seen them before?" She sank beside me and wiped her eyes.

"Of course," I said. "It's a certificate. It means you own a little piece of the company. You can cash them in for gold." I kept leafing through the pile, not even bothering to count. My heart was hammering. Each one read *500 pounds.*

"God-damn me, Rusala," I said. "Do you know what these are worth?"

"Yeah, I do, in fact," she said. "Do you recognize the name of the company?"

I forced myself to focus on the black gothic script. Half was in Russian, half in English. "DuChamp Railroad, Caucuses. I haven't heard of them."

She nodded. "DuChamp, that's what Vitya said. That's the *D*, right? He got some too. But this company's been bankrupt for ten years. I remember hearing about that scandal a few summers ago. A real fuck-up. Some say the company never existed. I hope Olga didn't buy these off someone."

"They sure look valuable." I lifted a bill to the light to see its watermark.

"People will sometimes try to sell these things, even after the company's gone bankrupt," she said. "Did you hear of that case in Chicago? A chorus-girl sold a pile of dead bonds to some old bloke. Made herself one thousand pounds, and he was left with fancy privy paper. Once he found out about it, he wanted to replace the money with one pound of her flesh. But she'd left the country by the time anyone realized anything."

Something in me was still circling, circling. Beauty and terror. Rusala watched me as I stood.

"Have you heard of Duino?" I asked. I crossed to the sidebar and poured myself a little whiskey. There was just enough for half a glass. "Maybe that would be a nice place for our cottage. Let's take a trip there sometime."

She watched me carefully. "Ain't you tired," she said. She stood to unbutton her skirt, then slid out of it. She pulled off her shirtwaist and underclothes, then leaned over to roll down her stockings. I stood watching, and it seemed the paintings all around us watched her too, expectant, lost.

She lay on the couch and rested her bare arm over her eyes. "Katie, please tell Lovorka not to mind me. Poor nervous little thing. She's become really attached to you, hasn't she? But I'm not accustomed to having maids. I find it damned unnerving. Fuck me, unnerving."

Maybe it was the cold, or the heat of running up the stairs, or the sight of her, or the stream of memories that still rushed in me, but I felt dizzy. It was worse when I closed my eyes, but then I couldn't open them again.

I heard her shift on the couch. "What is it?" she asked. "You've been so patient with me."

I heard her stand. I listened as she crossed the carpet, the floor.

Do you ever feel that you're circling and just about to fall? I wanted to ask her. I said, "I'm in a strange mood. It will be all right."

"Here, I'll mix up some sleeping powders for you," she said, and I felt her palm graze my cheekbone. "Poor old you. You deserve a little sweet relief, after all your work."

"It will be—" I said. She stopped me with her mouth, grabbing my hand and pressing it to her breast.

Chapter
Sixteen

TICK, TICK, TICK went the abacus. I counted one last time. Enough, conservatively, to last us another two months.

How strange, I thought, the closer you get to zero, the less you think about money. During the day, you hardly think of it at all, except as a kind of outrageous game. And at night, well, you might think of all kinds of rot at night, but that's what sleeping powders are for.

I ran my tongue over my teeth. Lately they ached in front, as if with a surfeit of sugar.

"Lovorka?" I turned and called into the bedroom, where Lovorka sat on the floor. She'd been out in the courtyard beating carpets all morning.

"Yes, ma'am?" She grunted as she straightened up. "Yes? Sorry."

"I expect to be moving soon." I looked down at my ledger. I found it hard to look at her face lately. Her eyes had changed, become bitter and recusant.

"I see," she said, a little pertly. I still didn't look at her. I was sure Amy's maids didn't speak to her that way.

"I'm going to give you a commission if you conduct some research for me," I said. "I need you to inquire about houses to rent on Istria. Someplace nice and quiet, on the coast. I haven't got any time for it, myself. Do you think you could manage that?"

"Yes, ma'am."

"And please have the place straightened up by noon. The packers are coming for the paintings."

"Of course, ma'am."

By the time I was downstairs putting on my coat, I felt a pang of guilt for being so brusque with her. I left a few lire on the hall table.

Rusala met me in front of the Ducal Palace. She had been sitting for artists all morning, and her hair was arranged in a heap of curls. She wore one of Olga's ermine cloaks. Her face lit up when she saw me. It was all I could do not to take her in my arms.

"You remind me of a little bear in that cloak," I told her. She kissed the corner of my mouth.

"I'm a bear with a pot of honey," she said. She took a pouch out of one pocket and shook it, raising one eyebrow. Looking around, she leaned close to me. "I sold a couple of the tiaras Olga left me."

"You're trying to buy me?" I loved standing with her in public, whispering. Any passersby would assume we were gossiping or deciding where to have lunch.

She licked her lips and pretended to consider. "Why would I pay for something I already have? You've been my own little pet lamb from the first day, haven't you?"

I watched her tongue. Between my legs, I felt my flesh swelling.

She saw it all in my face, and smiled wickedly. Her gloved hands found mine. "*Little lamb, who made thee?* Now you must behave in public, and not blush and pant that way, Katie. Anyone could guess what you're thinking."

A group of American tourists ambled by. "Shh, Rusala, stop that." I stood very still. I knew if I moved, I would feel the wetness on my drawers.

She looked out over the square. "If you can't contain yourself, Katie, I shall have to keep you safely fastened at home, in our bed."

The bells overhead sounded. A waiter had begun setting up tables near us.

"You bitch," I said. "I ought to slap you."

"Baa," she rejoined. The waiter glanced at us. We walked along the shop windows. "Do you know," she said, "we've been invited to the Bohemian Club for lunch. Want to go, for a laugh? It's the salon of some dollar duchess."

"No."

"There'll be food."

I looked around. We'd passed the antiquario and were nearing a bridge, where a gondolier sat reading. Rusala called out to him and waved. I was lightheaded. I'd got into the habit of skipping breakfast, to economize.

"I have little say in the matter anyway," I observed. The gondolier was setting up a tent of yellow lace over our seats.

"Correct." Rusala fished in her purse.

A BUTLER LED us through the hall, informing us in a hushed voice that the recital was just about to begin. He opened the door on a room so dark I thought at first he must have led us to the wrong place.

It was a parlor that had been stripped of all its furniture and paintings. Cushions lined the corners, and the walls were hung with velvet. The electric chandelier burned low, covered in a pink cloth. Only after a few seconds did I notice the quiet crowd of people sitting on the carpets. A few cigarettes flickered. Rusala took my hand and we crouched to the floor, while a tangle of dark legs moved aside to give us room.

Two girls entered from the opposite doors, holding candles that cast feeble tangerine light over their faces. Trails of melting wax oozed towards their nervous hands. They wore brief linen tunics, fastened around their waists with golden cords. They paused for a moment, then began a Greek dance, eyes lowered, listening intently to each other. Was one of them leading? I wondered. Or had they found some instinctive way of moving with one perfect impulse, like animals?

I rose to my knees for a better view. Maybe each thought she was leading the other.

When they finished, they curtsied and then stood together, hand in hand, while servants came forward to light lamps. The crowd began shifting and chattering, stretching out on the floor.

"The goddesses of cheesecloth," Rusala said, standing. "Here, I'll get us some sandwiches and chocolate. Try to be good."

I mouthed *fuck you* and she ran away.

"I thought that was you, Katie," came a deep voice.

I turned. Baptiste and Vitya sat against the wall. I crawled towards them. They were both smiling lazily, their eyes half-shut. As Baptiste leaned forward, his lambswool hair gleamed with burgundy lights. "Fancy," he said.

Vitya took another drag at his cigarette and ran his hand through his hair.

"You're still with that Rusala?" Baptiste said. "Now, don't mind me. I know she can be very sweet and charming, yet at the same time, she can flood your senses, overwhelm you." His accent made everything sound like a question.

I looked away. Rusala was talking to the butler.

"And what's wrong with that?" I said, glancing back at Vitya. He laughed. My eyes stung. I wanted a drink.

"Now, don't be offended, Katie," Baptiste said. You have to wonder when people keep saying *don't be offended, don't mind.* "It's only that I have seen other people become so enchanted with her that they go off-balance. Her old pal, for instance."

I jumped when I felt a hand on my neck. Rusala sat beside me. "No chocolate, but whisky and soda, which will warm us better. I thought we'd share a glass." She had a plate of cucumber sandwiches that she set on a cushion. "I tried to find the Duchess," she said. "I thought I could introduce you to her as Venice's exciting new painter. But she's repaired to her room."

"She got early start today," Vitya said. He closed his eyes and handed his cigarette to Baptiste. "Was dancing, literally, on the table, when we arrived."

"I don't believe it's that." Rusala held a sandwich and talked with her mouth full. "She can hold her drink. I suspect she's retired with her newest pal, that little Cuban poetess who always wears men's clothes. And I am scandalized."

"Indeed. I would expect more decorum at a salon such as this," Baptiste said.

Vitya burst out laughing. He slapped Baptiste's shoulder, then let his hand rest there. Baptiste turned towards him, smiling irrepressibly. I felt Rusala looking at me.

"AMY TOLD ME to wear something in red, though," I said to Rusala. "She said I ought to wear something pretty."

Rusala sat in our bathtub, smoking a cigarette in a long holder. I had all my gowns, and a few borrowed ones, piled on our bed. My showing was to be the next evening. It was a fine day; stripes of sunlight shone through the blinds. Rusala's smoke gathered above her, a cloud of violet light.

"I still like the gold one." She stroked her chin. "Olga's gown."

I drew it from the pile. It was sleek, made of stiff gold lamé and covered in paste jewels from its neckline to its hem. I needed two hands to hold it up.

"Do you really think so?" I asked, turning to the cheval glass and holding the gown to me. The jewels reflected little points of light on my face. "I'll spill punch on it or something."

Rusala smiled at our reflection. "You don't want *pretty*. You'll be a goddess in that."

She said it so matter-of-factly. I tingled all over with pleasure. "A goddess?"

"Conceited thing." She lifted her chin and blew smoke at me. "What are all those letters on the bed, with the pictures of houses?"

I took off my dressing gown. "Places on the coast. Maybe our house, you know."

The water sloshed. "Divine! Are they dear?"

"If I do well enough with the show, we might move right away." I unhooked the gown and stepped in. "Damn me, it's so touchy though. I have no idea how much I'll make, and I can't work up the nerve to ask."

"Don't forget, we have poor Olga's things," she said. "We

might vamp more of them."

I sneaked a glance at her. She looked down.

"We needn't sell any more of her things, if you don't want to," I said tenderly. "She wanted you to have them."

"Olga would understand," Rusala said. "I was just thinking we don't know how long it would last us, really."

I pulled the gown over my hips. It was snug; I'd have to tighten my corset to get it hooked all the way up. The beads tinkled as I put my arms in the sleeves, and the heavy cloth weighed on my chest. It gave off the scent of oriental incense.

"Or," Rusala mused. When I turned to her, her eyes widened and her mouth formed a small *o*.

"Or what?" I asked.

"My lamb in golden fleece," she said. "Mm-mm. Rum devil." Some ash fell from her cigarette into the bathwater.

"I was going to say," she went on, "or—we might sell those DuChamp bonds, mm? Can you imagine the heap of cash we'd make?"

"Shut up."

"Turn around," she said, and I did. Colored lights sparked and raced through the room.

She put down her cigarette and sat forward. Her nipples were dark as wine-soaked figs. She rested her chin on her hands and smiled.

"Vain, gorgeous thing," she said. "Take it off again, and come here."

Chapter
Seventeen

SOMETIMES IT SEEMED that the world fell away and there was only Rusala's face. Above me, her eyes were smudged with kohl, inhumanly black. Her tilting lips were wet. She lay on me, her breasts at my throat, and I inhaled her scent.

I'd always thought of beauty as something commonplace, or at least finite. I could recognize something as beautiful, perhaps try to commit it to memory, and then continue on my way, restored. I never knew this kind of terrifying, limitless beauty. I sometimes wished I'd never seen Rusala's face. I even fantasized of going away from her, breaking free for at least a day, to refresh my eyes. Then I thought I could never part from her. I wanted to have her always near me, like a talisman.

Her eyes were still emptied from coming. I felt that all my bones had been melted; I'd come so many times that each little death faded into another, and a paralysis had come over me.

"Your showing," she said, moving against me. "You ought to get dressed and get on your way."

She lowered her head and ran her tongue along my jaw. I fumbled, clasping her with my weak arms, but she jerked away and lifted herself on her elbows. "D'you want to be late?"

She rose to sit astride my hips. She reached for my breasts and held them, lightly.

"Your skin here," she whispered, moving her fingers, "is so perfect that I can hardly restrain myself from marking it, just making a few deep scratches with my nails."

I shivered, pressing my legs together.

"Shall I make some marks here?" Her voice nearly made me come again. Her nails grazed the tops of my breasts. "Some crimson little half-moons." She brushed my nipples with her palms. "So everyone might see you're mine."

"Come on, now, Ru," I said. "I have to go."

"Close your eyes," she said, reaching for something on the dressing table. "And stay still." When she saw me looking, she lightly slapped my cheek. I closed my eyes, feeling her shape shimmering in the air above me.

There were a few deft strokes on my belly, then the sound of her shuffling about the bed.

"Hey," she said, "your name is with a *K*, isn't it? Doesn't *K* look just like an *R*?"

I opened my eyes. With her stick of kohl, she'd drawn a careful *R* on my stomach.

AS I LEFT the house, my only thoughts were of Rusala, of the long, long time it would be before I could climb into the bed again.

She saw me off, wearing her white linen shift and holding a pillow to her chest. "Lovorka will take care of me. We're great friends now," she said. "You hurry up and make our fortune and come home."

As the gondola heaved into the canal, my stomach twisted. My paintings. Such a fine group of people would be looking at my paintings. I imagined them laughing, throwing their heads back and laughing, then saying, *I suppose the evening's not wasted. Let's go for supper.*

But no, I thought, they won't laugh. They'll smile thinly, and proclaim the paintings lovely. *Just... simply... lovely.* They'll give me kind looks before sliding away.

I shuddered at that last thought. If anyone called the paintings *lovely* I would scream.

Under the darkening sky, the canal was cold and still. A crescent moon was rising, bright as a razor. I watched the clouds move across it. The gondolier hummed to himself, sneaking glances at me. As I held my coat closer, my dress clinked and twinkled. He was going to expect a big tip.

When we arrived at the Seagroves Gallery, there was the sound of laughter, and a piano playing. The frosty grass crunched under my feet as I crossed the courtyard.

"All right, then, nice and early." Amy sat at a new piano in the front hall. She banged out a few more chords, then came to me. Her tight grey dress, with its blue satin collar and brass buttons, reminded me of a Salvation Army uniform.

The hall was lit more brightly than I'd ever seen, filled with mounds of white jasmine, Easter lilies, orange blossoms.

"Want to see your paintings, how I set it up?" Amy asked. She was radiant.

"No! No, I don't think I could bear it." A maid took my coat and hat. Amy whistled.

"The dress is a bit much," she said. "But why not? Good God,

you needn't look so damned green. Come and get a little food.
People should be here any moment."

She led me into the dining room, where William sat by the
fireplace. I tried to say hello but the sudden scents of meat and
chocolate made my throat tighten.

Another voice came from the hallway, and Greta swept in.
"Hoo, I'd been following you, Katie." She kissed my cheek, then
held my shoulders and looked into my face. Her own face seemed
so changed, longer and thinner, with parched skin and violet
shadows under her eyes.

"I knew you could do it," she said.

"Shh," I said.

Amy put her arm round my shoulders. She puffed her cheeks
and blew out nervously.

William stared into his book. He wore a turned-down collar
and a flowing jade-green tie that made him look younger and more
serious. He met my eyes and was about to say something when a
young girl came in.

"Signora," she said. The front door was opening.

"Amy," Greta said, "you go on out, and we'll keep Katie in
here until the crowd reaches optimal density."

I sat in one of the high-backed oak chairs that lined the walls,
tapping my slippers against each other. Laughter filled the front
room. Someone played a Scriabin piece on the piano, while two
male voices broke into a jocular quarrel. Amy's voice, high and
nervous, floated above it all.

I can't, I can't. I felt hot, then so cold that my teeth chattered. I
sat very straight on my chair.

William and Greta were staring at me.

"Isn't there any god-damned thing to drink?" I begged.

WHEN WE EMERGED again into the main hall, it was filled
with serene, richly dressed people. There was the subtle and
unmistakable scent of wealth — vanilla and bergamot and liqueur.
The men wore suits of midnight blue and black, of wool so fine that
it gleamed like velvet. Women wore gowns of layered chiffon, in the
season's newest colors of sugar-almond or celery or sweet-pea pink.

They all stopped talking and smiled at me as I passed.

By the entrance of the gallery itself, a plump girl stood next to
a poster that was half-covered by a red sash. Before I could read it,
she clasped her hands together and bounced to me.

"Thank you," she gasped, in a dainty British accent. She wore a
black choker very tight around her neck. "It's lovely of you, just
lovely."

"All right, I'm pleased you think so," I answered vaguely.

The gallery was quiet as a church. My dress chimed as I entered. My paintings stretched before me, with people gathered around them in groups of three or four. I could see for the first time how awful the paintings were, how intimate and messy and hysterical. I felt like a madwoman who'd gathered up some bits of trash and wrapped them as Christmas gifts for her friends.

This, I thought, is a nightmare. I'll back up now, and sneak out through the kitchen. I'll take two cups of sleeping powders and forget that this ever happened.

"Katie." Amy came up behind me. I turned, and she caught my upper arm.

"It's beyond my wildest dreams," she said. She looked around, then swallowed. "I must get hold of myself. I'm thrilled. They all came. Each critic, each collector I invited. You haven't spoken to any of them, have you? Tell me, because you must let me be the one who negotiates."

I couldn't answer. A fat man with a mane of frizzled white hair was gliding towards us, still gazing at the paintings, rapping his cane against the floor. A few smaller men trailed him, like dolphins trailing a yacht. I heard only fragments of their talk: "...a woman?"

Amy whispered, "Zolotov. Dealer." Then she sang out, "Dmitriy Ilyich."

Zolotov came to us. His smile was all gentle indulgence, as if he imagined us basking in his presence. "I've begged you to call me Dima. I thought Americans were non-formal that way."

"This is Miss Larkin," Amy said.

"Pleased to—" I said.

"I shan't tell you how outstanding these are, Miss Larkin," he began, "because you ought to know. I wish to buy three works, Amy. My good friends here will arrange it."

Stay calm, I pleaded with myself. No matter what, stay calm, don't act strange.

"Which do you want to buy?" I asked.

Zolotov held out his hands. Amy spoke up quickly. "There's also Constantini, who's said he might take at least four. I'm not sure if I ought to let you all clean me out on the first night. After all, there could be more buyers coming later in the week."

"Glass of wine, madam?"

I looked around. Hilda stood before us, holding a tray of drinks. She wore a white cap with black satin ribbons hanging round her cheeks. She squinted at me before she moved on.

I sipped at the wine. I wanted to sit down for a moment.

A few more dealers approached me, and Amy never left my side. I was grateful then for her hardness, her unreflecting, instinctual avarice. I could never have discussed the prospect of taking money for something I'd painted. There was evidently an entire language of negotiation, at once gay and deadly serious, that I'd never learned.

I finally left it all to her, and wandered about the gallery on my own, listening.

"See how the woman's flesh seems to be lit from within. And those eyes. She looks lethal. I wouldn't care to meet her in a dark alley."

"That glowing caramel color, with an ultramarine halo."

"And the ones with the orchids. Almost pornographic."

"I like the ballet-girls. Look at the little fat one."

"Of course you'll produce more," said a painfully thin German man. He seemed so affronted I thought at first he didn't like the paintings. He stood with his hands clasped behind his back, not taking his eyes from one of the largest paintings — the first nude I'd done of Rusala. She lay over the couch, legs splayed, her face turned towards the viewer. Her eyes were like two bullet-holes in the canvas.

"Might you paint another one like this?" the German man said.

"Yes," I answered. Confidence or wine made me more loquacious. "In fact, I'm considering a move to a quieter area, towards Istria perhaps, where I can concentrate more easily."

"Why, we have a villa near Porec," he said listlessly. "You must come and stay with us."

I imagined visiting with Rusala as my companion. We'd always be escaping the party to sea-bathe.

When I came out to the hall again, everyone applauded at the sight of me. Then I did sit down, holding the back of a chair, touching my hot cheeks. That only made them applaud more. On the far side of the room, I saw Amy pause for a moment and half-turn towards me, nodding, before resuming an earnest conversation.

An older woman, dressed in a frilled black widow's gown, sat beside me. "Brilliant," she crooned, patting my knee. Her accent was pure New York. "The orphans will bless you."

"Orphans?"

"Yes, dear." Despite her fine powder, her face was ruddy as a pig's, with tiny frenzied eyes. "Artists have a reputation for being so self-centered, and yet here you are giving."

"Giving what?" I asked, though I already suspected. Sweat prickled under my arms.

"A benefit showing, truly."

When she smiled, she pursed her lips as if she were tasting a lemon. She tittered, caressing my thigh. Amy passed by and I stood.

"Amy," I called out. The old woman kept merrily chatting and cooing to herself, gazing at my waist, my arms. Amy motioned for me to join her. She was talking with a group of Englishmen, just beside the red-draped poster. I approached and read: *All proceeds to benefit the Ladies' Collective for the Aid of Balkan Orphans.*

"May I speak with you for just a moment, Amy? If you'll excuse us."

Amy gave me a look of pure panic, but I turned and walked towards the kitchen. After a moment, I heard her footsteps behind me. The kitchen was bitter cold, reeking of fish. A boy stood sawing at a block of ice. I decided to ignore him.

Amy hissed, "Christ, this is not the — "

"All proceeds?" I watched her face go pale. I still hoped she might say something to explain it all, to show me I'd misunderstood.

"What's the problem? I need you to be frank and cogent here." Amy folded her arms.

I gestured back towards the hall. "Is this a benefit, then?"

"Yes, I organized it as a benefit. And? Yes? Do you object to orphans or something? Should I have donated it to the anarchists?"

I bit my lips and tried to speak clearly. "Am I to understand that I won't earn anything from my work of these past months, not a cent?"

Amy lowered her chin abruptly. She opened her lips but could only say, "Wha — wha — "

She whirled around and paced away from me.

"Why is it — " she began, very softly. "Really, indulge my curiosity. Why is it that talent seems to eradicate good sense? Couldn't I meet just one artist who isn't an utter fucking fool?"

"I'm sorry?" I hated my voice then, so shrill and childish.

"I'm going to hope this is merely a kind of shock, Katie, that you're overexcited and not yourself. Listen. This is a small gallery. This is my first major showing. Making it into a benefit was the only way to pull in this crowd. Zolotov is here, for Christ's sake! And do you realize that the woman who just sat and spoke with you is a duchess?"

"So, yes?"

"Yes, what?" she shouted, baring her lower teeth like a bulldog. The boy ran from the room, letting the saw clatter to the floor.

"Then your answer," I said, "is *yes,* I won't make a cent from this showing?"

She let her head fall back. "I'm not going to listen to another minute of this," she said, passing a hand over her mouth and smudging her lip rouge. "Most painters would do anything for such exposure. Yes, of the works you sell tonight, we'll be donating most of the proceeds to the Ladies for Balkans or whatever. But there's sure to be something left over, of course, for the gallery costs, and for you."

"What shall I do?" I said. It sounded so false and trite, like a line from a play, but I couldn't stop repeating it. "You have no idea. What shall I do? You might have told me. How are we going to live?"

She was so unnerved that her anger faded for a moment, changing to pure bafflement. "Live? You mean you need some money right away? Tonight?"

I sat on a low stool. An icy draft blew on my throat. "Or soon."

"Then William can take you to the telegraph office," she said, exasperated, "and you can cable home."

I didn't realize I was going to laugh. She might have thought I was sobbing, as I heaved forwards and pressed my palm over my mouth. When I looked up at her again, her face was dead calm. I realized she'd come to terms with it all, in her mind. She'd decided that she'd misjudged me, she'd soon be rid of me, she'd put all this nonsense behind her.

"I won't waste any time wondering about this," she said. "I've done everything for you, and you're still here going mad in a kitchen, humiliating me." She brushed her palms together, briskly, and looked at the space over my head as she continued. "I'm not stupid, Katie. I'm sure there are many excellent reasons why you need a heap of cash right this moment. And I don't care to know any of them. I'd like you to walk back into the lobby, smile mutely or gaze at the floor in your charming farouche way, and drink your free wine until it's time to go."

A maid came through, carrying some empty dishes. When I turned to her, she stopped and curtsied.

"Get my coat, please," I told her. "I'll leave from the kitchen door. Find a boy to get me a gondola."

"You may not go, Katie. I've promised several people they'd meet you. I need to cultivate these dealers, impress them."

"Wire home for some money, then," I said, "if you want to impress them. Throw them an even plusher party. That's the only reason anyone tolerates you anyway."

She was silent.

"You damned twit," I said. I stopped, as shocked as if a bird had flown out of my mouth. The maid returned with my coat and hat. I had to speak again. "The most important thing your money buys you is the belief that you're liked and respected, that any of these people care about you."

The maid ran out. "You little slut— " Amy began.

"That quiet voice you hear," I went on, "when you're alone at night, the one that tells you that you're unattractive and awkward and really rather stupid — that's the voice you ought to listen to."

I'd meant to say more, but I couldn't bear to spend another moment in the kitchen. My coat smelled of Rusala, and I hugged it to me as I left.

Outside, snow was falling in great soft flakes. I stopped and let it settle on my eyelids.

I DIDN'T WAIT for the gondola. I tried to walk home, but I quickly lost my way. The city was transformed again, shockingly clean, washed of every color but the soft azure of the snow. I found a young girl begging at a church and gave her two coins to lead me home.

Rusala was gone.

Lovorka had waited up for me. She was sweetly attentive, building up the fire, bringing me beef broth. I expected her to ask me about the showing, but she said nothing. I wondered whether she'd been crying. Perhaps Rusala had been scolding her again.

I sent Lovorka away and undressed alone. The gown had been so heavy that it was a relief to take it off. I felt as if my legs had been fused together and were now separating, becoming human flesh again. My thoughts came in little bursts: there was no more money for cigarettes; we'd have to dismiss Lovorka; we'd have to sell more of Olga's things. Might I get a commission? Yet how would I approach one of those dealers, who'd just spent so much, and ask for a commission?

And where was Rusala? Had she said there was a performance tonight? Or a photography session? I struggled to remember.

The church bells startled me. I was sitting naked before the fire, clenching and unclenching my fists. I counted, turning my ear to the window. Midnight already. The snow whispered shyly outside.

I lay down without putting out the lamps. Each time I closed my eyes, I jumped. There were children crying out with urgent joy in the alleyway below, let out past their bedtime. I remembered the girls' home in Boston, the exhilarating chaos of the very first snow. Adele and I used to sneak past the chapel to the back garden, where we'd make snow angels until our clothes were soaked through. Then, afterwards, we'd huddle under our quilt, still cold and wet, and tell each other ghost stories.

Adele, I've had the most horrible nightmare.

I woke and screamed. A spider lay on my belly. I swiped at it, thrashing, until it became a feathery *R*, traced in kohl.

Chapter
Eighteen

I WOKE TO find the room flooded with sunlight. I sat up right away, frowning. How strange the sunlight seemed, so weird and empty; I felt it rushing upwards, taking all the air with it. There were voices in the hallway, and the thump of boots. I suddenly remembered the night before and my heart leapt. Shivering, I tried to stand.

The door opened. Rusala stood in her ermine cloak, her hair pulled back as if for her ballet lesson.

"Katie." She was in my arms, climbing on the bed. Her cloak tickled my bare skin. "Oh, Katie."

"Where were you Rusala? I have to tell you something."

"I heard." She sat up. Her cloak fell open and I saw a purple gown. "I heard. Christ."

"You heard?" I asked, and she nodded and stood from the bed. She opened the wardrobe and took out one of her ballet practice dresses. My arms ached for her, but I only sat, chilled, watching her undress. Her gown was new, of thick aubergine plush.

"Yes, I heard," she said. "I saw Hilda on my way home last night. Tell me more about it while I dress, would you? If I'm late for rehearsal, I'll have my pay docked again, damn it. It's opening night tonight. Oh, fuck me." She stood still, looking down. Her cheeks were chapped and streaked with rouge. "Fuck me, I am so tired."

"I still can't believe it." I kept shaking my head. I stared at her, as if I could drink her in with my eyes, the only bit of color and substance in the strangely washed-out sunlight. I wished so that she would stop flying about and sit with me, and help me think.

"And you know how those ladies' clubs are," she said. "The money just goes towards grand excursions for the old bawds and their entourages. They caravan to poorhouses or hospitals and give out stale sweets and have their photographs taken. Bitches."

"Speaking of bitches, I lost my temper at that Amy," I said dryly. "I called her a twit, I think."

"I say." Rusala straightened up. The dimple showed in her left cheek. "But you didn't really call her a twit, did you? You might have come up with something better."

I watched her bend to take off her stockings. Her garters left deep red welts, as if she'd had them on all night. A bruise showed on her inner thigh.

"But now we are really on our backs, aren't we?" she said, and her laughter faded. She stood naked, turning her practice dress over and over in her hands, as if she'd forgotten how to put it on. "Flat fucking broke."

I swung my legs over the side of the bed. She wouldn't meet my eyes.

"Were you rehearsing late last night, then?" I asked her.

She stepped into her skirt, grunting as she pulled it over her hips. "Yes, and then I was at a miserable endless supper." The tarlatan rustled.

She turned from me and hooked up her bodice. "Perhaps, Katie," she said, "you might get a commission. Or a patron. Really, as talented and pretty as you are, you ought to be wallowing in it."

"How can you say that?" I cried. "A patron? Could I find one who'd give us enough privacy?" She half-turned to me and winced.

"Hell," she said, "we might both get patrons." Her voice was full of horrid forced jollity, and she suddenly lifted one palm towards me, warding me off. "There was, in fact, someone I met at the supper last night, an American painter. An heir, who paints. His family's fortune is from sewing machines. He said he crosses himself each time he sees a sewing machine advert. Ha, I thought you'd find that funny."

She was trying to smile, but her face looked awful, seizing and clenching. I thought she would be sick.

"You're joking," I said. "Stop that, stop."

"He wants to paint me, of course. Set me up in a place on the Lido." She fluffed out her yellowed skirt, breaking off some loose threads at its hem, then sat on the windowsill. The rooftops beyond gleamed with half-melted snow; my eyes smarted with the brightness. The edges of her seemed to disappear into the glare.

I covered my face. "Quit that, Rusala. You can't be serious."

"I am dead serious." Her fingers moved restlessly in her lap, fumbling over one another. "Perhaps it's time we were serious and stopped pretending like two little girls in a tree-house. Even if you were to get the ponciest commission imaginable, it wouldn't be enough for us to go on, not in the way we've dreamt. There are certain limitations to what we can do. That's the mark of intelligence, isn't it? To acknowledge the limitations?"

"Please, please stop." I tried not to rock back and forth.

"But I don't mean it must be all or nothing. We might still see each other, sometimes, here and there."

She stopped when she saw my face. I gripped the bed. Neither of us said anything, but the air between us went tense and acrid, like the puff of sulfur just after a fuse is struck.

The San Fantin bell rang. "Fuck me!" Rusala hit the windowsill with her fist. She took up her rucksack and stumbled out, tripping on the stairwell. She slowed when she reached the bottom, and there was a slumping sound.

I heard her fingernails scraping on the banister.

She pounded back up the steps, fell through the door, and clung to me, sobbing. I pulled her under the coverlet, clothes and all, and stroked her shuddering back.

She struggled to speak, hiccuping between sobs. "I've sold everything I possibly could from Olga's trunk. I hate myself so. I don't know what else to do. I don't have anyone to turn to. My father, if he lives, is still lying on his hip somewhere in London, selling his teeth for more opium. I know you haven't got anyone either. I don't want to live with some god-damned rotting bastard, I couldn't fucking bear it."

I could only say "hush, hush, hush." I promised her I'd think of something, I would. *Hush.*

"What shall we do?" she wailed. "I don't want to do terrible things. Other people don't understand. They think it's so easy to be good. Oh, Katie, how I hate myself, you can't know, you can't know, you can't know." She gasped again, then thundered: "And why — *why* must you be so loving, so lovely? Do you realize how impossible you make it all?"

I pressed my palms against her shoulders and held her to me, desperate to make her still and calm. She buried her face in my neck and her wails changed to moans.

In time she went limp, and lay languid in my arms. I remembered all the times she'd lain like that against me, after writhing against my thigh and gripping my waist.

"Oh, wanh, wanh," she said finally. She still hiccuped, but her voice sounded harder. When she sat up, her hair was mussed and her eyes were filmy.

She tried to smile. "Look at me," she said. "What a brat. I know we'll think of something. What good does it do to get hysterical?" She licked her palms and smoothed her hair along her temples, then blinked at the ceiling.

"Can't you take one day off from dancing?" I said. "Don't go off all alone. Stay home with me." I stroked her wet cheeks with my braid.

She put her fingers under my chin. "Not today, damn it all, or

I'll be sacked straight away. But come to the opera tonight. Just come late, and if someone gives you trouble, say you're Rusala's pal. We'll think of something. We'll think of something."

She stood and looked down at me, her lips still trembling. I thought, *I will always remember this.* I reached for her.

Her face crumpled. "Oh, Katie."

I stood to embrace her, but she slipped from the room.

I wanted to rush after her, and clutch her knees, and beg her to stay, but as soon as the front door slammed shut I heard Lovorka pattering below, hurrying to finish her chores. I knew I couldn't bear to talk to Lovorka now; if I saw her round bewildered eyes, I'd collapse into tears.

Just as I thought that, she approached the stairwell.

"Oh." I fell on the bed and buried my face in the pillow. As she ascended the steps, I pressed my palms over my ears.

Not now, Lovorka, I need to think.

She stopped just outside the bedroom door, and I watched the shadow of her feet as she fidgeted, skittish as a colt. She took a deep breath. When I sat up to listen, she went still. There was the only the drip, drip, drip of the melting snow, like a thousand clocks ticking, and the shadows of sparrows moving across the walls.

She knelt finally and pushed some paper under the door before running down the stairs. I thought I heard her weeping. I rolled to my back and rested my arm over my eyes. *Think, think.* I dressed quickly, distractedly, in some old suit from Boston. I sat on the floor to read the notes Lovorka had left.

The first was a stern brown stationery with a black border. On one side were the embossed initials GM, and on the other, a hand-scrawled note.

Did I ever tell you about my first big recital in London? I was sharing a trundle bed with cockroaches, eating nothing but potatoes and cabbage, and my manager so gaily made my first show a benefit. I still remember how proud he was. All that press. So much money we'd raised for the Girls' Home. Ah, my poor foster daughter. Amy gave excellent excuses, but I guessed. Look, these are times that try a girl's soul . . . and all that. To hell with them, Katie. Don't be frightened, but show them what you're made of. Meet me for lunch today, will you? At Florian's. Yours, Greta

The next was a note, on a scrap of paper, from William. His handwriting was large and angular.

Katie, you may count on me for anything. Amy's gone to Milan. I leave for America next week, but until then you're welcome to call any time.

"Ha!" I said. "Cheeky."

Suddenly I heard a voice. It was so clear that I started and imagined someone stood behind me: *Perhaps William has watched this whole affair unfold. Perhaps he sensed the woman's desperation for money, her hope, her disappointment. And now he takes full advantage of his chance to enter and contend and rescue.*

Before it finished speaking, I realized the voice was in my head. I marveled at its assurance. My stomach growled. I felt weak. When had I last eaten? I pressed at my eyes and swallowed.

I shuffled the papers, one after another. There was a thumping sound downstairs; I wondered whether Lovorka were moving the furniture in her room. Tick, tick, tick went the drops of melting snow.

I touched my braid, still damp from Rusala's tears. I heard again her sobbing that she had no one, that she'd sold absolutely everything in the trunk.

I was already trembling when I crossed the room and pulled the trunk from under the dresser. I opened it and inhaled its scent of incense and cigarettes. It was nearly empty now; against the black felt bottom there were only a few buttons, the china leg of a doll, and the pile of DuChamp bonds. There were more certificates than I remembered. Rusala had tied them into a neat little bundle.

I felt a chill, as if ice water trickled over my arms. I rubbed my shoulders and looked around the room.

"Oh, God."

"IT WAS RIGHT of you to come, Katie."

The marshmallow-soft couch in the Seagroves' parlor was covered with notebooks and German dictionaries. William cleared a space for me and sat himself at a chair, folding his ink-stained hands. A fire of pine cones and apple wood burned behind the screen.

I stared at my coffee cup and wiggled my toes in my damp shoes. I had stood in the slush for a long time before ringing the Seagroves' bell, watching the filigreed gate gleam in the sunlight.

It's like taking out a tooth, I told myself over and over. I ground my own teeth together. It's like taking out a tooth, or having a deformed limb chopped off. You have to do it swiftly, coolly, without reflection.

William smiled at me over his coffee.

"I ought to apologize for running off as I did, last night," I began, but he raised one hand.

"But I ought to have intervened," he said. "That is, I found out last week that Amy had arranged the show as a benefit, and perhaps I should have told you, or asked Amy to consider that you might not have the kind of means she imagines. Lord, this is so awkward. Or is that, in fact, why you left? Amy put a good face on it, but I sensed something was wrong. It's not your style to have a fainting spell, for God's sake."

"Indeed, that was true. I wasn't feeling well. I hadn't eaten all day, from nervousness, and then I was so overcome with the attention. And yet at the same time—" I sounded like an actress unsure of her lines. I gave a weird trilling laugh, turning my head to the side. My right hand, holding the portfolio in my lap, seemed to have turned to steel. I heard the bonds rustling inside and I gripped tighter.

I thought of Greta, the way she stood and walked with such compelling grace. Surely she never forgot her lines. I stood, resting my portfolio on the tea tray, and walked to the window. Along the opposite bank of the canal stood a row of palm trees, strung with scarlet beads.

Rusala and I will have a garden, I thought, with palm trees, and we'll decorate them at Christmas.

Focus.

"This is so embarrassing," I said. It was much easier if I didn't look at him. "As it happens, I may have been over-optimistic about ... about means."

I heard the chair creak as he settled back. "It's nothing to be ashamed of," he said gently. "Amy and I still get ourselves into tight spots. It's easy to do. And we've been living on our own for years. You've only been abroad for a few months."

"Mm, it's easy to do."

"I know you're so fiercely independent. I admire that about you. But it's still all right to ask for a little assistance, isn't it? Your family must be concerned."

"Ah, my family," I answered, thankful for the cue. "They are concerned, of course. They write me every week, to ask me whether I need anything. But my goodness, I'm twenty-eight. I hate to ask for their support. If only I could negotiate the banks here better."

My goodness?

"Yes, the banks here are a mess. I try to avoid 'em. We just get funds wired from home, and we use a safe here in the house. Do you need to withdraw from your holdings, or something?"

"Not exactly. I have, as part of an inheritance from my grandfather, some bearer bonds. Here, look." I crossed back to the table, feeling his eyes follow me. When I opened the portfolio, my hands were steady and warm.

I licked my lips before I continued. I'd rehearsed this part well. "Now, I'm no banker," I said, "but I thought I'd be able to keep these with me as I traveled, and then cash them as needed at any international bank. Yet when I went into—oh, what's that big bank near the Rialto? Anyway, when I went there, I had to meet with three different men who barely spoke English, and they kept asking me to sign a whole heap of documents, and there were all sorts of taxes and fees. After an hour of that I gave up and just left in pure bewilderment. I don't believe they're accustomed to the patronage of eccentric female artists."

"That's a shame."

"And so I thought I'd ask for your advice. Could you, maybe, come to the bank with me, and help me sort it out?"

I looked at him then. He rested his chin on his fist, staring at the bonds. "I wish I could help," he said. "But my Italian is probably no better than yours. I think all we'd do is add another layer of intrigue to the affair. They'd want to know my relation to you." He blushed, laughed. "And so on."

"I'd tell them you're my best friend in Venice." I walked again, this time to the fire. *That's enough walking about,* I warned myself. *Relax. Calm.* I rested my hand on the mantel, where there stood a little golden statue of a Buddha.

"You're right, though," I said. The fire was warm on my skirt, my stockings. The smell of cooking came from somewhere in the house, and my stomach growled again.

"I suppose you're quite right, quite right," I repeated, sighing. It felt exactly like one of those awkward moments in a play, when one actor forgets his lines and the other prompts, waits.

"I've got it!" William snapped his fingers and I turned to him. His eyes sparkled. "Hey, here's a simple idea. Why don't you let me buy up some of those bonds? I'll give you the cash for them now, and then when I'm in New York for Christmas, I can sell them to my bank. Dad's got a whole swarm of bankers. They'll work it out."

My heart stopped, then lurched twice. "Oh, for God's sake, are you drunk? I didn't come here to ask you for money." I rested my palm on my flaming cheek. "How could you even say that? Now I'm embarrassed."

"Why?" he cried, raising his eyebrows. He looked pleased with himself, tapping his ring on the arm of the chair. "Don't be silly. You're being a stubborn Yankee now, aren't you? You're being a tragically austere *artiste.* Are you going to make me beg you to accept my money?"

"No!"

"Heaven forfend. Friends helping friends, can you imagine? You just wait right there. No, don't move."

He jumped from the sofa and tugged at the bell-pull. I'd never seen him so animated. Within seconds, a valet appeared at the door and they consulted together. The valet lifted his dark, canny eyes to mine for a moment.

I turned away and studied the golden Buddha.

"William, please, please don't," I said, after the valet had left. "Maybe you'd better not, after all."

"Maybe I better had. Let me help, won't you?" His voice was softer. "I'll just spend all that filthy lucre anyway, if I have it lying around. This will force me to budget a little until I'm home again. And then wouldn't Dad be proud?"

He came to me and took my hand, pressing it. He smelled of coffee, and the firelight made his hair and his lashes glow. *No*, I almost said out loud. I remembered Jeffrey's embrace, when we were first married. How solid and safe he'd seemed at first, a sun-warmed boulder. William's eyes took on a sort of dull, unseeing look that gave me a shock of memory, and made me swallow and pull away.

"William, I—"

The valet came in again, holding a leather binder. William opened it and nodded with contentment.

"More than I thought," he said. "Almost three thousand pounds. That should buy most of them, eh?"

I'd been so desperate about this moment. Would I scream at the sight of the money, or lose my nerve and bolt outside? Yet William barely noticed me in his glee. Flushing with pleasure, he was a young St. Nicholas, wrapping the notes and putting them carefully in my portfolio. He didn't even try to keep me, as I stuttered something about a lunch appointment. He was all delicacy, letting me make my modest retreat, taking my coat to put tenderly around my shoulders.

He kissed my cheek, wishing me a merry Christmas, and I exited to the bright alleyway.

I stood dumbly for a moment, then began walking, so quickly that I stumbled and nearly fell. I was afraid to breathe. There was a moment of intense dread—the breathless moment after a tooth is pulled, or a limb severed, or a deep slash made with the finest razor. The terror just before the pain arrives.

But there was no pain. Instead, when I breathed again, the world was full of color, and texture, and music.

I walked more slowly, letting the crowd eddy around me. A man sat under a parasol, playing Spanish songs on his guitar. Only a few yards away, a woman made a bear cub dance, while a crowd of children howled in terror. The sunlight felt comforting now, soft and fine as a cashmere mantle, and the city was filled with the richest colors I'd ever seen: acidic yellows, pure blues, and crimsons you could fairly taste.

I stopped at a fruit stall and bought a piece of coconut. I had to bite and suck hard to take the meat from its rind. Some girls walked by, arm in arm, singing Christmas carols in French.

I covered my mouth, because I couldn't stop smiling.

"Fuck me," I said, sounding just like Rusala.

Chapter
Nineteen

THE MONEY RESTED in my portfolio, quiet and hot; I felt it
bunting against my thigh with each step. Its heat seemed to burn
through the leather and cloth, moving through me, surfacing
finally in my eyes.

It's curious, I thought, how natural it feels to have money, so
much money. It didn't feel shocking at all. It felt rather as if the
money restored me, as if I'd had something cancerous removed, or
as if my mind and my lungs had been clogged with teeming worms
that were now blasted clean away.

My heart beat out a quick rhythm, just a little quicker than my
step, reminding me of the need to keep moving. How hot it had
grown. My coat was stifling. Even my sweat seemed cleaner, with a
scent I hardly recognized. I walked along an unfamiliar passage, by
a butcher's shop with a grinning pig's head, and emerged by the
Ducal Palace. The boutique windows gleamed so brightly I thought
I could hear them humming.

I stopped in a book store and bought a children's reader for
Rusala, a doll-sized book covered in russet calfskin. There were
illustrations of red-cheeked English children sitting in a garden,
holding large, fine, flower-strewn letters. Later in the book, the
children told contented stories about their cat, and Jane, and milk. I
bought another copy of *Innocence and Experience*, one she might
soon be able to read on her own.

I knew I ought to buy paints before we traveled, and a new flat
brush, but I wanted to purchase our tickets right away. I started
towards the nearest bank, hoping to hire a sandolo or a motor-
launch to the station. Where should we go first? Perhaps straight to
Porec, or somewhere else on Istria, or perhaps all the way down to
Spalato, or even on to Greece? I knew only we must leave the city,
keep Venice to our backs, and go, go, go.

I slanted my shoulders, murmuring apologies, working my
way through a herd of somber-dressed German ladies. I resolved to
buy tickets for the first ship to leave the next morning.

"Katie!"

I stopped so quickly that a man behind me sputtered.

"Hey, Katie!" There was a flash of white across the square. Greta stood before Florian's, waving a handkerchief. "Hey!" she shouted again, then blushed, putting a hand on her collar. I couldn't hear her laughing, but I watched her cover her mouth while her eyes narrowed and glittered. Her hat drooped with ostrich feathers.

"Will you look at me," she said when I reached the shelter of the awning. The musicians were setting up on a felt-covered platform, ducking as the pigeons swept by. Greta looked around, still laughing and blushing, breathless.

"I guess Americans are supposed to be brassy and loud and everything," she said, tugging on her hat brim. She leaned in to kiss me, then stopped.

"Whoa. Are you all right?" she asked. The ostrich feathers brushed my cheek. "You look so queer and pale."

I shifted the portfolio and scratched, absently, where it had rested against my hip. "I can't stop." My legs burned with restlessness, and when I looked to the fondamenta I saw half a dozen idle sandoli. The German tourists were approaching them. There wouldn't be any boats left for me.

"What?" she cried. "I thought you were here to meet me." Her brows drew together. "Can't you stop for just a cup of coffee?"

Of course. Her note. It seemed days ago that I'd read it.

"I can't. I'm sorry, Greta." I took both of her hands. My gloves were drenched with sweat. "But do you have any idea how your note inspired me? What was it you said? To show what I'm made of?" I thought of Rusala saying *Little lamb, who made thee?* and I had the urge to giggle.

"Inspired you to what?" she asked. She noticed my half-bitten smile and attempted to laugh herself, but her forehead was still wrinkled tight. "Won't you come in?" she added. I must have been talking very loudly; the musicians had stopped chattering and were sneaking glances at me.

"No." I swallowed. I felt suddenly naked in the sunlight. "All right, let's go in, I have some time." I was careful to speak very quietly. She had to turn her head to hear me better.

Once we were seated at a red bench, I took off my gloves and grabbed her hands again. She started at my touch. Of course, it must have been so strange for her to see how changed I'd become, how liberated.

"Can you keep a secret?" I asked.

Her eyes darted. The hair at her temples had become the color of tarnished silver.

"Depends," she said finally, drawing her hands away and looking for the waiter.

"I'm leaving Venice. But, really, don't tell anyone."

"Oh," she said, turning back to me. "That might not be a bad idea. Where?"

"Can't say, can't say. And promise me you won't tell anyone about it. Promise, Greta." My heart fluttered so violently I had to put both hands on my sternum and press down. "Promise."

Her face became solemn. "Very well, I promise. But is it for a good reason or a bad reason?"

"A good reason, of course," I nearly shouted. "I know you'll be happy for me, but I can't tell you about it, just yet. Maybe—"

Maybe someday, I was going to say. My eyes smarted. I didn't know when I would see her again, or feel her soft strong arms around me.

She was watching me intently. "You're going away with Rusala?" she asked, speaking deliberately as if I were deaf.

I nodded, not trusting myself to speak. She pursed her lips.

"That Rusala?" she asked again, her voice growing sharp. "I knew it. I knew there was something about the way she latched on to you. Are you sure?"

The words seemed to pierce something. I felt some numb, filmy barrier around me break and bleed, like a blister. I watched her eyes darken, her pale mouth fall at its corners. She would have looked stern but for the way her eyelids darkened and twitched. She twitched with fear, I thought suddenly. She envied my courage. She wished she'd had more daring in her own youth.

I'd been wrong to stop, and I was desperate to get moving again. "I'll write you," I said. "I have to go. I'm sorry. I have so much to do before we leave."

She lowered her chin and shook her head slowly. The ostrich feathers waved so comically I almost laughed. The waiter brought two cups of espresso on a gold tray.

"Now," I said, not bothering anymore to hide my smile. "Won't you kiss your foster daughter, before I go? Can't you see how happy I am?"

I closed my eyes and felt her cool, slack lips on my cheek.

I left her, zig-zagging through the alleys. I stopped at an artists' supply shop, and heard my own voice, as strident as a true Yankee's: "But don't you have anything brighter, more vivid? I must have the deepest violet there is, and a bright orange. No, not that. I mean a blinding orange, a radium flame. And that shiny, arsenic green, like a pigeon's throat."

I raced home to find the house quiet and calm, as if we'd already moved out. Lovorka had cleaned thoroughly that morning.

Even Olga's trunk, where I'd left it gaping open, was tucked neatly away. I wasted more than an hour pacing, packing my shoes, then wrapping my new paints and packing those as well. I wrote out a partial list of tasks: *pay up grocery bill, leave reference letter and money for Lovorka, buy gift for Greta, postcard to Boston?*

I set off to buy tickets and got as far as the alley's end before I remembered I might need our passports. I ran back and fished through Rusala's tin trunk, finding a paper portfolio tied with twine. Inside were photographs she had posed for, tinted the colors of semi-precious stones. There was Rusala embracing men or other women, dressed as a maid or a school-mistress or a sort of girl-pony. In one series, Rusala wore only the jeweled waist-chain of an odalisque and posed on a zebra skin, cupping her breasts and leering towards the camera. How strange and tense she looked, holding a stretched grin, her feet blurred where they must have twitched with impatience.

Towards the bottom of the trunk, there were just some childhood treasures: an ivory cross, a pair of red crystal earrings, a thin braid of pale hair wrapped round a plaster-of-paris heart. I decided she must carry her passport with her, in her rucksack.

The room had become dark and cool. I went to the glass and smoothed my hair, looking at my electric-white face and black, black eyes.

THE SKY WAS covered in a lace of peach-colored clouds that darkened to scarlet as I reached La Fenice. The show had already begun. I heard the scream of the soprano and the rumble of the cellos as I paced around to the artists' door. I'd put all the pound notes into a belt, just under my drawers, and I felt it like a band of hot iron round my hips.

Stagehands slouched near the stage door, tilting their heads to watch the sky. I caught Vitya's eye and he grinned, holding his cigarette in his teeth and ruffling his sweaty hair. He let me in, ushering me to an empty box that smelled of sambuca.

"It's Du Lac's box," he said. "I know he went to Paris today, so you're safe. Only don't show your face." He pointed to the brocade drapes. "But if someone sees curtains moving, it's all right. He likes to have guests here, and sometimes they forget to watch opera. Maybe you'll find knickers under chair."

The music started again and he looked up. "Oh-pa. I have to be in the electrical box. Be good, Katie. Careful. Knickers." His laughter faded as he limped off.

I felt my way along the cushions and found a pair of opera glasses. Leaning forward, I peeked through the curtains to the burning stage. The second act had just begun. The soprano lay on a couch, in a purple dressing gown and a crown of gold foil, I supposed some sort of Eastern queen. She began to sing, her eyes widening, her throat pulsing with cobalt veins. When her aria ended, I sighed with relief.

A warm current passed through the crowd, and I risked a look around. The other boxes held rich people in gloves and gold chains, but the floor seats were filled with people in plain dress — women in faded shirtwaists, men wearing kerchiefs knotted at their temples. The very first row of seats, right before the orchestra, held a group of young women, all of them aggressively pretty, with upswept hair and naked shoulders. They were seated as if to highlight their variety, like flowers in a box: red-head, blonde, brunette, red-head, blonde. I remembered Rusala telling me how the managers hired girls for this, so that there would be a guaranteed minimum audience at even the dullest shows.

As the conductor raised his baton, the stage filled with dancers, all smiling ecstatically. Rusala was at the center of the line, wearing trousers of blue chiffon and an Indian blouse that showed her bare stomach and her arms. Sleigh bells hung from her anklets and bracelets.

She stepped forward and danced a sarabande, creating a slow chime with her footsteps and her undulating arms. The only other accompaniment was a celesta and a flute. She spread her arms wide, rolling her hips, sometimes lifting one leg behind her in an acrobat's pose, sometimes turning and bending backwards so far that her upside-side down face gazed at the audience. It was strangely transformed face — a snake's face, with steady human eyes.

The crowd stared, their eyes glassy and still, their heads pivoting slowly to follow her movement. They would look for her again tomorrow, I thought. They scarcely realized the subtle alchemy that had already started in them. They would dream of her tonight, and be distracted tomorrow morning, remembering the dark, round-cheeked girl who'd danced a solo at the opera. By tomorrow afternoon they would decide that they must see her again, if only one more time. Perhaps they'd decide to come alone, the better to savor her. They'd come early and mill around the artists' door, the richest of them sending flowers and peremptory little cards.

How shocked they'd be to find her gone. Because, of course, she'd be with me, the only one of them who knew her, who'd risked everything for her, who deserved her.

When the show ended, I waited in the dark box until Vitya came for me and led me backstage.

The dressing room for the ballet-girls was little more than a
storage closet, with a watery stone floor and two cracked mirrors. A
gramophone played while a few of the girls danced, gasping and
flushed. Every few moments one of them shouted, "It's a bear!" and
they would embrace as if wrestling.

Rusala sat before a mirror. She looked at me with one eye, then
the other, as she drew off her false eyelashes. I sat beside her,
feeling serene as soon as I was near enough to touch. I wondered
whether she might divine the whole story by looking at my face.
She certainly seemed to try. She squinted and turned her head.

"Well then, Katie?"

I leaned in, putting my lips to her ear. The maelstrom of
shrieks and laughter and complaints continued all around us. I
couldn't hear my whispered voice, but only felt my lips forming the
words against her skin, my breath stirring her hair. I didn't get
half-way through the story before she pulled away, breathing in
sharply, fussing innocently with her make-up kit. She seemed so
unperturbed that for a moment I thought she might not have heard
me.

Then she looked up and our eyes met in the mirror. Her jaw
clenched. "Well done," she said levelly. "Well done."

"And for tickets?" I said, wondering at her calm.

She gave a slow smile, but her eyes remained wide and fierce.
"No," she said. Someone was calling her name, yet she went on.
"You've done enough. Now you rest, and leave everything to me."

"Hey, Rusala!" It was Hilda. She soaked her feet in a pan of
water. A girl beside her was changing into a gaudy pink hobble
skirt. "You stole the show, old girl. Don't you think so, Katie?"

A blonde girl sniffed, and leaned to say something to her
neighbor. They both scowled at Rusala.

"Ah, she's not listening," came Vitya's voice. I turned to where
he sat on the floor. I hadn't known he'd followed me in, but the
other girls seemed unbothered by his presence as they streaked by
him, barefoot and half-dressed.

"Rusala has that look in her face, like she is planning,
planning," Vitya continued. He poured some gin into a cracked
teacup.

"We're all planning stuff, sweet Vitya," Hilda scolded. "Oh, if I
could freeze my feet in a block of ice, I would. You've got to plan,
plan, plan, all the time, to get on. Remember, Rusala, when we
planned to try for the Theatre Slav?"

"What about acting?" Frannie offered. She was brushing out
her curly hair so swiftly that it crackled around her like a black
storm cloud. "Easier than dancing, and besides, I get too fat now.
Who cannot act?" She opened her mouth in a silent scream, then bit

her hand.

"I heard Aga Khan's in Venice, looking for a sweet young friend," Hilda countered. Another girl broke in, speaking Italian, and they all began arguing about films, and operas, and where to go for supper, and who had been in the audience, and who had which plans, and whose feet hurt the worst.

Rusala said nothing. When she stood to undress, I didn't dare look straight at her. Instead I watched her shadow as it writhed around her feet. I imagined, when we were finally settled in our house by the sea, I would do nothing but hold her close for days.

Chapter
Twenty

RUSALA TOOK HER time dressing, backing into an alcove she'd made for herself between the rough wall and the costume rack. The gramophone played on while the girls fixed their hair and scrubbed their faces and groused. Hilda tied the ends of her corset strings to a doorjamb, then leaned away, grunting. Vitya found a pack of cards and dealt himself a circle of kings.

The girls dressed in cheap, sparkling gowns of chintz, the kind that resembles silk from far away. They used swags of tulle to cover tobacco stains and rips. Their costumes were hung along the walls, under a piece of grey oilcloth. In the center of the room stood a shallow tub, where they rinsed the blood and grime from their feet.

After a few moments, there came a rumbling from the hallway, the tick and crunch of new shoes on the sandy floor. The girls went quiet, exchanging smirks. Someone knocked at the door. When Vitya undid the latch, a boy stuck his head in. Behind him were the coal-black suits of gentlemen. A monocle flashed in the shadows.

"Shut the door!" Hilda squealed. Her voice was full of girlish outrage, but her face remained placid, even bored. She was sewing the hem of her skirt, biting off the threads.

The boy squeezed in and pulled the door shut. He wore green livery with braids of gold on his shoulders. He began handing out notes to the girls. He brought several to Rusala and prepared to read them aloud to her, but she shook her head without lifting her eyes.

When Frannie finished dressing, she came to sit by me. Across the bridge of her nose, tiny pearls of sweat showed through her powder. Her gown was the color of orange taffy, with a shawl of black Spanish lace. She had rolled her hair into a towering pompadour. She panted so hard I could hear her corset creaking.

"Are you speaking more Venetian lately?" she asked, wiping the back of her neck. "Ah, you only need more practice. Maybe you'll come for Sunday lunch at my aunt's house sometime. We teach you Venetian, you teach us American."

"Of course," I said, smoothing my skirt. I looked around, imagining all of them months from now, years from now, gossiping as they washed their feet. *That Katie, Rusala's pal. They just took the money and disappeared.* They would say we'd disappeared, not that we'd been caught, or were in prison. The belt of money squeezed my waist.

Frannie popped a white mint in her mouth and clicked it against her teeth, watching me. She drew on a pair of long black satin gloves and fumbled with their buttons, frowning. Her breasts were mottled red and white.

"Here," I said, pulling one of her hot arms towards me. I fastened the two pearl buttons behind her elbow while she fanned herself. The gloves were too big for her.

"Thank you. So, you'll come?" She looked towards Rusala's back. "Rusala will be here for another hour, dressing, won't she? She is lucky to have a friend so patient."

She winked and stood. Most of the girls had exited to the hallway. Frannie sighed deeply before she joined them. As soon as the door closed behind her, I heard her voice rise in a falsetto compliment.

I turned back to where Rusala sat in her chemise, her legs bare. She grimaced at her feet.

"Don't look," she said. "I've lost another damned toenail." She pulled at her big toe, where the nail had turned dark as rotted sea-shell. I saw the pink pulp of flesh beneath it before I turned away, shivering.

"I said don't look." I heard her hiss with pain, then stand. "But do you know the very best thing about it?"

I turned towards her. Her shoulders were high and tight.

"The best thing is that I'll never wear these again." She had both of her hard little slippers in her fist; she wound up and threw them across the room. When they hit one of the gin-filled teacups, the crash made me scream.

The chatter outside paused. "Quiet," Rusala said. She clapped her hands and threw her head back. "Shall we go? Let's go, let's go, let's go, let's go, before I break every one of these looking-glasses."

"Stay calm," I said. "By tomorrow morning we'll be far away. When we find our house you can smash things whenever you want."

She pulled up her stockings and pushed her hair out of her face as she stepped into her shoes. She didn't bother with a gown, but threw on my old grey cloak.

"You're right," she said. "You're right. Take me out of here."

When we ventured to the hallway, the crowd had moved towards the lobby. We went the opposite way, back towards the artists' door. My legs were jittery under all the layers of clothes. The belt of money itched like wool.

It was a balmy night, with a humid, insistent wind. I was amazed at how alive the air seemed, how full of activity. Where my nerves had been dulled before, by sadness and medicines, they were now alive as electric filaments — tiny tentacles reaching out into the darkness, finding the trickle of a fountain, the flap of canvas, the scent of burning garbage. And just beyond what I could sense, a pool of imaginary things widened. I could feel them gathering strength, as if they longed to finally burst through the night. I thought of the buildings shattering around us; or the stars splashing into the canal; or burly, fantastic creatures lumbering out of the seawater and rolling into the squares, struggling to speak.

We turned a corner. I saw two black figures coming towards us. I jumped backwards. I wanted to run but my legs were weak.

"Katie!" Rusala gazed at my face, then turned to where I'd been looking. "Oh, lord, oh, damn you," she said, and I watched the smaller black figure take the arm of the taller one. "Those are our shadows. You're nervous as a witch."

The torchlight behind us sputtered and flared. The alley looked commonplace again. When I started to giggle, Rusala did too. I scratched at my skirt.

Rusala squeezed my wrist as we reached the house. "We'll pass one quiet, quiet night," she said. "I told Lovorka to take a holiday. We've only a few things to pack."

"No, we have to leave now," I said. We were already in the vestibule, but I kept whispering. When Rusala reached for the lamp, I grabbed her shoulder.

She shook me off. "Will you quit that? Relax." She lit the lamp and turned to glare at me. The light wavered over her hair, the fine down of her cheek. There was a streak of cold cream just above her ear.

"You relax," she said, more mildly. She exhaled. "If we panic, we'll only end up doing something strange, something that draws the neighbors' attention. Like skulking and whispering around a darkened house."

"I'm not —" I cleared my throat. "You're the one whispering."

Her teeth flashed. She stifled her laughter quickly. I wanted to laugh again, but I couldn't catch my breath.

"Now then," she said, coming close to me and leaning her cheek against mine. We both struggled to breathe more slowly. "Now. We must stay calm. We must stay here until morning. Think of it. Nothing draws suspicion more than a midnight departure. We'll go to the harbor tomorrow morning, looking bright and fresh and innocent as a pair of bluebirds. We'll buy tickets for the first ship available out of Venice. First class, since they ask fewer questions there. Once we land, we'll get ourselves new documents. Then we'll go on to buy our little house on the sea."

I felt her voice buzzing under my cheekbone. She had been gripping my shoulders, but now she turned her head, slipped her arms around my waist, and stepped closer to me. I rested my chin on her hair.

"But I won't be able to rest," I said. "God, I'm so nervous, I want to scream."

She leaned back to look up into my face. "But it will be weeks before William might notice anything about the bonds," she said. "Or probably months. No one will even think of us until we're safely tucked away somewhere. What are you nervous for, tonight?"

"You're right," I said, "but suppose he shows them to someone? What if Amy comes home and sees them? But no, that's not even what I'm nervous about. I'm about to panic. I want to run. I won't be able to stay in one place all night." I let go of her waist and gripped myself. I wanted so badly to undress, or to pace, or to hit something.

"Aha, I see," she said. She took my hand, all business, then led me up the dark staircase, still carrying the lamp. The house seemed larger than ever. The stairs popped and whined under our weight.

"Let's take some drops, this last time," she said. "Come on, pack first." She drew me into the bedroom.

It took us only minutes to roll up our underthings and lay our gowns into our trunks. Rusala didn't pack any of her ballet shoes or practice dresses, leaving them instead in a corner with my books. I tied my paints, brushes, and knives into a hatbox and laid them on top of my traveling cloak.

We tucked the belt of money into the bottom of Rusala's rucksack.

The sight of our stacked bundles made me shake again. "All right," I said, hurrying into the dark studio. "And how much do you think we should leave for the grocer? And for Lovorka? Don't you have any small bills? Lord, it all looks like play money to me." I opened the windows and gulped in the air. A vase of almond blossoms stood on the sill, perhaps left there by Lovorka. The mint in my flower box was all overgrown. Its leaves — dark, hoary little tongues — still held clumps of snow.

Rusala followed me in. She set her rucksack in the corner, saying, "Let's keep this near." She sat on the low stool by the fireplace, holding the lamp in her lap, keeping very still. Only her eyes moved, following me as I paced uselessly before the window.

Finally she sighed and stood, setting the lamp on the mantel.

Her face grew softer. "Shall we try and sleep?" she said, in the
meek voice she'd used the first day she came to my house. I
remembered her oversized umbrella, her purple evening gown, her
hands blue with cold. Without waiting for my answer, she
unfastened her cloak and crossed to me. If anyone had watched
from outside, they would have seen only a gold-edged shadow
slipping through the dark.

She lifted a bottle of shiraz from the sideboard and it sloshed
quietly. "Now," she said. "One last time, let's take some of your
drops and sleep."

As she spoke, my desire for the medicine grew sharp. How
sweet the anticipation for it could be. Even the most cutting grief,
the hottest rage, would become in an instant bearable. She picked
through the bottles at my desk. The drops plashed into the wine
with a soft, deferential sound. Already I could feel the pull of the
drug on the backs of my thighs.

She smiled. "I heard that sigh. Here, won't you feel better in
the morning?"

I undressed, lying back on the couch and holding out my
hands.

"Let me sleep here," I said. "I can't stand to look at our trunks
in the bedroom. Let me pretend it's just another late night of
painting, and I've collapsed onto the couch." I started to cry, and
she hurried to my side. The glass was very heavy, and the wine had
a metallic, piney taste. I could only manage two swallows before I
had to stop, licking my lips.

Rusala undressed and knelt beside me. She stroked my arms,
then rested her fingertips on my face. "Sle — ee — eep," she said, in a
deep voice like a hypnotist's at a carnival. "Droop, crimson petal."

As she stroked my hair, I slurped at the last gritty dregs and
winced. "Ukh. What crimson petal?" I put the glass on the floor and
she trailed her fingers over the back of my neck, over my shoulders
that were still twitching with nervousness.

"You know," she said, reclining beside me. "That poem you
read to me once, with the cypress and the peacock."

"Right," I said. "Clever thing." I rolled towards her and put
my palms on her waist. Her calm radiated up my arms. I recited:

Now folds the lily all her sweetness up,
And slips into the bosom of the lake:
So fold thyself, my dearest, thou, and slip
Into my bosom and be lost in me.

By the time I finished speaking my lips were numb. She rested
her head on my chest. I struggled to stay awake. I tried to speak
again, but her fingertips moved between my legs until they cupped
my center. "So warm," she said. Her fingers slipped inside me,

gently. Her palm pressed into the softening flesh above. She ran her tongue once over my nipple. "Oh, Katie."

The bed seemed to float. I tried to whisper, *don't stop*. I must have slept, for suddenly I was startled by her ragged voice at my ear, her hips rocking against me. Her tiny fingers circled and swam inside me. "Katie, I must, Katie."

I tried to answer but I'd become heavy as stone; only my cunt was warm and quick. When finally she went quiet, I slipped back into sleep, but it was a restless, panting sleep, full of painfully bright dreams. Sometimes I dreamt it was broad daylight and Rusala was fully dressed, shaking me awake, sobbing that the money was gone. Then it would be evening again, and I was trying to find my way to the theater. Then I dreamt of the canal below, simmering with insects. Fish hurled themselves to the banks, shouting with outrage, shrieking nonsense words over and over.

I woke sitting up in darkness, heart racing, streaming with sweat. A square of moonlight lay across the floor.

"Rusala?" I said. She must have been down at the privy.

Then I heard a voice, a clear, piercing sound like an icicle falling: *piz-do-bol-su-ka*. After it came a defeated wail, and the furtive slap of a woman's slippers on the cobblestones.

I crept to the windowsill, edging along the square of moonlight. I rubbed my eyes and looked outside. The drug made everything waver, as if I were looking into a dirty well. Two women stood at the canal railing, just at the corner of the bridge where the shadows were thickest. One woman was fair-haired and disheveled. She looked insane, or sick, shaking her head every few seconds. The other was smaller, wearing a hood; she stood tense and guarded, sometimes lifting her arm in self-defense.

The fair one pounded her fist on the railing and screeched, louder than before: *pizdobol!* Then she stepped forward so suddenly I thought she meant to jump into the canal. Instead, she slapped the hooded woman—awkwardly at first, with a shaking arm—then again, harder. She lifted her hand a third time, but the hooded woman grabbed her wrist so hard that she went still.

Then they were close together, cleaving and tottering. I couldn't see whether they struggled or embraced. The mad voice sobbed, and nearly rose, but then all at once was choked into a furious, airless wheezing.

The air around me collapsed and I screamed. I stepped back from the window as my voice echoed over the alleyways. When I looked out again, the fair woman was running alongside the canal, clutching a purse. Her hair flashed white and green behind her. She listed from one side to the other as she ran, tripping on her skirt, her path uncertain and frantic as a moth's flight.

Downstairs, our front door slammed shut. I couldn't stop staring at the fair woman. She looked familiar, or would have, if she hadn't seemed so mad.

Then she looked back towards the house. A streetlight shone in her face. I cried out, "Lovorka?"

The studio door burst open and a shadow rushed at me. A small hand pressed at my mouth.

"You shut up," Rusala panted. "Hush, hush." She'd brought the night's chill on her clothes. "Hush."

"What happened?" I broke away from her and leaned outside. The alley was empty.

Rusala lit the lamp and turned it low. Her face was chalky, her eyes rimmed in scarlet. She patted her rucksack, staring into the corners of the room.

"Get away from the window," she said. "You need more medicine, sweetheart?" She kicked off her slippers, pulled off her cloak. She wore nothing underneath. She found the shiraz and the vial of drops. Her hands shook, and the bottle scraped against the glass.

"What was that?" I said. "Did I see Lovorka?"

She laughed sharply, her chest hitching. "I need some drops myself. Yes, you saw Lovorka, and heard Lovorka too, as did fucking everyone else on the street, no doubt. Fuck me. Fuck." She slammed her fist into her thigh.

"Right now, steady," she said. She looked up at me. "Right, we'll keep to the plan, we'll not leave until dawn."

"What did you say to her?"

"Be quiet." Rusala closed her eyes. She pounded the floor with her heel, twice. "We'll stay calm. I said nothing to her. She came stealing in, and she saw our things all packed. And then she fell into hysterics. Fuck if I know why." She rubbed her palm violently over her forehead, her eyes. "You know how maids can be sometimes. They're soft-hearted as old whores. They believe they're members of the family. They get sweet on their mistresses and feel jilted if they're dismissed. I told her you'd written a fine reference letter but—" She scratched her scalp, making her hair wild. "Must we talk about her any more?"

"What was she saying? What does that mean, *piz-do?*"

"Who knows what that slap-rat was going on about? She speaks her own language whenever it suits her. I'm sure it means she wanted money. I gave her a god-damned heap." She held her breath for a long time, turning towards the window. She lifted her head, and when she spoke again her voice was careful and low. "I dipped into the stash of bank notes and then threw in all the coins I had with me. So don't worry, proper Katie. She's been taken care

of. And we'll leave some money for your landlady, for the grocer.
We'll do all of that in the morning."

"But did she hit you? It looked as if she did." I touched my hot
forehead. I thought of the white-green hair, the rippling skirt.

"Hey, Katie," she said. Her voice was nearly calm but she
didn't turn towards me. "Were you sleepwalking again?"

I wanted to approach her but her shoulders seemed brittle in
the darkness.

"Now, no more nightmares," she whispered. I'd once had a
dream of her whispering. My head was so heavy. I wanted to lie
down. She was already walking towards me with the wineglass in
both her hands. The medicine swirled inside, like fronds of sea
grass.

I lay back and took three gulps as she watched. She turned the
lamp down as far as it could go, and lay beside me. When she
rested her palm on my eyes, I plummeted down into a perfectly
dreamless sleep.

A BABY WAS shrieking. There was the sound of a slap, then
another. The shrieking stopped, then turned to a keening whine.

It took all my strength to lift my eyelids. The ceiling was
bright. The sunlight was strangely clean, like milk mixed with
bleach. I breathed deep and moved my hands around the sofa. I
was lying on my back. I pressed my enormous meaty tongue
against my teeth, trying to say *Rusala*. "Ru," I croaked. I tried again
and my voice was a muffled squeak.

Mid-day noise rose from the street below. "Rusala," I said,
quite clearly. I turned my head and my temple throbbed with pain.
Nausea crept up my throat. Rusala's rucksack was gone, and in its
place she'd propped a postcard of herself posing with a giant
poppy.

I smiled at the picture. I knew just what it meant: it was her
way of reassuring me. She must have found me impossible to wake,
and so she set off on her own for our tickets.

When I tried to sit up, I felt sick again. My guts gnawed on
themselves with hunger. I would have to run out for just a little
food. I stood, and the floor heaved beneath me. I stumbled against
the half-empty wineglass, shuddering at its scent. It took me a long
time to dress. Each time I tried to button a shirt I was off-kilter. I
finally gave up and put on a tunic and a straw hat.

Outside, it was another fine day, warm and spring-like. It was
perhaps even later than I'd first thought; the shadows by the
Campo Manin wellhead were long, and the cafés were still. How
strange to walk about, not even knowing the time, like a child. Men

stared frankly at me. I thought I must look unwashed and still drunk, as if I'd slept under a bridge. From the corner of my eye, I saw a man leaning against a lamppost. He lifted his head and threw down his cigarette as I passed. I pulled down my hat brim, trying to walk more quickly.

I avoided the cafés and found a stall that sold paper cones of roasted chestnuts. I peeled them quickly, burning my fingertips. Leaning against a railing, I dropped the shells into the oily water as I ate. The reflection of my face was pink and bloated, like a cake that had been left underwater.

A shape appeared next to me and I jumped.

"Just me."

I turned to Vitya's face.

"Hungry?" He looked at my crumpled paper. I wiped my mouth carefully. Before I could answer he said, "Will you come to restaurant and help manage overstock?"

He watched my face warily, but smiled.

"Hey, you look sad again," he said. "Don't, now. You see, I was waiting in your neighborhood here. I hoped I might see you or Ru. Don't be cross. I know you two like to feel private here, but I had to come. I worried for you." He looked around. "I know everything, Katie. But don't worry, I tell no one."

"You know?" I said. "You know we're leaving?"

He looked down at the floating chestnut hulls. "Leaving?" He nodded, raising his eyebrows. "I didn't know that. Probably not a bad idea. Although I think by now Larisa's left Venice for good."

I thought the drug had dulled my hearing. "Larisa?" I stared hard at him.

"Rusala's old pal." He leaned in close to me. "I thought she told you."

I did remember, but I didn't feel any less confused. "The injured girl? The one who left her and went back to Russia?"

"I thought, too. We all were thinking she's in St. Petersburg." Vitya's voice rose. His accent thickened until his words all slurred together. "But she was in Venice, for a long time. All the time. And to think I never believed Baptiste. He always said he saw her, sneaking in the market, carrying vegetables or bundles of laundry."

"Vitya, no, Larisa wasn't here, certainly," I said, stepping away from him. "She wasn't here in Venice. She couldn't have been. We'd have known. You were all good friends." I wondered whether he'd just come from smoking with Baptiste, yet his eyes looked perfectly clear. He held his hands before me, palms turned up, as if he hoped I could offer some clue.

"She's been in Venice," he repeated, when he saw I couldn't say more. "And I saw her, today, before dawn. Really I thought I was seeing a ghost. She looked mad, I mean perfectly mad, like a madwoman in opera. Witch hair, gown with holes. Talking to herself."

"No," I said.

"She almost did not know me." Vitya patted his vest pocket and drew out a cigarette case. "And so I think I'm mistaken. But then I said something in Russian, and she rushed at me, answering, talking."

"What did she say?" I wondered whether I should fear for Rusala, or for myself. Was Rusala back in our rooms now, waiting for me?

"She spoke about Rusala. I don't understand. She said that she and Rusala for a long time were planning to leave Venice together and go to St. Petersburg. When they had enough money, then they would go. Then they were supposed to go last night. Larisa says she was waiting at station all night, got on the train to wait for Rusala, train was almost leaving. Then she go—went—to find Rusala." He struggled with the words, the tenses, finally giving up and opening his cigarette case with trembling hands.

"She's delusional, the poor thing," I said. "Rusala hasn't seen her in years."

"No?" Vitya fumbled with a matchbook until I took it from him and lit his cigarette. He puffed, shaking his head. "But Larisa said she just came from seeing Rusala. God, she looked ready to kill. She scratched, you know, her own arm, when she was talking."

Vitya clawed at his forearm. I slapped his hand away.

"You don't think she knows where we live?" I said. I thought of Rusala's insistence on keeping her friends away from our house. Had she suspected something, feared something? "Vitya, this is nonsense, this can't be." I jumped away, turning to leave, but then I turned back and stared at the water. Why would this girl resurface now, of all times?

I pressed my stomach against the railing. "Do you think," I said, "that she's looking for Rusala, that she might have been following her? Following us?"

"But she says she talked with Rusala," Vitya said. "She says she just talked to her, only a few hours before dawn."

"She's crazy as a roach, of course. What am I doing here? I've got to go. Rusala might be all alone at home now." Still my hands were tight around the railing, and I looked up at Vitya's haggard face.

"You did not see her, then?" Vitya closed his eyes and seemed to resign himself. "Larisa has an idea that she was fighting with Rusala. Rusala threw money at her, and told her to go away or else—"

I scarcely understood him. His words dropped here and there in me, like scattered hailstones: *money, fighting, did not see.* I meant to kiss his cheek and run away, run home and hold Rusala to me. We might leave before the day got any longer. Yet all the same, my feet remained still. There was something hypnotizing about Vitya's story. I imagined a bright thread winding around my wrist, and I had the desire to grasp it and pull. The water underneath us was strangely loud. Had it been so loud, the whole time we'd been talking? Why had I just heard it?

"Or else what, what?" I demanded.

He breathed out smoke. The water reflected on the wheat-colored stubble of his chin. "You're right," he said, "Larisa's mad. She kept cursing. She called Rusala a bad name. Called her a liar. No, worse than a liar."

"What are you talking about?"

"There's a word in Russian, a terrible word that means something like pain, pain in cunt." He blushed and looked away. "Yet it also means something like damned liar. Pizdobol. Lovorka kept calling Rusala *pizdobol, pizdobol.*"

As he spoke, I saw again the fair-haired woman running along the canal. Her crippled gait, her face at once familiar and utterly transformed.

"Stop, Vitya, stop."

He might not have heard me. The water below had become deafening. The bridge buckled and spun under us. I crouched and clung to the railing, the way a cat clings to the wind-tossed branches of a tree.

ONE AUTUMN NIGHT, long ago, Adele and I spoke of Alexandria. It was a city for artists, Adele had insisted. The ashes from the burned library still made the sunsets so vivid you would think you'd landed on another planet. She'd been reclining before the fire in her aunt's library as she told me this, warming her bum. I'd always warned her that her skirts would catch fire. She'd read me some lines by a poet who lived in Alexandria:

Days to come stand in front of us
Like a row of lighted candles.

I whispered the poem to myself now, watching my dark mouth move. My lips looked bruised.

Rusala had left her make-up kit. The sun was setting, tipping its slow gold light into my room one last time. I sat before the smudged mirror, leaning so close that my breath made a mist.

It had been a different woman, the one who arrived here three hours ago, whose sobs were like belches of flame; who rocked and scraped her fingernails along the carpet, braying as if giving birth; who tore at the curtains and bedclothes until her hands were numb. It wasn't me.

For the fifth time, I tilted the bottle of morphine and pressed it against my tongue. It had been empty for a half-hour, yet I still hoped some drops might trickle out. It was just as well. Too much morphine would make me insensate, but taken in small amounts it seemed the very substance of valor. I went back to painting my face. I tweezed my eyebrows into arches, brushed powder over my cheeks, spread a tacky carmine paste over my lips, shadowed my lids with kohl. I saw for the first time how a plain face could be honed, sharpened, made bright as a poisonous beetle. I pressed my fingernails into my cheek, leaving pink crescents. I didn't feel a thing.

On the back of her postcard, Rusala had written *new york* in a quaintly serifed font, as if she'd copied the letters from a newspaper advertisement. Underneath she'd drawn a plump heart, and then *by. R.*

Rusala had abandoned her tin trunk, with its cheap gowns. Just inside my own trunk, I'd found a cloth bundle tied with ribbons that held five hundred pounds and a false passport with my physical description. With the money, she'd made it clear that *new york* was not an invitation. I knew she wouldn't bother to taunt. Simply, those were the only words she could write, and she wanted to fix something of herself for me, a dead moth on a pin.

I brushed my hair. Time kept halting, as if I were caught in a broken watch. Each time I closed my eyes, I might live an entire day in memory. I saw Rusala practicing a pirouette, or stealing out of the bed on those nights she couldn't sleep. I saw the paintings I hadn't dared make, the ones with harsh, straining forms and clashing streams of color.

My skin still smelled like Rusala, like the back of her neck. I remembered her sumptuous breathing as she slept. Once, I'd bent over her at midnight and kissed her eyes lightly; they'd trembled like warm fruit under my lips. I'd wanted to fill myself with her, saturate all my cells with her so that they'd never contain anything else.

I should have injured her when I'd had the chance. I should have given her a scar to wear on her cheek, or her collarbone, for remembrance. I closed my eyes again, and the drug made me pitch forward. Ah, I saw Rusala injured. I had a quick dream of running to her and saving her.

I swung between rage and desperate, frenzied tenderness. I wanted to find her and hurt her. I wanted to embrace her knees and promise her anything, anything, if she'd only come back. My fists tightened until the bones crunched. All these impulses were edges, facets, of desire. Like a diamond gathering light, desire can't be looked at all at once. It might sear your eyes. You can only see it in fragments, in relief. You can only sense its light, pulling you forward.

I stared at my bending reflection and let the kohl stick drop to my lap. As the daylight faded, my skin glowed mauve. My teeth were blue-white. How quick my pulse was, in my throat.

I listened to the footsteps beneath my window. Any minute now I'd hear the young girl calling. I'd found her in the square an hour earlier and given her a lire to fetch a boat for me, one that would take me to the harbor. There I would buy a first-class passage to Alexandria. There were plenty of jobs there. Adele and Jeff and I had discussed the issue many times. I might teach, translate, manage accounts. I saw myself walking in the bright streets, steady as a sleepwalker, smiling when needed.

And at night, I would paint until my arms gave out, filling my room with Rusala's colors, with her shape. The paintings would sell, or they wouldn't. I'd have to paint them, all the same. I could already see them: warm, repellent, irresistible, so saturated with color that they gave the illusion of emitting light. I'd have no peace until they were painted, and I would never be able to paint enough.

Nervous footsteps pattered along the pavement below, stopping just before my house. I turned to the window. Sparks of red and violet ricocheted across my ceiling, reflections from the jeweled crowd passing below. A girl's voice called me, and I rose.

The End

The Odd Couple
by Q Kelly

Morrisey Hawthorne and her four-year-old son, Gareth, have a pretty good life. Then one day they meet Charlene Sudsbury, who is trying to move on from the suicide of her son, JP, three years before. Gareth is nearly the mirror image of JP, and Charlene connects instantly with him. Not quite so with Morrisey, who can't escape fast enough after Charlene shows her a picture of JP. Charlene is convinced Morrisey is hiding something and sets out in search of the truth.

Despite the circumstances, the two women form an unusual bond and end up with a lot more than they bargained for. But when an old friend of JP's resurfaces, he challenges the fragile trust Morrisey and Charlene have been building.

Can these two women overcome the obstacles that separate them from the happiness they seek?

ISBN 978-1-932300-99-4
1-932300-99-6

OTHER REGAL CREST

Be sure to check out our other imprints,
Yellow Rose Books and Quest Books.

About the Author:

L.E. Butler, a former dancer, lives in England. *Relief* is her first novel. Her website is www.lebutler.net.

VISIT US ONLINE AT

www.regalcrest.biz

At the Regal Crest Website You'll Find

- The latest news about forthcoming titles and new releases

- Our complete backlist of romance, mystery, thriller and adventure titles

- Information about your favorite authors

- Current bestsellers

- Media tearsheets to print and take with you when you shop

Regal Crest titles are available from all progressive booksellers and online at StarCrossed Productions, (www.scp-inc.biz), or at www.amazon.com, www.bamm.com, www.barnesandnoble.com, and many others.

Printed in the United States
141011LV00004B/67/P